POP-UP DINNER, DROP DOWN DEAD

D.B. ELROGG

A MILO RATHKEY MYSTERY

Pop-up Dinner, Drop Down Dead

A Milo Rathkey Mystery

Copyright © 2025 Alyce Goldberg, Harvey Goldberg All Rights Reserved

ISBN 979-8-9872032-1-7 (eBook)
ISBN 979-8-9872032-0-0 (Paperback)
ISBN 979-8-9872032-2-4 (Hardcover)

No part of this publication may be used, reproduced in any manner, or published in any form or by any means, electronic, mechanical, photocopying, recording or otherwise, without the prior written permission of the publisher, except brief quotations to be used in the production of critical articles and reviews.

If you wish to contact the authors, you may email them at authors@dbelrogg.com

This is a work of fiction. All characters and incidents are totally from the minds of the authors and any resemblance to actual persons, living or dead, or incidents past and present is purely coincidental.

Cover Art by John Edgar Harris

Dedicated to Quinn Rose, Whose Smile Delights

SPECIAL THANKS TO

STAN JOHNSON
JODY EVANS
NICK GOLDBERG
DR. ELENA CABB
DOUG OSELL
ROB RAINEY
SUZETTE FORD
PIPER GOLDBERG

1

January in Duluth is cold, snowy, gray, and dark. For some people, such as Mary Alice Bonner, the month is a time to seek warmth and light from the sun. This year, her island of choice was St. Croix in the US Virgin Islands.

Following Mary Alice's New Year's Eve Gala, Agnes and Sutherland McKnight scampered off to Hawaii for two weeks, where just a year ago they were married by a charter boat captain—unexpected, impulsive, and for Sutherland, uncharacteristically rash, but by all measures, a happy coupling.

Police Consultant Milo Rathkey tried the fun in the sun route with Mary Alice for a few days. He enjoyed Blue's company, but then flew home. Milo loved the cold, the snow, and especially the dark. He found relaxation and enjoyment in the comfort of Lakesong and the warmth of the roaring library fireplace. If Lakesong's two cats, Annie and Jet, had a vote, they would clearly be in the Milo camp. Curling up by the fireplace as a blizzard or two roared around outside the house, the cats purred their contentment.

Friends were incredulous with Milo as to why he didn't stay in St. Croix with Mary Alice. The unsaid portion of that question was: "She is so beautiful, and you are…well you. Aren't you afraid she will find someone better?" Milo maintained he hated the sun. In truth, this was also Mary Alice's vacation time with her son, Richard. Milo's unclingy nature made Mary Alice comfortable in their relationship. He was her something *different*. That description of him always amused Milo.

January was a busy month for Martha Gibbson, Lakesong's chef. Her younger sister, Breanna, was preparing for a second trip to the Chilean telescopes in the Atacama Desert. Next in line, Jamal had a new girlfriend and a new basketball season. And finally the youngest, Darian, was starting work on a major science fair project involving the telescope on the roof of their cottage.

Martha, along with her good friend Gabby Nguyen, head chef at VaVena, a popular Italian restaurant in Duluth, had their own project—pop-up dinners. Pop-ups were something Martha dabbled in when she was a culinary student in the Twin Cities. She loved them, so the dinners continued after graduation, allowing her to experiment with different cuisines—stretch her culinary skills. New flavors and food combinations kept her fresh and excited about food.

Five years ago, after her parents were killed in a car crash, leaving her younger brothers and sister orphans, everything changed. The dinners ended abruptly, and she knew she would have to leave her job. Martha never knew how her good fortune came about, but within days of their loss, John McKnight offered Martha the chef's job at Lakesong. The job included use of the cottage on the estate grounds, perfect for her and her new charges. They would all have a home together. She would have to move to Duluth, but her sibling's school life remained the same.

The loss of their parents was still with them, but stability and a new normal sustained them and brought safety and balance. Martha, with friend Gabby, felt safe enough to venture into the world of international food and flavors.

Not only was Milo alone in Lakesong, but he had to fend for himself when it came to all meals that weren't breakfast. So, after his morning swim in the heated saltwater pool, his lumberjack breakfast was waiting for him in one of the warming drawers. Sated, Milo would retire to the library.

The cats also preferred the windowless library, free from the unwelcome sounds of blowing snow, freezing rain, or frigid cold. Curled up in front of the warming fireplace, they kept Milo company until it was time for lunch. Luckily for Milo, he had a long list of favorite restaurants. Today was Nonies and their outstanding Devil's Delight sandwich with French fries and cheese curds.

The Devil's Delight consisted of pastrami and corn beef on a baguette with melted pepper jack cheese and a healthy swath of just spicy enough mustard. From time-to-time Nonies removed the Devil's Delight from the menu, which prompted complaints from Milo. He guessed other patrons also complained because it always reappeared quickly.

When dining solo, Milo's favorite table at Nonies was the one in the back by the kitchen. He enjoyed the hubbub—thought it homey. Servers coming and going, cooks yelling out orders that were up, and a few shouting matches kept Milo entertained. As a topper, there was an occasional fistfight.

Today, he was in luck. Sounds of a serious argument intrigued him as he began to remove his overcoat. He glanced into the kitchen. All was peaceful and productive there, yet he still heard yelling as he sat down.

Milo startled. Something was thrown against the wall behind him, followed by louder screaming voices. Milo leaned back, trying to catch the gist. He scooted his chair closer to the corner, trying to get a better view in case anything or anyone was thrown out into the hallway.

"…money Kick. I need money and you owe me!"
"I don't owe you shit! I…"

"Money," Milo said to himself, "always a good reason for a fight."

The argument behind him was overridden by an order disagreement at full volume that radiated from the kitchen. Adding to the commotion, the server ran past Milo into the kitchen to snatch up her orders. Quiet descended, allowing Milo to continue listening to the more interesting fight behind him.

"We tried that once. You blew it. Don't you dare threaten me!"
"I told you it was just a misunderstanding."
"Get out! You're ruining my life. Get out!"

Milo's waitress, the ponytailed target of the chef's anger, delivered his menu. "We're not very busy today sir, would you like a better table? This one is noisy. I don't know why they put you here today."

Pop-Up Dinner, Drop Down Dead

Milo inhaled the aroma of the pastrami and corn beef wafting from the kitchen. "Thanks, but I like this table."

A thud like a body hitting the wall behind him drowned out his explanation. Seconds later, a disheveled, pudgy man literally flew into the hallway, landing hard on the floor inches from Milo and his server.

The man used his heavily tattooed arms to force himself up. Stumbling to a nearby empty table, he grabbed a handful of napkins and wiped blood from his mouth. He stared at Milo and the server, cursed, and fled.

"Friend of yours?" Milo asked the stunned girl.

The question snapped her out of her shock. She refocused on Milo. "I'm sorry. What?"

"Friend of yours?" Milo repeated.

She looked at Milo strangely. "No. He's a friend of the owner."

"Who threw him out here?"

"The owner. That's his office. What would you like to eat?"

"The Devil's Delight and a Diet Coke, please."

Milo enjoyed a certain amount of chaos, and today's activity at Nonies provided it. The restaurant was calmer now. The victim of the fight had fled. More people were arriving for lunch. The kitchen was humming with calm activity. His Devil's Delight was set down in front of him when a tall man wearing a black sweater and jeans emerged from the hallway. He stood to the right of Milo, rubbing his knuckles, staring out over the restaurant.

He turned, noticing Milo for the first time. "Oh, hello. Welcome to Nonies. I'm Kick DeJong," he offered his hand. "Did you see all that?"

Milo nodded after taking the first bite of his sandwich.

"I'm sorry for the disturbance. Of course, I insist on comping your meal and getting you moved you to a better table."

"I like this table!" Milo mumbled after swallowing. "Thanks for the floor show."

Kick smiled. "Yeah, it won't be repeated. That guy is forever banned from my restaurants, Mister ah?"

"Rathkey, Milo Rathkey. I do have one request, though."

"Sure."

"Stop taking my sandwich off the menu. I'm tired of complaining."

DeJong looked at Milo's plate. "Devil's Delight? I know. You and a lot of people. When we created that sandwich, we thought it would be a one month special. Now we can't lose it."

"Why would you want to?"

"We like to turn over the menu, keep things fresh."

"Fresh is overrated."

"Well, Mr. Rathkey, enjoy your lunch." Kick stepped back into the hallway between the kitchen and his office and motioned to a young man in too-tight jeans and suit coat, who hustled over from the bar area. "Raf Bianchi, the guy I just threw out, is to be kept out of the restaurant. If you see him, muscle him out, then call the cops."

"Yes, sir."

Milo smiled to himself. The kid didn't look like he could muscle a third grader.

Kick returned to his office. Milo's server reappeared and announced his meal was on the house. He left a generous tip, bundled up, and went back out into the cold.

Pop-Up Dinner, Drop Down Dead

Milo thought he should have ordered a dessert just in case that Raf guy returned for round two. He cranked the Honda, enjoying the warmth of the heater. Edging out into the street, he steered toward Lakesong and his fabulous old library to continue reading about murder and mayhem.

2

The excited chatter of patrons' voices grew as bundled guests arrived, took in the beautiful multicolored banyan tree, and were escorted to their tables. This was the third and final night of Martha and Gabby's pop-up dinners they called Travels. Breanna, Martha's sister, escorted Milo to his table.

"I'm earning money for my Atacama trip," she told him.

For a moment, he sat alone. Lakesong's co-owners, Agnes and Sutherland, were flying in from Hawaii on their private jet. Financial advisor Creedence Durant and author Ron Bello were also expected but had not yet arrived.

Milo ordered a vodka gimlet from Breanna, glanced at the menu on the table, and began to check out the crowd. Not easy as plants and bushes around the tables afforded privacy with a tropical feel in the middle of a Minnesota winter. The multicolored leaves of the banyan tree gave the illusion of dining in a tropical rain forest. The lights filtered through the leaves as soft drumbeats completed the theme of the evening. *Well done, Martha.*

A different waiter brought Milo's drink. "Where's Breanna?" Milo questioned.

"Her twenty-year-old self is not old enough to deliver an alcoholic beverage in Minnesota," the waiter snipped. "Order takers wear t-shirts with the stars of the Southern Cross. That's all they can do. Full waiters, such as myself, wear glorious birds of paradise on our t-shirts." He swept his hand over his colorful shirt. "We take alcoholic orders and deliver them."

Milo took a sip. "Well, she ordered correctly."

A loud, angry shout from behind took Milo's attention away from the waiter, who flew away to another table. Milo stood to check out the ruckus, only to see Creedence being escorted to his table by Jamal, Martha's brother.

"Is somebody yelling at you, Milo? Do they want you to leave?" Creedence asked as he arrived at the table.

"I was just checking it out, but I can't see crap through these ferns. I know it wasn't directed at me, but I'm not so sure about you."

Creedence stretched his portly frame. "I can see over the ferns. If the shout came from the people at the table behind us, they all seem calm now. I don't like my pop-up food with chaos."

"Your drink order, sir?" Jamal asked.

"Whiskey neat. Ah, Milo, I see your housemates on the horizon."

Agnes and Sutherland rushed into the building, stopped, and began to search for familiar faces. Breanna rescued them, leading them to their table. Milo turned. "They look tan but crazed. I doubt they've even been home," Milo said.

"We made it!" Agnes said, breathless, as she reached the table. "I didn't want to miss this. Look at everything! It's beautiful! So tropical, like we never left Hawaii. I know the theme is Papua New Guinea, but…"

Milo turned to Sutherland, who was helping Agnes with her coat and chair. "Did you know the theme was New Guinea?"

"Of course. Everyone knew that," Sutherland said.

"I didn't know. Creedence, did you know?"

"I don't want chaos, Milo, but I would suggest you read the menu more carefully. You need to read things people give you, such as my financial reports."

Milo picked up his menu. "Let's see what the evening has in store."

Full waiter, Mr. Snippy, took drink orders from Agnes and Sutherland before flying away. Milo questioned the whereabouts of Ron, but no one knew. Everyone commented on the menu, discussed their choices, and tried to keep an eye out for Ron, but it was tough over the tall plants. Drinks were delivered. The catch-up conversation was jovial. The evening was off to a great start.

The lights flickered and the soft, rhythmic background sounds stopped. Chefs Martha and Gabby stepped up onto an elevated area in the center of the room; their eyes met in an *it's time* gesture. Looking out over the room, they were thrilled to see a third night of seats filled with eager patrons. Martha looked at the microphone in her hand and attempted to hand it to Gabby, who shook her head. Each had taken one night to do the welcome speech and Gabby just elected Martha to do the third night.

"Ladies and gentlemen, I'm Chef Martha Gibbson, resident chef at the Lakesong Estate, and this is my friend, Chef Gabby Nguyen. You know her as the culinary magician at Va Veni."

Gabby took a small bow to scattered applause.

Martha continued, "Welcome to the final night of Travels, our pop-up dinner and something new for Duluth. Tonight, we hope to transport you out of the snow and cold to the southern hemisphere, where some of the delicacies of New Guinea await. Gabby?"

Chef Gabby Nguyen took the mic. "Forget the nasty weather outside. Tonight, we find ourselves under the constellation of the Southern Cross."

She looked up, as did the patrons. As Gabby's arm glided across the ceiling, a sparkling light display came to life, showing through the leaves of the banyan tree. There was a collective, "Ahhh."

"We start with a Papua New Guinea staple appetizer, Kaukau, the southern hemisphere's version of chips and salsa. A mash of sweet potato, coconut milk, orange juice, ginger, garlic, and a touch of smoked paprika."

Servers dressed in birds of paradise and southern crosse t-shirts began quickly placing dishes in front of the guests. The rhythmic soft sounds began again as Martha and Gabby moved from table to table, chatting with guests, and thanking them for coming.

The front door opened, creating an unwelcome wind tunnel of cold air. Ron Bello stepped in. Darian, Martha's

Pop-Up Dinner, Drop Down Dead

youngest brother, was given the job of door monitor. He rushed to slam the door shut against the cold air.

Unescorted, Ron spent the next five minutes pinging from table to table, trying to find Milo and company. Breanna retrieved him and guided him through the foliage to the Lakesong table just as Martha arrived. Ron, in his larger-than-life manner, grabbed her around the waist with one arm and kissed her hello while sliding into the only empty chair. "Forgive me for being late. I took a wrong turn at Indonesia, but Breanna saved me."

"All of my favorite people!" Martha exclaimed. "Even the late ones like Mr. Bello. Ron, I'm sorry, but we do not have the Rathkey-McKnight Scotch."

Sutherland held up his hand, produced a small silver flask, and asked for glass.

"How? We haven't even been home," Agnes said.

Smiling, Sutherland said he stashed it in the car before they left for Hawaii. Two glasses were provided, and Sutherland poured for both him and Bello.

"Well, Mr. Rathkey. How have you been faring in my absence?" Martha asked.

"I was called upon to sample a number of unique Chinese dishes, making sure each was seasoned properly. I am exhausted."

"You picked up takeout from the Chinese Dragon." Martha shook her head.

"I did not!" Milo insisted. "They delivered."

Sutherland smirked. "In Milo's mind, that makes it not take out."

"Do you know you have a tree in the middle of your restaurant?"

"Yes, Mr. Rathkey. This place used to be an Asian restaurant with big bowls of food that were supposed to be shared. Good idea, wrong time," Martha said. "Covid. The people who own the building were more than happy to rent it out to us for our dining experience."

"It doesn't explain the tree," Milo insisted.

"It's a banyan, a fig tree native to many Asian countries. Asian restaurant, Asian tree."

Sutherland laughed. "Years from now, Milo will solve a murder based on the knowledge you have given him about this banyan tree."

"Well, this is all spectacular, Martha," Agnes said. "The lighting, the tree, the music, everything. Loving the first course."

Gabby had moved to a table that was reserved for one of her best customers at VaVena, Kick DeJong, and his crowd. She spied four empty seats. "Who's missing?"

Kick drained his drink and looked over his shoulder. "They're here. They travel in herds."

Gabby turned to see the three women making their way through the crowded room. She recognized Jess, Kick's wife, and Emma, her younger sister. The third woman was a mystery until they reached the table, and she wrapped her arms around Reese Winterhausen's neck. "Reesy Peesy, I missed you so much!"

Reese, another member of the group, untangled himself. "Poppie, you were only gone for ten minutes."

Pop-Up Dinner, Drop Down Dead

Without an introduction, Gabby deduced that Poppie was Reese's latest young thing. The group often frequented VaVena and usually came with drama.

Raf Bianchi flagged a waiter, ordered a drink, then approached the table. Sizing it up, he decided that Emma would be his first conquest tonight.

"Ah, the lovely Miss Emma," Raf called, hoping she would turn away from her sister Jess to greet him. She didn't.

Rushing around the table, pushing ferns out of his way, he stumbled on the pretext of pulling out her chair, but his free hand moved down the young woman's back and began inching around toward her breast. Emma turned, grabbed Raf's arm, and wrenched it behind his back.

"Ow!" Raf yelled. "What the hell!"

People at the adjoining tables stopped their conversations to look. Reese Winterhausen stood, pushing his chair back with his legs. "Raf! Time for you to go!"

Emma loosened her grip on his arm and pushed him back before letting go. Raf toppled as he lurched away, knocking over a small fern. "I was just trying to be a gentleman, bitch." As Raf shuffled to the empty seat next to Kick, all eyes followed him.

Kick gave him an angry stare. "Raf, shut it down!"

Raf shrugged, slapped Kick on the back. "Sure, old buddy." He steadied himself with the back of Kick's chair, dropping something into Kick's jacket pocket.

Jess snapped at her husband. "Shut it down? That's it? This predator fondles my sister in front of everyone, and that's all you have to say?" Jess stood and moved to the back of her husband's chair. "This is now my chair. Move over," she ordered Kick.

Kick sighed, stopping Gabby as she walked past. "Gabby, I'm going to need a double shot of whiskey…yesterday."

Gabby raised her hand, and the waiter assigned to the DeJong table nodded.

Kick scraped his chair back, then shifted one spot over. Jess remained standing, preparing herself to endure a dinner with her inebriated husband on one side and Raf Bianchi, a man she despised on the other.

Poppie, clearly miffed at being ignored by Reese's lack of attention, turned and leaned into Bob Young. "Would you mind if we changed places? You sit next to Reese. He's so annoying tonight. I'd rather put space between us and talk to you."

"That will put you next to Raf, and he's a pig," Young warned.

"I can handle myself. Besides, I know he's a nobody. I don't know you that well. You might be a somebody."

Bob wondered how he got so lucky. She was gorgeous. He couldn't move over fast enough.

"Jess wants to be close to me, Kick," Raf sneered, stand-ing and offering to pull Jess' chair back from the table. "You should be jealous." He stumbled, falling up against Jess. She pushed him away, giving him a *drop dead* look.

"Aw Jess, you don't love me?" Raf reacted to Jess' obvious rebuff.

One of the servers arrived with two drinks. Kick grabbed his whiskey and downed it in one gulp. Raf motioned for his drink to be placed by his plate as he sat down.

Pop-Up Dinner, Drop Down Dead

Gabby, attempting to defuse the drama, stood behind Poppie to introduce herself.

Jess smiled. "Oh, Gabby, we know you. This appetizer is delicious, as usual."

"It's just sweet potatoes," Raf grumbled. "Any peasant can do this."

Gabby kept smiling.

"Raf, shut up!" Bob Young barked. "You cook swill, and you're a freeloading bastard."

Raf continued his belligerence—his volume increasing. Bob stood and grabbed and squeezed Raf's shoulders. "Shut up before I shut you up."

Reese, having had enough of everyone at the table, peered over at the twisted branches of the banyan tree. "Gabby, how long do you have this space?" he asked.

"We have it through the weekend, Reese."

"I'd like to come in and sketch some things here. I'm designing a new logo for a client and I'm getting ideas from this tree."

"I know all about banyan trees," Raf claimed. "The leaves are edible, and the sap is used for gum." He puffed up, expecting this bit of knowledge to impress the table, especially Emma. "You gotta watch out for the gum, though. Some people are allergic. You know, fall over and die stuff."

On the other side of the green fronds, at the Lakesong table, Sutherland's phone erupted just as the appetizer plates were being collected.

"Emergency mortgage?" Milo joked, referencing Sutherland's real estate business.

Agnes laughed and hugged Sutherland's arm.

"Ha ha, very funny," Sutherland admonished, looking at the caller ID. "It's the Duluth public works department."

"Emergency sewer repair?" Milo couldn't resist. "Glad to see that second job is paying off."

Sutherland pressed the green button. "Hello? Yes. Yes. No one." There was a pause. "I understand. I'll head that way now."

Agnes groaned. "Nooo!"

Sutherland hung up. "I know, but the city's worried. The rain is about to freeze."

"And they're calling every citizen to encourage them to ice skate home?" Milo asked, looking at his phone. "No call yet."

"They called to borrow Goliath," Sutherland stated firmly. "The agreement between Dad and the city when he bought Goliath was that the city could use it when they deemed necessary."

"Your father bought a half-track? Why?" Ron asked.

"My father thought it would be fun for the estate. The city no longer had room for it. They only used it once or twice a decade. My dad had a lot of whimsy. We McKnight men are known for our whimsey," he said, locking eyes with Agnes.

Agnes nuzzled into Sutherland when Milo piped up. "I know I have New Guinea food written all over me, but duty calls. One of us must sacrifice for the good of the city. I'll go and get Goliath out of the utility garage."

Sutherland narrowed his eyes. "You just want to drive the beast on the hills, don't you?"

Milo feigned shock. "Me? Drive Goliath? On hills that could become a frozen death plunge into Lake Superior?"

"They won't let you do it. I read the insurance package. If the city is using it, only city personnel can drive it."

Pop-Up Dinner, Drop Down Dead

"I, sir, am a consultant to the Duluth CITY police department."

"It won't help."

Agnes began to rub Sutherland's back. "Let him go! You stay." Agnes insisted. "But Milo, be careful."

Milo sought out Martha to explain his absence and ask her to bring one beef entrée home. On his way out, he passed the large round table that had the outburst earlier. He did recognize the owner of Nonies and the scruffy guy who he hit and kicked out. Odd, he thought, but Milo was on a mission.

§

City officials were right to be concerned. The pelting rain was gaining heft and morphing into sleet as Milo reached the gates of Lakesong. He left the gates open for the city truck, tucked his Honda away in the garage, and did a quick change of clothes, scrapping his dress shoes for boots. He grabbed his Air Force parka on the way out to wait under the garage overhang for the city truck.

The truck arrived minutes later, with Milo stepping into the driveway, flagging the driver by the steps. Hopping into the truck, Milo said, "Drive around the house to the back."

"I'm Ted," the driver said.

"I'm Milo. Have you driven Goliath before?"

"Nope, any tricks?"

"You have to double clutch it into second," Milo said, looking at the man. He appeared to be in his fifties. A good age to know about double clutching.

"Not a problem," Ted said.

"Also, it's best to let Goliath warm up."

Ted nodded.

"I can drive it," Milo offered.

"No can do. Insurance."

§

The waiters began taking dinner orders—entrée choices of either Raining Fire Stew or MuMu. The menu had described the stew as containing short ribs, peanut butter, carrots, taro root, sweet potato, onion, thyme, and cayenne pepper served in a deep wooden bowl. MuMu was seared chicken and pork belly, with pineapple, sweet potato, taro root, carrot, sweet plantain, coconut milk, and lime juice cooked in banana leaves, all served in a pineapple half.

"What? Are you trying to kill me?" Raf charged at full volume. "Peanuts are a death food. Allergies. No real chef uses peanut butter." He downed his drink, then turned to their assigned waiter and ordered another.

Gabby heard the yelling, cringed, and rushed over to the DeJong table, trying to defuse yet another outburst. "That's why we have two choices, Raf." Gabby placed a large plastic yellow number two by Raf's plate, indicating he was to get the MuMu. "We wouldn't want you to perish."

Jess immediately ordered the peanut butter ladened stew while throwing a death stare at Raf. "It sounds delicious."

Bob Young, amused by Jess' taunting of Raf, ordered the same, echoing his love of peanut butter. Poppie did the same.

"Great," Raf blustered. "I'm surrounded by peanut butter. This is bad. I may have to move over and sit by my lovely Emma."

Pop-Up Dinner, Drop Down Dead

Bob sneered. "Not on your life. Read the table, Raf. You're the only one with entrée two. We must all be trying to kill you, even your lovely Emma."

After being served, everyone savored the stew, making overly loud comments about how the peanut butter *made* the dish. Kick did not join in the joke. He drank another double, pushed his full plate of food away, and closed his eyes.

After downing his seared chicken, and fourth whisky, Raf received a text message on his phone. "I..I..gotta go. I gotta go now," he told the table as he tripped over his chair in an effort to race to the exit. Without waiting for a response, he rushed out the door of the restaurant, pushing Darian aside.

"What's going on?" Kick jerked awake.

Jess snarled. "Nothing."

Raf ran to his car. He was unlocking his door when two large men came up behind him, each one grabbing an arm.

"Hey! Hey! Watcha doing?" Raf yelled, breaking one arm free.

"Shut up!" One of the men yelled, slapping him across the face hard enough to knock him to the ground. The other man picked him up, punched him hard in the midsection, and pushed him into the back seat of a waiting car. His head slammed into the door frame before he landed.

§

Martha and Gabby huddled together as guests devoured the main course. Martha was looking at her phone. "This storm is getting close. The city says people should be off the roads within the hour. I hate to do this, but I think we need to call it so our guests can get home safely."

"Give me five minutes. Entrees are finished and being cleared. We can box the desserts to go. We have the containers," Gabby said. "I'll get going on that now."

Martha nodded and set her timer. At the alarm, she climbed to the raised platform, turned on her mic and announced that unfortunately the Duluth weather was going to interrupt their evening in the tropics. "Ladies and gentlemen, we have loved having you at Travels. The city has informed us that the rain is beginning to freeze. A sweet ending is being boxed for you at the back table as you leave. Please enjoy Talautu, shredded coconut, pineapple chunk, lime juice, coconut milk and sugar, served in a coconut shell. Enjoy it in the safety of your homes."

As the crowd began to leave, some people rushed out. Others leisurely came up to Martha and Gabby to tell them how wonderful the evening had been and to please include them in the guest list for their next Travel experience.

"It's so cold. Start the heater," Poppie chirped as she followed Reese and jumped into his car.

A dejected Bob Young slid into his truck alone.

Within fifteen minutes, the entire desert carrying pop-up crowd had cleared the parking lot. Martha and Gabby joined them, agreeing to leave the cleanup until after the storm.

As the wind-blown snow swirled around the empty parking lot, only Raf's car remained.

3

Disappointed by Ted's 'no-can-do' reply in Milo's bid to drive Goliath, Milo brandished his police consulting badge just in case it threw more weight. It didn't. It did help in his bid to ride shotgun, however. As Ted and Milo crept along, the streetlights glimmered on the icy road. The half-track turned onto Superior Street as the sleet turned to snow—wet, heavy snow, falling temps, and increasing winds.

Because of Ted's careful creep, several cars zipped past them.

"Idiots! What's wrong with people?" Milo shouted over the roar of Goliath's engines. "There's ice under the snow!"

"People are crazy. They'll be decorating the ditches soon," Ted yelled back.

Ted's radio burst into life. "Kimble, what's your ETA?"

Ted pressed the microphone pinned to his jacket. "We're on Superior Street at Third Avenue East, almost there."

"The plows are waiting for you. The barrier is up at the top of Mesaba to stop anyone dumb enough to drive down."

"10-4."

Ted drove past the sign that in normal weather directed Superior Street traffic up the Mesaba Avenue hill. Milo was about to say, you missed your turn, but stayed quiet watching Ted turn up the hill on the wrong side of the street. He stopped Goliath.

"We clear the down lanes first. We worry about the up lanes later."

Going up the down lanes played well with Milo's need for a bit of chaos.

One of the huge street graders with the plow in the middle pulled up behind them. "We break the ice, and Margy, that plow behind us, will throw it off to the side of the road."

"Margy?" Milo questioned.

"Goliath?" Ted shot back.

"Does something as big and heavy as Margy really need Goliath?" Milo asked.

Ted pointed up the hill. "There's Bert and Ernie."

Through the fog of snow, Milo spotted the hind end of two graders that had slid off the road. "That's why you were called, or rather, your machine. This is just the first street we need Goliath for tonight. We have about twenty roads that are even steeper than this one. I love Duluth, but we are a city that plunges into the lake."

"Let's kick this pig!" Milo yelled.

Ted laughed as he dropped the plow and let out the clutch. Much to Milo's disappointment, Ted continued his creep up the hill. At Lakesong, yelling 'kick the pig' meant flying snow, ice chunks, and wild wind tunnel effects. It was fun.

Tonight, the engine roar was followed by creep, clang, crunch and more creep, clang, crunch. After about ten minutes, they were only about a quarter of the way up the hill. Milo sat back, regretting his eagerness to ride along.

"Not as exciting as you thought?" Ted shouted.

"What are you talking about? I'm ready to pass out from all the action," Milo yelled back as he continued to look up the hill, measuring the lack of progress. A dark shape appeared to be spinning toward them. Milo pointed.

Ted peered through the wiper blades on the window. "What the hell?"

§g

Martha and Gabby had their feet up on the ottomans with their heads back on the overstuffed chairs in Lakesong's family room. Three empty coconut shells were sitting on the coffee table. Agnes was still working on hers. All three ladies were snuggled up in fuzzy throws, watching the falling snow sparkle off the uplighting on the Lakesong terrace. Even with the shortened evening, they declared the pop-ups a success. They had received only positive reviews and empty plates coming back to the kitchen.

"Ladies, let's toast to your new business venture, Travels, and its continued success. A right and proper Lake Superior ice storm calls for Tom and Jerrys. We are in luck. I had some delivered this afternoon."

As Sutherland put dollops of batter into waiting mugs, Martha said, "I remember your father saying he bought his batter from a bakery over in Superior."

"Connolly's," Sutherland said. "The best Tom and Jerry batter in the country." He added a shot of rum and a shot of brandy to three of the four mugs before pouring hot water into the mix. "Connolly's is gone, but someone still makes the batter, and we have it here at Lakesong tonight to celebrate."

Agnes, Martha, and Gabby eagerly accepted the white foamed topped mugs. The sticky mustache that accompanies every Tom and Jerry sip caused yums and giggles all around.

"There is no neat way to enjoy this," Gabby proclaimed.

"I'm starting to relax. It feels wonderful," Martha said. "Gabby, we can't forget to clean up our messy rental restaurant tomorrow."

"I don't know if anything will be moving tomorrow," Sutherland said. "It's snow on ice—couldn't be more slippery. Lots of salt and sand trucks need to do their thing before we mere mortals attempt to drive."

"Gee, we may have to stay here all snuggled up, drinking these cartoon drinks all night," Gabby said, holding up her mug while snuggling deeper into the fuzzy throw.

"Cartoon drinks?" Agnes questioned.

Gabby, who was older than Agnes, laughed. "Tom and Jerry were cartoon characters once upon a time. Tom was the cat, I think, and Jerry was a mouse. They fought all the time, in a friendly manner."

"Sounds like Sutherland and Milo," Agnes joked.

"I am the mouse, shrewd, evasive," Sutherland insisted as Annie the calico stood up, giving Sutherland a strong meow.

Pop-Up Dinner, Drop Down Dead

"She's saying you just described a cat, not a mouse," Agnes laughed.

§

"Car!" Ted yelled on his radio. The dark spinning shape careening toward them was sliding and gaining speed.

Milo braced for a collision. Goliath held strong, barely yielding to the oncoming car. The car grazed the plow with a crunching of metal and bounced away to the left, eventually wrapping itself around a power pole.

Ted's eyes were wide. "You okay?" he asked Milo.

"Yeah, yeah. I expected to feel the crash, but I don't think it damaged us at all," Milo said.

Ted turned and looked down the hill at the twisted metal. The grader operator behind them dropped out of his cab onto the ice in an attempt to cross Mesaba. He didn't make it two steps. He slipped, his entire weight falling backwards.

"Oh, crap!" Ted shouted as a power pole began to lean. It snapped and smashed the car, caving in the roof. The broken power lines began sparking and whipping like electric snakes. An explosion briefly lit up the street and then there was darkness.

Milo leaned across Ted to survey the scene. "Well, that was unexpected. I hope your grader buddy is okay."

"I gotta help him," Ted said.

Milo grabbed him. "Whaddaya gonna do? You can't stand on that ice. He fell down. You gonna join him? I'd have to drive Goliath."

"I can't see him," Ted said. "It's too dark."

Milo unbelted himself, turned, and lifted the top to a utility bench behind the driver. "It's still here!" he announced.

"What's still here?"

Milo handed him a large spotlight, plugging it into an auxiliary power slot.

Ted grabbed the floodlight and began to make a sweeping motion on the now blackened street, looking for his buddy. "I found him," Ted said, watching the grader operator sit up, shaking his head for clarity. The man waved his thanks for the light and scooted backwards on his butt, away from the downed power lines until he reached the grader. Using the plow for stability, he lifted himself up, got his footing on the already plowed section of road, and climbed back into the cab.

"You okay Larry?" Ted asked over the radio.

"Yeah, I think so, just kind of stunned. Dumb move. I don't think the guy in that car is okay, though."

"Guys, what gives?" the public works dispatcher asked.

Ted briefly explained the situation, asking for an ambulance, firetrucks, and the power company. He advised he was going to turn around and clear a path down Mesaba so the emergency vehicles could get up to the smashed car.

"Are the power lines sparking?" the dispatcher asked.

"They were big time. Then a transformer blew. It's blacked out here. I don't see any sparks, but I think they could still be live."

"Stay away from them."

Ted rolled his eyes. "I'm not twelve," he said without keying his mic.

§

Pop-Up Dinner, Drop Down Dead

The day full of fabulous food topped off with Tom and Jerrys was making everyone drowsy. They all agreed multiple times it was late, but no one was moving from their cozy spots in the family room.

Agnes was the first to stand, shaking off the sleepy buzz in her brain. "Gabby, you will love the pink bedroom. It has a great bathtub."

"Bathtub?" Gabby mumbled drowsily. "I was hoping for a bed."

Agnes laughed. "Yes, the room has a bed, too. Oddly, I now judge bathrooms by the availability of a bathtub." Needing to talk to keep herself awake, she continued to share. "When I moved into my husband's bachelor quarters here at Lakesong, they did not include a bathtub forcing me to tippy toe down the hall to the Pink Room. Wonderful for soaking."

"After three days of pop-ups and two Tom and Jerrys, a warm soak fits the bill," Gabby said, smiling at the thought of Agnes tiptoeing down the hall. "Do you still want to use the tub tonight?"

Agnes didn't understand at first, but then smiled. "No, it's all yours now. We remodeled the other side of the house. I have my own bathtub." Agnes beamed with a Cheshire Cat smile.

"My wife made us all assemble on the back lawn and salute the crane as it hoisted the mighty tub up and into the bathroom," Sutherland teased.

Agnes hugged his arm. "No, they brought it up in the elevator. I loved the clapping, but there was no hoisting or saluting."

"It was a glorious day in the history of Lakesong," Martha said, yawning, as she reluctantly joined the mass movement to the pink room. "Gabby, you're in good hands. I'm going to make my way to the cottage. See you all in the morning. Brunch for all. Tenish?"

"You're going out in this weather?" Gabby was shocked. "We can share the Pink Room."

"Thanks, but Lakesong has underground tunnels," Martha said. "One of them leads to my cottage."

"So cool! How can I get a tunnel? I want one."

"The tunnels came with the house," Sutherland said.

"I would love to see that listing," Gabby joked.

Sutherland went into real estate agent mode. "Tidy little Jacobean house, sixteen bedrooms…"

"Not anymore. We took some for our place," Agnes corrected.

"Twelve bedrooms, numerous fireplaces, a lot of bathrooms and, of course, tunnels."

"I'll take it," Gabby said.

"Oh, come on Martha," Agnes said, "have you ever seen the Pink Room?"

Martha laughed. "No, Mrs. McKnight. I don't wander the mansion at night, checking out the rooms."

"That's not you?" Agnes joked. "Sutherland, I think we have a ghost."

Sutherland shook his head. "No ghost, just two cats."

§

Without electrocuting himself, Ted had crunched and plowed enough of Mesaba to allow the fire trucks and power vehicles to reach the crash site. Maneuvering Goliath in front of Margy, Larry's grader once again, he informed dispatch and waited on word to continue his ice breaking up the street.

Pop-Up Dinner, Drop Down Dead

"That car must have been going at least sixty," Milo said.

"This street has a ten percent grade. There's a formula to figure out miles per hour, but I forget what it is. Spinning on its way down didn't slow it, either. I bet he slammed on his brakes to get that spin."

"Idiot."

"Absolutely."

Milo had no desire to continue Goliath's creep, clang, and crunch up the hills of Duluth. The firemen and power crews were out of their vehicles, maneuvering around the crash site.

Milo saw his chance to escape. "It's been fun, Ted. You've got the double clutching down, and I'm really more attracted to lights and sirens. I'm jumping out here."

Ted laughed. "Suit yourself. I avoid lights and sirens. I'm a crunch guy."

As Milo dropped out of the half-track, an ambulance and two police cars were pulling up. He grabbed and hung onto the side of Goliath as he made his way hand-over-hand around the vehicle. Even though the street had been plowed, it was still slippery. Milo's steps were halting as he started to cross the street.

Edging his boots like skis, Milo was making progress when suddenly a tach light blinded him, causing him to falter. "You're somebody, right?" the cop with the tach light hollered.

Milo steadied himself and lifted his consultant's badge.

"Oh, I've seen you around the station. What are you doing here?" she continued to holler.

"I can hear you," Milo barked. "I came from the half-track. We were plowing Mesaba…"

"Why?" she asked, taking out her notebook and pencil.

"Why what?"

"Why were you in the half-track?"

"It's my half-track," Milo said.

She stared at him for more than a comfortable amount of time. "People say you're odd."

"They do? That's odd."

The cop shook her head as if trying to get Milo out of her ears.

"What are you and your tach light doing here in the middle of an ice storm?" Milo asked.

"I'm keeping order."

Milo looked around. "Good idea. Those firefighters can get rowdy."

"I'm also taking witness statements. So, you were in the half-track. Were you driving?"

"No, Ted's driving. I was consulting."

"Consulting what?"

"The double clutch between first and second. That car over there crashed into us." Milo pointed to the car with a pole laying on top of it. "It was spinning down Mesaba."

The cop held up her hand to stop Milo from saying any more. She keyed her radio. "This is one-seven. Is the barricade at the top of Mesaba still in place?"

"Negative, one-seven. Someone crashed through it. We're stationing a patrol car up there now."

"Looks like our victim went through the barricade," she said to Milo. "Did you get a look at the driver?"

Milo thought back to the crash. "It was snowing. We were creeping. Then…"

"What?"

Pop-Up Dinner, Drop Down Dead

"Something was off."

"Did you recognize the driver?"

"Maybe, but there were airbags. It might come to me. The back of my brain has to talk to the front of my brain."

The cop smiled. "See, that's odd. I don't know if I should include that in my notes."

One of the firefighters spotted Milo. "Rathkey! We meet again," he said, shaking Milo's hand.

"Chief Kutka, plane crashes, car crashes, I just can't stay away. This time, I'm a witness. I was just explaining to the officer who is keeping the crowds in order that the car came spinning down the hill, bounced off my half-track, and crashed into that pole over there."

"Your half-track?"

"Yeah, mine. Keeping up my rep. Word on the street is that I'm odd," he said, looking at the cop.

"Mr. Rathkey said he saw the driver for a split second," the cop explained, "but he hasn't talked to his brain yet, so he doesn't know if he recognized the driver."

"You're right, officer," Kutka said. "He is odd."

"I'm standing right here," Milo said.

"I'll catch you later," Kutka said, getting the sign that his crews were beginning the extraction of the body.

The ambulance backed up but drove away. Ten minutes later, the body bus arrived.

"That's not good," the cop said, waving her notebook. "I didn't finish with your version of the accident. You were sitting in the half-track…"

"With Ted, the driver."

"Ted who?"

33

"Ted the driver. Check with public works for more."

"You drove with this man but didn't know his last name?"

"We weren't eloping, just crunching ice. Besides, I'm odd, remember. Everyone knows that."

The policewoman looked at Milo, not sure if he was kidding or not. "Then what?"

"We were moving up the hill, slowly, crunching ice when we saw the car spinning down the hill towards us."

"Did you move to get out of the way?"

"It's a half-track in a snowstorm, not a vespa on a lovely spring evening." Milo's determination to avoid sarcasm had dissipated.

"So, you were crunching when the car hit your vehicle."

"The car bounced off us, traveled sideways across Mesaba, and hit that pole. It was like a pinball game."

"Did you try to assist the driver of the car?"

"No, Larry, behind us, tried but fell when the pole fell. Then Ted No-Name was going to join him on the ground. Being odd but sane, I stopped him. We called it in and now you and I are standing in a snowstorm, and you are taking my statement."

§

Sutherland began his migration to bed. He headed towards the front stairs, his usual way to the second floor.

"I'm not taking the stairs tonight," Agnes said, leading the trio to the hallway by the kitchen. "We're taking the elevator."

"Elevators and tunnels?" Gabby asked.

Pop-Up Dinner, Drop Down Dead

Agnes opened the door to the elevator, causing Gabby to take a step back. "Oh, I forgot to warn you. It's a turn of the last century elevator. Works well and is safe, but is scary when you first see it."

As Gabby walked into the black cast iron cage, she said, "This is creepy. I can see the walls of the shaft."

Agnes closed the scissored gate of the elevator. "I think we are going to have to install a more modern elevator. I don't want little fingers getting caught between the elevator and the shaft."

"Darian and Jamal already know to keep their fingers…"

"We could have guests, Martha. Guests with little children and tiny fingers," Agnes interrupted.

The elevator shook to a stop. "No one knew this helpful iron prison even existed until Milo moved in," Agnes said.

"Milo? Milo Rathkey? So, he lives here too?" Gabby asked.

Agnes nodded, opening the door to the second floor. "Long story, but he owns half this house and the estate. Don't you tell your friends anything, Martha?"

"We talk food."

"Wait," Gabby said, following Agnes. "How did Milo know about the elevator, but you didn't?"

"Part of the long story," Agnes said. "His mother was a cook here. He grew up in this house."

"He also knew about the large catering kitchen in the basement," Martha said, following Gabby. "It's a beauty."

"Oh my, you have to show me," insisted Gabby.

"First, let's show you the Pink Room," Agnes said. Opening the door to the room, she clicked on the light, which flooded the room in a dusty rose hue.

Gabby took in the pink flowered wallpaper, the dark, carved, fourposter bed, and the fireplace along one wall. "This is not my house."

"Please feel free to use my old friend, the lovely clawed soaking tub in the en suite," Agnes said.

"You're tiny like my sister, Breanna," Martha said. "I will send her over with a change of clothes for the morning. We're going to be trapped here until the roads are cleared."

"Oh, gee whiz. Poor me," Gabby joked. "Can I help with brunch?"

"No, you are a guest."

Gabby glided further into the rose hue.

"The clothes will be left outside the door," Martha said.

"There are towels and night clothes in the dresser. Oh, and we have two cats, Annie and Jet. They're friendly but they wander. Just keep your door closed."

"Remember. Sleep in. When you wake, your first mission is to find the kitchen and the Morning Room," Martha said. "If you get lost, text me. One hint. It's off the family room." Looking at Gabby's blank face, Martha was clearer, "The Tom and Jerry room."

Agnes and Martha left their guest and walked to the elevator, where they bid each other goodnight. Martha descended to the basement, taking the tunnel to her cozy cottage. Agnes turned and walked to the new apartment, opening the double doors. "Sutherland?" she called.

"In the bedroom," he answered.

Agnes crossed the new living room, still not believing the home they created. She jumped on the bed and snuggled up to Sutherland. "Big day."

Pop-Up Dinner, Drop Down Dead

"Oh, I've started your bath if you still want it."

She kissed him. "You know me so well. Will you marry me?"

"Sure. Loved doing it the first time," Sutherland said, stretching out on their California King.

As Agnes got up and crossed to her bath, she said over her shoulder, "Those striped pajamas are the cat's meow."

"Cat's meow? Are we hankering back to the twenties?"

"I don't know," Agnes shouted from the bathroom. "Ask those pajamas."

"I thought you liked these. You gave them to me for Christmas."

"Oh, Sutherland. I got them as a joke!"

"Good. I don't really like these pajamas. I'm changing back into my sweatshirt and shorts."

Agnes stepped into the tub. "Nice and warm. Perfect temperature. I'll come out when the water begins to cool," she said.

"The heater is on," Sutherland laughed. "You could become a prune."

After a half hour, Agnes re-emerged from the bathroom, snuggled under the covers, and laid her arm across Sutherland's chest. "Have I told you how much I love you today?"

"Yes, this morning, on the way to the pop-up dinner, and now. But you can keep saying it because I love to hear it," Sutherland said.

Agnes snuggled closer and mumbled, "Words of affirmation."

"What?"

"It's my love language to you," Agnes said.

"You've mentioned that before. What's my love language to you?"

"Acts of service. You started my bath. I didn't ask you, but you knew I would love it. You did it because you love me, and I keep saying I love you because you love hearing it."

"Well," Sutherland said, "this works out quite well. I do nice things for you, and you tell me how wonderful I am."

Pulling the comforter up to her chin, Agnes whispered, "Let's listen to the storm. I love feeling safe and snuggy warm in our own little house, within our big wonderful house."

For Sutherland, who grew up in Lakesong, the security of the house had always been a given. However, he realized that Agnes, growing up in other people's houses, had never had that security.

They listened to the whistling wind blow snow against the windows.

He hugged her. "Lakesong loves you, and I love you always."

4

Milo's feet were cold. This was not his warm Lakesong bedroom. As he began to move his hip and shoulders ever so slightly, he found them to be stiff and cranky. He squinted one eye open. Midcentury orange and large happy plants assaulted his senses—definitely not Lakesong. He edged up to a seated position, put two cold feet on the floor, and blinked several times. Outside the glass doors, the storm was still at full strength with high whistling winds and blowing snow slapping up against the windows. Running his fingers through his curly brown hair, he stretched out his shoulders, then stopped abruptly, thinking he was turning into Gramm. A friendly voice distracted him.

"I'm charging you with vagrancy," the desk sergeant joked.

"Fine. Are the cells warm? Do I get breakfast?" Milo asked as he put on his boots.

"Yes and no—warm cells. You just missed breakfast."

"How did you get here?" Milo asked.

"I never left. As soon as you get off that couch, I have dibs on it."

"Looking at this mess, we may be the only people in today," Milo said, watching the storm out the window again.

"The snowmobiles are out picking up key personnel. They scheduled you for the second shift until I informed them you were already here."

Standing and continuing his Gramm stretches, he announced, "I'm going to the vending machines; can I get you anything?"

"Already been. That was breakfast. I only said you missed it to make you feel bad."

Milo grabbed his parka and trudged his way down the hall to the lunchroom. He was thinking waffles. He would save his favorite vending machine food, burritos, for lunch. Luck was on his side. One machine held small cartons of waffles. He opted for two of those and rued the fact there was no butter. They came with small packets of syrup, but to Milo, butter was king.

After nuking the waffles, he walked into the empty bullpen area and was pleasantly surprised to find freshly made coffee. He poured a cup and sat down at the desk he had claimed more than a year ago—squatter's rights.

"Oh, good! I wasn't sure if I made an entire pot only for myself," Officer Kate Preston said as she walked toward Milo.

"How did you get here?" Milo asked.

"I'm part of the snowmobile brigade first shift. I took a snowmobile home. How about you?"

Pop-Up Dinner, Drop Down Dead

"I slept here last night after getting dropped off by a squad that had been called to the accident."

"You were in an accident?"

"I wasn't. Goliath was."

"Goliath?"

"A World War Two half-track with a plow. The city borrows it from time to time."

"Borrows it? You own a vehicle from World War Two?"

"Yes. Well, me and Sutherland. Wait, me and Sutherland and Agnes. We own Goliath."

As they talked, more personnel began to dribble into the bullpen, delivered by the second shift platoon of police snowmobile taxis.

"I was assigned to pick up the deputy chief," Preston said. "He was pleasant. I never met him before."

An extremely ill-tempered Lt. Gramm shuffled into the room with both hands on the small of his back. Dressed in a large, light gray snowmobile suit, he looked like the smiling dough boy's evil twin. "I hate snowmobiles!" he shouted.

Following him, Sgt. Robin White walked in and shed her bright yellow gloves and matching snowmobile suit. "It was a most gentle ride. I stayed on soft snow, avoided all ice, and didn't go fast. A baby could have slept on that snowmobile."

Gramm grunted.

"Why does Ernie get the boring snowmobile suit?" Milo asked. "If he fell off, we wouldn't find him until spring."

"Gray is departmental issue. A similar one would have been delivered to you if you had needed to be picked up," White said. "Speaking of that, how are you here?"

"He came in after his half-track was in an accident," Preston said.

Gramm was pulling his shoulders back against the open-door jams of his office, loosening his neck and shoulders. "This day is so wrong. Somebody get me coffee!" He disappeared into his office.

"Milo? You had an accident?" White asked.

"Well, yes and no. But first, let's watch Gramm try to get out of his snowsuit," Milo suggested.

"It could be amusing," White agreed.

White and Milo walked in and sat down in their usual chairs. Preston brought Gramm a cup of coffee, left to get a chair, and returned. For the next five minutes, the trio silently watched Gramm extricate himself from his snowmobile suit and stretch every muscle in his body. Finally free, he sat down at his desk, looked at the three, and asked, "What?"

"Milo's half-track was in an accident last night," White said.

"Why should I care?"

Before Milo could answer, Gramm held his hand up. "Wait. Is that half-track enclosed?"

"Correct," Milo said.

"Half-track. Tracks designed to go through mud and snow."

"Right again."

"The next storm, you pick me up."

White rolled her eyes but said nothing.

"This accident of yours. Any fatalities?" Gramm asked.

"Yeah, but not me." Milo explained the accident and the subsequent squashing of the car by the power pole. "I only saw the driver for a second. It was odd."

Pop-Up Dinner, Drop Down Dead

"Milo, with you, everything is odd," Gramm said. "What was odd this time?"

"Not a clue."

"Good. We're investigating it not as odd, but as suspicious," Gramm was about to explain when his phone rang. It was the deputy chief. "Yes sir," Gramm listened for a few minutes. "Yes, Officer Preston is a safe and efficient driver."

White's eyes widened, remembering Preston's dangerous flight through the air on a motorcycle, ramming into a fleeing suspect.

"She does have motorcycle experience," Gramm added. "Yes sir," he said again. "Well, sir, we'd love to help but we're investigating a suspicious death last night on…" he looked at Milo.

"Mesaba." Milo mouthed.

"Mesaba Avenue. A car busted through a barrier and careened down the hill, running into some plowing equipment. Preliminary investigation points to a homicide."

Milo looked at White, who shrugged.

Gramm hung up. "Okay then. We are officially investigating Milo's accident, unless we all want to jump on snowmobiles and respond to missing cats and motorcycles up a tree."

"Oh," White said. "Yes! We have to investigate a car slipping down a steep hill in an ice storm. After all, our esteemed consultant thinks something was odd."

"I think the snowmobile thing sounds like more fun," Preston objected.

The silence was deafening.

§

Gabby was too exhausted for a tub soak last night, but found it relaxing this morning. After the soak, she peeked out of her door to find light blue leggings, a soft, white sweater, and fuzzy Ugg boots neatly placed in a shopping bag. She looked at herself in the mirror and thought Martha's sister could be her personal shopper. Before conquering the massive mansion, she downed two Tylenol for minor muscle aches from three days of pop-up dinners. By the time the adventure of finding breakfast was over, she would be good to go.

Gabby made only one wrong turn in search of the morning room. She found herself in an old library. Turning back on her heels, she roamed around the gallery for a few minutes, watching the snow pelt the windows as she took in the park-like room. "Blowing snow outside, summer inside, birds that looked real, and one calico cat in a Guiana tree. Incredible," she said to herself.

As if to guide her, a sleek black cat cut her off, weaving in and out of her legs before walking straight in the opposite direction through the gallery.

"You must be one of the friendly wanderers I was warned about. Should I follow you?" she asked.

Jet responded with a squeak.

Gabby followed the cat into the family room. She recognized this room from last night. Jet, being a kind soul, turned and squeaked again. Again, Gabby followed.

"This must be it! Thank you furry fellow with yellow, golden eyes," she said to Jet upon arriving in the hearth room and the roaring fire. This time, she and Jet both followed their noses to the kitchen, where Martha was frying bacon.

"Good morning," Gabby said.

"You found us." Martha smiled.

"I had a friendly furry guide," Gabby said, looking around. "He's gone!"

"That would be Jet. Annie would have ignored you. She's a calico. Jet may have wandered back into the gallery, although the sound of the wind whistling around the dome scares him. He's probably curled up by the hearth room fire. If you turn around and go back, passing the fire, you will find Agnes, Sutherland, and coffee. But before you go, what would you like for breakfast?"

"What are you offering?"

"I normally eat earlier, but I slept in today too, so I'm pampering myself with eggs Benedict."

"Oooh, that sounds perfect."

"Eggs benedict for two. Would you like juice?"

"Just coffee. Thanks Martha." Gabby, as instructed, turned on her heel, walked back through the hearth room into the morning room.

"Good morning; you found us!" Agnes said.

"The eternal coffee urn is over there on the cart," Sutherland said.

Gabby helped herself to the coffee, two sugars, and a spot of cream.

"Sit anywhere," Agnes said. "Milo is not with us this morning."

Gabby sat down next to Agnes. "Where is he today? Milo, I mean."

Sutherland leaned forward and whispered, "There is no Milo here. He's Agnes' imaginary friend."

"He is my friend—our friend, but not imaginary!" Agnes protested.

"Who's not imaginary?" Martha asked as she arrived with a plate of eggs Benedict with smoked salmon.

"Milo…"

Martha feigned concern and said to Sutherland, "So, it's happening again. I thought she was cured."

"Martha! You're supposed to be on my side!"

Martha laughed and said to Gabby, "The imaginary Mr. Rathkey sent me a text: *Won't be back for breakfast. Car crash. Goliath is fine.* He is probably at the police station."

Gabby did a double take. "He's arrested?"

"No, he does the arresting," Sutherland said. "He's a detective and a consultant with the police on murders. His solutions are rather…there was a book…"

"Oh, my goodness. That book about Harper Gain? Milo Rathkey is the guy who figured it all out!" Gabby said. "I knew Harper Gain. He ate at the restaurant."

"So, Sutherland, what does *car crash, Goliath is fine* mean to you?" Agnes asked.

"I can't translate Milo into normal human discourse. I'm not going to worry about it."

"Martha? Where are you going?" Agnes asked.

"To eat my breakfast," Martha said.

"Bring it in here. Sit down," Agnes said.

Martha hesitated, then left, returned with a second plate of eggs benedict. She poured a cup of coffee and sat down next to Gabby.

"Will you people adopt me?" Gabby asked. "This place is way more fun than my house."

Sutherland's phone rang. He excused himself to take the call in the hearth room.

"I'm glad Breanna's clothes fit," Martha said.

"Oh, thank you both. The soak this morning and these cute warm clothes have perked me right up. I feel twenty again."

"Do you swim?" Agnes asked Gabby.

"Yes."

"Good, after breakfast, if you feel like it, we'll go swimming."

Gabby looked out the morning room windows. Snow was still being hurled against the glass by the wind. "Not quite my kind of pool weather."

Agnes smiled. "It's indoor and heated."

Martha added, "It's lovely. Saltwater…needs to be experienced, especially in a snowstorm."

"I suppose you have suits too, just like nightgowns and robes."

"Yes, we do. Suits, towels, and a coffee bar. Well, a bar, but the main liquid is water and coffee these days."

Sutherland returned. "The city needs to use Goliath another day. I got the full story about Milo's cryptic message. Somebody broke through a barrier on Mesaba and bounced off Goliath. Then got crushed by a power pole."

"Oh, that's bad," Agnes said.

"Agreed."

"Who's Goliath?" Gabby asked.

"Not a who, a what," Martha said. "It's another long story. All I know is that Jamal and Darian can't wait for snowstorms and Milo's call."

"Yeah," Gabby said, taking a sip of coffee. "A lot more fun than my house."

§

"If we're investigating this *murder*, let's start at the beginning. Gotta name?" Gramm asked, looking at Milo.

"Nope," Milo said.

"You kill a guy and didn't catch his name?"

"I didn't kill him. Death by snowstorm."

"Unfortunate accident or suicide?" Preston asked.

"No!" everyone chorused together.

"As your boss, I order you not to say accident or suicide out loud. Both get us directing traffic or waist deep in snow saving squirrels. Now then, Milo, you killed a guy, but don't know who he was."

"I wasn't driving, Ted was."

"Ted who?" Gramm asked.

"Don't have a clue."

"Ted's your accomplice and you don't know his last name? Did you buy him off of Amazon?"

"Ted works for the city. Goliath was being rented by the city. I was along to teach Ted how to double clutch into second."

White broke in. "What we know so far is Milo killed a guy and is making up some lame story about a guy named Ted."

"Couldn't we give him a better name?" Preston asked. "Maybe something French like Antoine."

"I like that," White said. "Milo and this French guy, Antoine, were recklessly careening up Mesaba…"

"Careen up?" Milo questioned. "How do you careen up?"

"He's French. They do weird things," Gramm said, picking up his phone. "Now I'm going to do some real work." He pushed the quick call button for Doc Smith, the medical examiner.

"Smith here," the Doc answered.

"Doc, you're here. Who brought you in?"

"I have my own snowmobile. What can I do for you?"

"Doc Smith on a snowmobile," White whispered to Preston. "Sweet."

"Last night there was a fatal accident and fire on…"

"Mesaba Avenue. I know. I have the body here. Kinda smashed, I'm afraid."

"Any ID."

"Not yet. Why?"

Gramm explained that they were treating it as a suspicious death.

"Ah, snow duty looms and you guys grab onto the first dead body you can find. Looking at the report in front of me, I see your consultant was in the military vehicle at the time of the accident."

"You think Milo killed the guy just to get out of snow duty?" Gramm asked, enjoying the tease on Milo.

"Sure," Smith said.

"Unfortunately, we still need an ID."

"The license plate is missing. I've asked the forensic people to snowmobile out and look for it."

"It's still snowing," Gramm said.

"Flurries don't kill. Forensics sent Handy, the guy who takes a million pictures."

"He's actually pretty good," Milo said.

"Explain to me how this fantasy homicide happened," Doc Smith requested.

"Milo here. Ted, from the city, and I were crunching the ice going up Mesaba when this guy comes ripping down the hill, slams into the plow, and bank shots into the power pole that fell on him. The officer assigned to keep order called me odd and said the guy had broken through the barrier at the top of the street."

"A real barrier like portable concrete walls, or a flimsy sawhorse?" Smith asked.

"Sawhorse is my bet."

"I need to finish the autopsy. Good news for you, there are some irregularities."

The good doctor hung up.

5

The delightful, lazy, snow day continued after the long, leisurely breakfast. The group moved into the gallery to talk and watch fat flurries hit the glass dome. Fog blanketed the back lawn hiding the lake.

Martha broke the reverie, wanting to crunch the numbers on the pop-ups and start thinking about the next Travel gastro experience. Gabby begged off the number crunching, wanting to experience the swimming pool in the snowstorm for inspiration, she claimed.

Agnes was tired and fine with just spending the day resting and reading in the gallery, but Gabby really did seem excited about the pool. After all, Agnes did offer. She led the way from the morning room down to the basement. They walked past the furnaces, past the wine cellar, and trekked up the three steps to the indoor pool. "Sorry for the circuitous hike, but it is a basement to a very large house. There is a more direct way, but it requires going through one of Milo's closets."

She began explaining all about Sutherland's parents, John and Laura, and how Laura recreated the pool and gave herself direct access. She was the swimmer.

"Why does the closet belong to Milo?" Gabby asked.

"It came with the master bedroom. Sutherland has always claimed the second floor since he was a teen, so he offered the master to Milo after Sutherland's dad willed Lakesong to both of them. Milo did offer it back to us after we married, but we wanted to create our own home within Lakesong."

Agnes opened the pool door, letting the smell of saltwater sweep over them. Gabby stopped, her attention being taken by yet another glass dome and the flurries swirling above it.

"This is unreal!" she exclaimed.

"The closets on the right have suits, towels, and pool toys."

"Toys?" Gabby questioned.

"Yes, some are from little boy Sutherland, some from Martha's sibs. Use them if you like. The changing rooms are next to the closets."

Agnes quickly changed into her usual turquoise tank suit. She left Gabby to filter through the many swimsuits. Agnes was alone as she stepped into the pool, letting the warm water flow over her shoulders—a stark counterpoint to the snow swirling outside the glass dome.

Gabby emerged from her changing room in a fuchsia and neon-green two piece. "I found one in my size!" she shouted as she descended into the pool, using the blue tile steps. "I'm small. My parents were small. I thought I would have to wear a suit with bunnies or daisies, but you had an adult double zero."

"I'm glad you found one, although a few bunnies or daisies are fun sometimes," Agnes quipped. Agnes always thought that suit belonged to Ms. Petite—her pet name for Sutherland's prior fiancé. "This house has hosted many people," she said to Gabby. "No telling how that suit came here."

The two swam, then drifted, pausing for storm gazing. "As much as I'd like to stay in the pool, I'm getting thirsty," Gabby said.

"Me too," Agnes agreed. "Coffee or water?"

"Whatever is easiest." Gabby flopped into one of the lounge chairs. "It's so cold and blustery out there, but my bikinied butt is here swimming in the Caribbean. How can this be?"

"I know. It never ceases to fill me with awe." Agnes handed Gabby a bottled water. "Biscotti?"

"Oh, definitely. You said this house was Sutherland's. Did you grow up in this sort of house, too?"

Agnes' thoughts darted to her vagabond orphan life, but all she said was no.

The two were silent for a bit, sipping their water, crunching on their biscotti, and watching the snowfall. The snow filled the glass panes then slid off, awaiting another collection of snow.

"I'm sorry your dinner was cut short last night by the storm," Agnes said absently. "We really enjoyed the food and the atmosphere. I think you have a winner idea there."

"Thank you. Travels was not interrupted Wednesday or Thursday by foul weather, and we got through enough of last night to declare all three nights successful. At least we've gotten good feedback. I'd like to do it again. Martha will triple check those numbers, but at first glance, we think we made enough to provide a little profit for ourselves and our backer."

"You have a backer?"

"Yes, a great guy. Martha's find. A writer."

"Ron Bello?" Agnes guessed.

"Yes, that's the name. Martha said he had some extra cash and was expecting some more from a new book. He and Martha go way back, I guess."

"Ah, he is a nice guy. My renter."

"Your renter?" Gabby asked. "Does he live here too?"

Agnes laughed. "No, not here. My old house. A cute little bungalow in Lakeside. When Sutherland and I were married, I couldn't say goodbye to it, and Ron needed a place to stay."

"So, you two had to choose between your bungalow in Lakeside or this hovel with an elevator, tunnels, and tons of fun," Gabby joked, looking up to the domed ceiling.

"You joke," Agnes smiled, "but my place had a bathtub in my bathroom. I didn't have to walk the halls to take a bath."

The intercom lit up. "Attention all young residents of Lakesong and surrounding area. This is Goliath speaking. I have two hours before the city needs me again. I am currently parked outside the utility building. All young residents be advised it's first come, first served. Some driving by young residents of Lakesong and surrounding area may be required. Don't tell Martha Gibbson."

"That voice would be Milo's," Agnes said.

The intercom lit up again. "Milo, this is Martha. It will be Darian."

"What about Jamal?" Milo asked.

Pop-Up Dinner, Drop Down Dead

"He's got KP."

"So, now that Goliath thing is back, and Martha's brother gets to ride in it?" Gabby asked.

Agnes gave her a side eye. "More than that, I bet. Darian, who has had a considerable growth spurt since last winter, will be driving that Goliath thing. I know it. Darian knows it and Martha knows but pretends not to."

§

Kick DeJong woke up in the emergency room. He was hooked up to an IV, and he heard beeps. *Where was Jess?* He called out for Jess. A nurse popped through the curtain and in a calm, measured tone, explained where he was. His wife was okay, also being treated. She added the doctor would be in soon to talk to him.

Kick laid back and tried to remember the accident. They were driving home. The snow was really sleet, slapping against the windows. The wipers were trying to keep up, but the weight made it hard.

His Nissan GT-R's all-wheel drive was doing great staying on the road. They were almost home. He cruised through a yellow light. He remembered that. Then some fool t-boned Jess' side of the car. Kick remembered being slammed against the door and airbags punching him from everywhere.

He couldn't see anything. All he heard was Jess groan. He maneuvered his hand to his phone, called 911. Then he blacked out.

Kick's head and body ached. He buzzed the nurse and asked for more pain meds. She left but was gone for too long a time. He needed something now. Raf had slipped him some oxy at dinner. He fumbled in his front pocket until he found two pills and downed them quickly.

A young doctor swung open the curtain. "I'm Dr. Mehta, Mr. DeJong. How are you feeling?"

"I'm achy. I asked the nurse for some pain meds, but she hasn't returned."

"According to your chart, you've been given a significant dose of pain meds."

"Well, they aren't working."

"Where do you feel the pain?"

"All over."

"Mr. DeJong, do you take pain medication regularly?"

"No! Why would you ask?"

"If you're overusing, you could build up a tolerance."

"No, no, nothing like that. I just slammed around that car more than you think I did. What about my wife? Where is Jess?"

§

Satisfied, Gramm tossed his second burrito wrapping in the trash and declared it to be a three pointer as his phone rang.

"Gramm, is homicide having a warm, leisurely day?"

"Yeah, Brenda, nice of you to check on us. What does the head of traffic want with us?"

"I hesitate to interfere with your powerful murder investigation, but I have something you might actually have to investigate." Gramm did not take the bait. "Some woman called us and said she witnessed a traffic accident at the top of Mesaba, Friday night."

"That's terrific, Brenda," Gramm said, suddenly shouting. "Preston, where is that autopsy report?"

Preston looked at White and mouthed, "What report?"

White rotated her hand as if to say, "Play along."

"Got it here, boss!" Preston shouted.

"Is this acting just for me? I'm throwing this call to you, Gramm, because a crash at the top of Mesaba, and a crash at the bottom might be related."

"Related by what? The road?"

"Sure, why not? You're sitting in a warm, dry office, and I'm heading out in this storm for a second time because some idiot thought they could cruise down 24th Avenue West on bald tires."

"I bet that didn't end well," Gramm said.

Brenda Peinovich laughed. "I've been told he bounced off of three parked cars, took out a porch, and finally came to rest on top of a stop sign."

Gramm stretched his neck. Holding his phone to his ear this long made it ache. "Those stop signs aren't cheap," he joked.

"That's what you came up with? Keep enjoying your made-up murder."

"We're busy here, but go ahead and text me that woman's number."

"Already did." Peinovich hung up.

White took a sip of coffee from the communal pot. "Ugh! This stuff is bad!"

"All of your fru fru coffee shops snowed in today?" Gramm smirked.

"We should go over to Milo's place and work. I bet they always have good coffee. Where is he?" White asked.

"He was here," Preston said.

"Some guy from the city hauled him home in that half-track they own. We get drafty snowmobiles, but Milo gets chauffeured in a half-track with a heater."

Preston looked at her phone. "You forwarded a name and number to me, Lieutenant?"

"Yes, I did," Gramm said, stretching his back.

"You should get some physical therapy for that back," White said.

Gramm stared at her. "I'm married to a nurse, thank you very much. If I need medical advice, I can get it at home."

"And what advice does Amy give you?"

"Get physical therapy," Gramm mumbled.

Preston raised her hand.

"What?" Gramm shouted in Preston's direction.

"I have this name and number you forwarded. What am I doing with it?"

"Oh, yeah. I guess you would need that info. Peinovich from traffic called and said this woman witnessed a possible accident at the top of Mesaba Friday night. Might be our guy. Call her. Get the particulars. Report back."

"Got it," Preston said, leaving for her desk.

Gramm's phone lit up. "You know, for a pretend murder case we've got a lot of interruptions. Hello Doc."

"Have I told you how much I love working on a Saturday?"

"You mention it every time you're working on a Saturday."

Pop-Up Dinner, Drop Down Dead

"Good. We have an ID on the car. Handy found the license plate in a snowbank. We have about two hundred and forty pictures of it. The car, a 2009 Prius, belongs to a Ralph Bing." The Doc hung up.

Gramm turned to White. "Get a number for a Ralph Bing. Tell him his car died Friday night."

"Shouldn't we assume that Ralph already knows that, seeing as he was probably in the car when both he and it died?"

"Friday night, a guy crashes through the barricade. I'm thinking there's a chance that car is stolen."

"Got it." White left to make the call.

§

Agnes was still tired. She gave Gabby a brief tour of the wine cellar while securing several bottles of Sutherland's best for dinner. Outside the wine cellar, Agnes caught her heel on the mat. She stumbled and bumped her arm against the outer wall of the hallway.

"Ouch!" she shouted. "What the…?"

One of the bottles shattered against the concrete floor.

"Oh wow. Give me the wine. Check your arm."

Agnes held out the two remaining bottles. Gabby grabbed them to let Agnes check her arm.

"It's scraped but not bleeding. I hit it hard, though. I think it's going to leave a bruise. I didn't really need that today. Let me call Sutherland to come down and clean up this mess."

"I'm glad you're okay, but I wouldn't say the same for the basement. It looks like your wall is coming apart."

Agnes turned to check out the damage. Moving her good arm over the wall, her hand hit a line of bricks that were jutting out. Agnes wiggled her fingers into a small opening that stretched from floor to ceiling. "That's more than a crack. I think it's a door!"

Agnes tugged on the wall with one hand, lost her grip, and fell back.

"Oh, my!" Gabby exclaimed, still clutching the two bottles of wine. "Are you all right?"

"I've been better!" Agnes said. Kicking the broken glass to the side, she steadied herself. Inserting the fingers of both hands, she tugged hard on the wall. Peering into the gap, she mumbled, "Those are steps."

"Steps to where?" Gabby asked.

"Maybe the staircase to the elusive third floor on the south side."

"Can I see?" Gabby asked, as she put the wine down on the concrete floor.

"Sure." She backed up to give Gabby a peek.

"What now?" Gabby asked.

"I'm bushed, bruised, and not really dressed for full on exploration, but help me open the door a little wider."

With Gabby on the bottom and Agnes on the top, they pulled the brick door until the opening was wide enough for Gabby to squeeze in. Once inside, Gabby pushed while Agnes pulled. Once Agnes could squeeze in, using her phone as a flashlight, Agnes scanned the opening and the wooden stair.

"This is filthy, and the stairs don't look safe," Gabby said. "Certainly not as fun as discovering tunnels and elevators."

Pop-Up Dinner, Drop Down Dead

Agnes tried anyway. Her climb up the stairs ended as quickly as it began. The bottom step cracked, and the railing came loose from the wall. Gabby reached up and tried to steady Agnes as she backed down. "That's it. I'm done. These stairs are awful. We need Tee."

"Tea?" Gabby asked. "I was thinking about a bath and a glass of wine."

"That's funny Gabby. Not t-e-a. Our builder, T-e-e." Leaving the brick door open, both brushed themselves off. Gabby picked up the unbroken wine bottles. Agnes led the way. They wound back through the basement, past the furnaces, to the elevator.

"What about the smashed wine bottle?" Gabby asked. "I can go back and clean that up."

Agnes shook her head. "Sutherland's wine. Sutherland's mess."

Martha was preparing dinner. "Have a good swim?"

"Yes and no. We found it! Maybe," Agnes announced.

Martha stopped slicing carrots and asked, "The pool? I hope so."

"No. The missing staircase to the third floor."

"What? We searched all over that basement for it," Martha exclaimed.

"Gabby, a broken wine bottle, and my bruised arm will testify to an opening on the outer wall opposite the wine cellar. Agnes pulled a cold pack from the freezer and put it on her scrapped arm. "The staircase is not solid like the library staircase and yours in the cottage. This one is all cracked, broken, and narrow. It also goes straight up," Agnes said, grabbing a bottle of water and sitting on Martha's desk chair.

"Tee will make it safe, then," Agnes motioned her hand to include Gabby, "we can all explore."

"I'm going to assume it's filthy."

"It was nasty." Agnes fluffed her hair, trying to remove imaginary cobwebs.

"After Tee finishes," Martha said, "have it cleaned. Then I'll join the expedition."

"I have a question," Gabby said.

"Sure."

"Have you never been to the third floor of this house?"

"Yes, our new apartment includes the third floor on the north end of the house, but the whole third floor was cut in two by the big glass dome when Sutherland's mother had the gallery built. Maybe access to the south end of the third floor wasn't needed, so it was forgotten."

"Who would go into the basement, through a brick wall, up the stairs to get to the third floor?" Gabby asked.

"When we discovered Sutherland's Aunt Lana, another long story, she told us that servants and gardeners lived up on the third floor. Gardeners and outbuilding workers must have used that staircase because it went straight into the basement and then outside. I'm guessing, but someone at some time closed off the staircase with that brick wall we discovered. That's really a door in a solid wall. So confusing."

"How did you find it?" Martha asked.

"I stumbled and fell into it. It found us," Agnes said.

"Of course," Martha laughed, "it's Lakesong."

"The house may like me, but she isn't always gentle," Agnes said, looking at her scraped arm.

"You have to promise to call me when you're ready to explore," Gabby said.

"Of course. You reached out and saved me. You are now one of us—an official member of the Lakesong Explorers."

"We need t-shirts," Martha suggested.

6

Goliath purred, waiting to roar. Darian suited up in Jamal's air force parka and raced into the tunnel system, ready for some fun. He ran into the basement of Lakesong before making a sharp right into the utility shed tunnel. Bursting through the door, he easily jumped up into Goliath's passenger seat. Milo had noted Darian getting taller over the past year, but his unassisted jump into Goliath was a major benchmark.

Last year, Milo let Darian sit in the driver's seat. He pretended to steer but couldn't reach the pedals, so Darian didn't drive.

"Do you think you can drive this thing this year?" Milo asked.

The young boy looked at Milo, trying to assess his seriousness. Darian bounced to the ground, ran around the vehicle, and met Milo leisurely descending Goliath. Impatiently, he waited for Milo to get out of the way before jumping up into the driver's seat. Milo sauntered to the passenger side and hoisted himself up. Once settled, Milo clapped his hands together. "Okay, any questions?"

Darian knew this was the fun part, clearing out the maintenance shed road. He adjusted the driver's seat, depressed the clutch, and forced the stick shift into first gear.

"Good on first gear. I will talk you through how to double clutch it into second," Milo yelled over the roar of the engine.

Darian nodded as he let up on the clutch while giving the monster some gas. Milo was impressed. No balking, no jerking. Goliath's roar increased as it sped down the road, throwing chunks of ice and snow past the side windows.

"Slow down or you are going to have to shift…" Milo stopped yelling as Darian deftly double clutched into second.

Darian turned his head and grinned at Milo. "Jamal showed me. We practiced," he shouted.

Milo did a thumbs up as Goliath picked up speed. "Watch the road, and slow down. We're plowing, not racing." Milo turned and looked out the side window to hide his smile. John McKnight's words had flowed effortlessly out of his mouth. John, Sutherland's dad, was the man who showed a young Milo the tricks of Goliath. Milo knew John was laughing too.

Darian pushed in the clutch. Goliath rolled to a stop. "What's next Mr. Rathkey?"

"Start with plowing out the garage area, but leave the circular drive in front of the estate for the guy with the pickup truck."

"The usual. Got it," Darian said as shifted back in first, let up on the clutch, and rounded the corner to the garage.

Pop-Up Dinner, Drop Down Dead

He took the tall snow drifts out in three passes and stopped again. The snow was neatly piled into a long, tall mound. "Will the pickup plow guy mess with the snow mountain I just created?"

Milo remembered hollowing out the snowdrifts for forts. He and his friends would play in them until the April thaw. "Those mountains are yours. I'll have Sutherland text his guy to leave them."

"Now what?" Darian asked.

"Follow the road over to your cottage and plow out your parking area. Don't knock down the house."

"You're funny, Mr. Rathkey."

While Agnes was in the kitchen making herself raspberry leaf tea, she happened to look out the window. "Goliath is barreling for your house, Martha."

Gabby ran over to the window. "Oh, that thing is huge."

"Martha, I'm serious. You may want to take a look," Agnes insisted.

Martha was adding vegetables to the McKnight crudité. "Seen it," she said.

"Well, you may have seen it with Milo driving, or you may have seen it with Jamal driving, but in this case…"

Martha rushed over to the kitchen window just in time to see the half-track pass. Milo was in the passenger seat, leaving just enough room for Martha to make out a smiling Darian at the wheel. Martha mumbled to herself, "He's only eleven, Milo."

Sutherland walked into the kitchen, grabbed two carrots, and joined everyone at the window. "Is that Darian at the helm?" he asked.

"Yes," Martha said. "My eleven-year-old brother is driving a tank toward the cottage!"

"Ah yes," Sutherland smiled, "the torch has been passed."

"The torch was passed to Jamal, not Darian," Martha said.

Jamal, who was quietly peeling potatoes, looked up. "I passed it to Darian. I showed him how to shift and double clutch into second."

"When? How?" Martha demanded.

"There were times when everyone was gone. We may have taken the beast out for a spin."

"Are you kidding me!" Martha's eyes went to Sutherland. "Did you give permission for this?"

Sutherland put his hands up in mock surrender. "I knew nothing."

"I am so sorry, and these young men will be apologizing, too."

Sutherland nodded his head, but remembered when he and two of his buddies did the same thing. The torch had indeed been passed.

Sutherland went back for the tray of veggies. "Those big snowbanks over by the garage will make great forts. I'll leave a message for Perkins to make sure he doesn't remove them."

"I'm sure you, Milo, and Darian will have a good time," Agnes said. "Tomorrow is Sunday…all day."

"Don't forget me," Jamal insisted.

"Keep peeling," Martha demanded. "You may never stop. Your brother is eleven years old and driving a tank! I'd like to see him make twelve."

§

Pop-Up Dinner, Drop Down Dead

"I went through the stolen car list, no Priuses yet," Preston reported to White and Gramm as they had one last meeting before calling it a day. "I also talked to Pearl Landrum."

"Okay," Gramm mumbled. "Who the hell is she?"

"You gave me her name. She has a living room window that looks out on the top of Mesaba Avenue. She told me that a dark car, maybe the Prius—my words, not hers—traveling fast rammed through the barricade and kept going."

"I think we should pay her a visit to look out her window to see what she actually saw," Gramm said.

"What time did she see all this?" White asked.

"Shortly after ten."

"It was dark and snowing. Why was she just happening to look out the window?"

"It's her entertainment. She told me she enjoys sitting by the window with her brandy and watching the traffic. When the brandy takes hold, she knows it's time for bed. She said she had just started her brandy, no buzz."

Gramm, all suited up in his snowmobile suit, reached for his boots, anxious to get home. "Robin, what about the driver, Ralph Bing?"

"An arrest for illegal gambling," White said. "I called the number on his vehicle registration. It was out of service."

"Do we need to be in tomorrow?" Preston asked.

Gramm thought about it. "No, not you, but I'll be working tomorrow night, keeping my nose to the grindstone."

"Kate, the grindstone is the Sunday night card game," White said.

"I learn a lot at those card games," Gramm defended himself. "Also, this week, you, Sergeant White, will be joining us since Creedence Durant, financial advisor to the rich, is out of town. I hope you're up for this. We're almost professionals."

Preston side glanced at White.

White smiled, waited for Gramm to look away and gave Preston the sign to be quiet, a finger to the lips.

§

The mid-January storm slowly diminished and was only a memory as the Lakesong residents sat down for dinner. Martha had found two chickens and prepared coq au vin with mashed potatoes expertly peeled by Jamal.

"Gabby and I picked the wine," Agnes bragged.

"Well, picked might be an exaggeration," Gabby admitted.

"Okay, we found and carried most of the wine Martha said she wanted."

Sutherland picked up one of the bottles. "Clos de Tart Grand Cru Burgundy 2011. Good choice."

"It's always a good choice," Milo complained. "Just once, look at the bottle and say, 'Not this rot gut, go get some Mad Dog 2020.'"

Sutherland smiled. "It's my cellar. All the wines are a good choice, and I can assure everyone that there is no Mad Dog 2020. Although from time to time I find myself craving a glass of Mateus."

"Mateus?" Agnes questioned.

"Good wine after skiing," Sutherland said. "Great with onion rings. College days."

"Onion rings!" Milo echoed. "The Pickwick!"

Pop-Up Dinner, Drop Down Dead

"Stop!" Martha ordered. "Coq au Vin! Mashed Potatoes! No onion rings but peeled baby onions, cooked in butter, then added to the sauce."

"So far so good," Milo said.

"She had you at butter," Sutherland mocked. "You'd eat my left shoe if it was cooked in butter."

"You are joining us. Right Martha?" Agnes said.

"I am. Jamal will serve."

"KP and serving. What did he do?" Milo asked.

"He taught Darian how to get that monster half-track to move, and he wants money for the new Dune video game," Martha said.

"I played Zelda once," Milo said. "Go left, go right, pick up the sword."

Jamal entered the family room with a salad cart. "Do you still have it, Mr. Rathkey? The Legend of Zelda?"

"I had it on a Game Boy."

"What's a Game Boy?"

"It's a magical device that you use when you're young so that someone can make you feel old later in life," Milo said sarcastically.

Martha looked at Jamal. "You're here to serve, not to take part in the conversation."

Jamal did a quick bow as he dressed the salad, then used two tongs to toss and plate. Each guest was served, except Milo. As instructed, Jamal reached down to a lower shelf on the cart and produced a blue cheese wedge of iceberg lettuce. Placing it in front of Milo, he said, "Your salad, sir."

Milo laughed. "Thank you, Jamal."

Gabby looked quizzically at Martha, but Sutherland answered.

"Milo was frightened by mixed greens as a child, from which he never recovered."

"I like iceberg lettuce and blue cheese. Why should I eat anything else?" Milo asked.

"I never have this much fun at my house," Gabby said, picking up her salad fork. "Of course I live alone."

"The fun will only increase. Sutherland doesn't know this yet," Agnes said, "but we're going cross country skiing tomorrow in Patterson Park."

"I was thinking of a nap on the couch," Sutherland protested.

"After skiing," Agnes added.

"Will the streets be plowed out?" Gabby asked.

"Probably not, but it's just across the road. We have a tunnel that goes under the road," Agnes said.

"Of course you do. Who doesn't have a tunnel to their favorite park?" Gabby laughed.

"If you're not into skiing, stay and help me look at the video from the last three nights of Travels," Martha said. "We can see what did and didn't work."

"Too bad there's no audio. We could get some gossip," Gabby suggested.

"Milo?" Sutherland questioned. "What do you have planned?"

"Now that there's an opening on the couch, I lay claim to it for a few hours."

"It's a plot," Sutherland said.

"I have to rest up for tomorrow night's poker game," Milo added.

"If I don't win, wife of mine, I'll blame you," Sutherland said.

"If you don't win, don't come home. Sleep on the back lawn with the possums," Agnes joked.

"The possums are hibernating. They won't let me into their den," Sutherland protested.

"Do possums hibernate?" Milo asked.

The answer came from Jamal as he picked up the salad plates. "No, on the hibernation."

"How do you know?" Martha asked.

"Biology," Jamal said.

"Am I the only one here that worries about the wait staff knowing all about critters like possums?" Milo asked. "What exactly is in this cocoa van?"

"Coq au Vin," Martha corrected. "Means rooster with wine, not possum!"

"That's a relief. One of the back lawn possums and I have become very close. His name is Bert."

"Is there another one named Ernie?" Gabby asked.

"That would be so predictable—no, the raccoon is named Ernie," Milo said with a straight face

"Possums are beneficial," Jamal said. "They eat ticks."

"Ernie just hisses at me. I think it's personal," Milo said.

"Wildlife waiter, no talking, just serving," Martha admonished.

"I texted Tee," Agnes said, changing the subject. "When the roads are clear, she's going to check out the basement stairway to the third floor,"

"Or you could simply close the door and ignore it," Sutherland said, knowing he was poking the bear.

Agnes stared at him. "The house invited me. I do not ignore an invitation. I may not get another. Lakesong is sensitive and one must be in tune with her many moods."

"The house invites you?" Gabby questioned, looking at Martha.

Martha shrugged. "I'm just the chef."

Jamal began serving the coq au vin. "It talks to my brother, Darian," Jamal said

Gabby's eyes opened wide.

Martha closed her eyes and said, "Serving, no talking."

"The house talks to Darian?" Gabby asked.

"Ignore Jamal. He plays basketball and gets hit on the head—concussions," Martha said, turning to her sibling. "Continue your serving, silently."

Jamal bowed…smiling.

7

Sunday morning arrived bright and sunny, but bitterly cold. Sutherland insisted that Martha not make breakfast, Sunday being her normal day off. "Ilene said her bakery snowmobile delivery service would be up and running today. I ordered extras," Sutherland called behind him as he left, hoping to find the box on the front steps.

"Nice," Gabby said. "Home pastry delivery. I get the snowmobile delivery, but how does the delivery person get past your front gate?"

"They have the code," Agnes explained.

"Is that safe?"

"Extremely unsafe," Milo interjected. "It has been proven that in situations where every member of a household has been bludgeoned to death with a cake knife, chances are someone got loose with the gate code."

Gabby began to laugh.

"Welcome to Sunday morning at Lakesong," Agnes said, joining Gabby's laughter.

Sutherland returned with a huge yellow bag which held an equally huge box of Ilene's best pastries.

"Check him for knife wounds," Milo said. His phone's *da dunk* ringtone told him Gramm was calling. "I gotta take this. Gabby, you and only you can have my creampuffs."

"I ordered extras," Sutherland said.

Milo moved out of the morning room to the hearth room to take the call. "What's up, Ernie?"

"I need to bring you up to speed on our fake murder," Gramm said.

"Okay?"

"We have a woman who witnessed a car crash through the barricade at the top of Mesaba about the time your half-track killed that guy."

"Self-defense. Goliath was attacked."

"Yeah, yeah, yeah."

"How credible is this woman?" Milo asked.

"Drinking brandy, looking out a window in a snowstorm. You tell me."

"Have we interviewed her?"

"Preston talked to her on the phone yesterday, but I'm thinking we have to talk to her in person. You and Preston get to go to her house today."

"Mesaba is blocked off, still an iced over ski hill."

"Not anymore. The main arteries have been plowed, salted, and sanded."

"Pity."

§

After being fueled by several crème puffs, Milo spent thirty minutes trying to put the Lakesong SUV into four-wheel drive. He finally gave up and called Sutherland, who joined him in the garage. Peering into the vehicle, Sutherland extended the fingers on both hands and proclaimed, "Abracadabra,"

"Cute, but I need this car today. You have to do this," Milo insisted.

"I did," Sutherland said, turning around and starting to leave.

"You did nothing. You said abracadabra."

"Well, that and coming all the way out here and noticing that it already was in four-wheel drive. That's what that lever in the center does."

Milo looked at the lever. "It's not labeled. How would I know that it's in four-wheel drive?"

"That icon on the dashboard that looks like four wheels tells you."

"I thought that was about tire pressure."

"Why would it show you tire pressure?"

"Tire pressure is important…I think."

"Fine. Tire pressure is important, but it's Sunday. Where are you going?"

"To bludgeon a witness with a rubber hose who may or may not have killed the victim of our make-believe homicide Friday night."

Sutherland crinkled his forehead, trying to figure out Milo's rambling. "I don't see a hose?"

"I don't have a hose. I was hoping to find one on the way, and before you start on about the green hose hanging on the wall over there, can't use it. It doesn't look like it's made out of rubber. These witness beatings over fake homicides are very specific—rubber hoses, nothing else."

Sutherland had run out of witty responses and his head hurt after spending too many minutes with Milo's banter. He wished him luck, told him to be careful out there, and watched him drive away.

Once back inside the house, Sutherland rejoined the group in the morning room. "Milo is off to bludgeon a witness to a fake homicide," he mumbled. Sutherland walked to the coffee urn and poured himself a cup, sprinkling the liquid with cream and sugar.

"Is he okay?" Gabby asked.

Agnes shrugged. "With Milo, we have no idea. Is Sutherland okay? I sense my dear husband has gotten trapped by Milo's mind lint imaginings and now he's trying to share. They can rot your brain and leave you with a headache."

"No, mind lint is when Milo solves a crime. This is…"

"Look," Agnes whispered to Gabby, "Sutherland never drinks two coffees in the morning."

Sutherland looked up, then back down to his cup. "I don't want coffee."

"Sometimes talking to Milo will do that to you," Agnes murmured.

§

For Kick DeJong, being released from the hospital in the middle of a blizzard simply meant changing rooms. He exchanged the emergency room bed for a recliner in his wife's hospital room. The room was quiet. Jess mostly slept throughout Saturday night.

Kick had updated Reese and Emma, assuring them Jess was doing fine. Glancing up to make sure Jess was still sleeping, he texted Raf. *I need another delivery.*

There was no response.

Kick downed an oxy, leaving one pill left. He texted Raf again. *Whatever you're asking, I'll double it. Get here! Room 237.*

No response…again.

A middle-aged doctor came in and nodded at Kick. "I'm Doctor Levine. How's our patient?"

"She's sleeping now. She woke up a couple of times during the night for the nurses to take vitals. Doesn't seem to remember anything about yesterday. Not the accident, nothing," Kick said.

"The scan we did of her brain was negative for any serious injury. The memory loss could be caused by the trauma of the accident. Her memory should return over time."

"Do you know where my car is?"

The doctor was somewhat taken aback by the question. "I…I have no idea. I assume the police towed it. The roads are not fully plowed in case you were thinking of going somewhere."

Kick glanced at his phone. Nothing.

§

Driving out of the Lakesong garage, Milo squinted. The bright winter sun reflecting off the new snow blinded him.

He stopped at the main gate to rummage in the glove compartment to find a pair of sunglasses. Sutherland 'the ready' to the rescue—he found sunglasses—dirty sunglasses. He attempted to clean them by rubbing the lenses with his shirt. He only succeeded in smearing them beyond all use.

Still in the morning room, Sutherland received an alert that someone was at the front gate. He checked the camera with his phone. "Milo is outside parked in front of the gate. He's getting out of the SUV."

Gabby looked at Agnes.

"I don't know," Agnes said.

Sutherland continued. "It looks to me like he is shoving my old sunglasses in the snow."

"More mind lint?" Gabby asked.

"Not mind lint," Sutherland corrected. "Now he's using his shirt to clean the glasses."

"It's winter. Isn't he wearing a jacket?" Agnes asked.

"He is, but he unzipped it. Now he's done with that, and he's put on the sunglasses and gotten back into the SUV."

"Are those your old tortoise shell sunglasses?" Agnes asked.

"They are."

"Do they look better on Milo than on you?" Agnes laughed.

Sutherland feigned hurt. "No, they do not."

"I should take notes," Gabby said.

Martha laughed. "That's what Ron Bello says every time he's over here."

§

Pop-Up Dinner, Drop Down Dead

Preston arrived at the top of Central Entrance and Mesaba Avenue five minutes before Milo. She was looking for his old Honda and didn't notice the SUV pull up behind her. Milo knocked on her driver's side window, causing her to jump.

"Kinda nervous," Milo said as Preston opened her door and stepped out onto the street.

"You shouldn't sneak up on people like that," Preston admonished.

"I trained in sneaking. It's a hard habit to break. Where are we going?"

Preston pointed to a three-story, white Victorian house on Mesaba Avenue. "We have to walk down the hill a bit. It's probably still slippery. Be careful."

"I left my cane and seeing eye cat in the other car."

"Cute. Pearl Landrum lives on the first floor."

A snow-filled ramp led up to a wide porch. Both Milo and Preston opted for the shoveled stairs. Seeing no doorbell, Milo knocked on the large wooden door. No one answered. He knocked again. Same result.

"Maybe it's apartments," Preston said. Milo turned the doorknob, pushing the door open to an outer foyer.

Three doorbell buttons were stationed alongside three mailboxes. The lower box was labeled *Landrum*. Milo pressed that button and waited. He pressed it again.

"Press it again," an irritated voice yelled. "It won't get me there any faster!"

Preston spoke up first. "Duluth police officer Kate Preston and Consultant Rathkey to see Pearl Landrum. I talked to her on the phone."

"I figured!" Pearl barked. "I'm not gaga."

Milo laughed as Pearl pushed the unlock button to the inner door. The buzzer was exceptionally loud.

Inside, there was only one apartment on the ground floor and a stairway leading upstairs. Milo knocked on the lone apartment door.

"I'm not getting up again! The door's unlocked!" Pearl yelled.

Milo pushed open her apartment door to find Pearl sitting by her front window in a modern reclining chair.

"Coffee's on the table by the couch," Pearl said, putting an old pair of binoculars up to her eyes.

Preston and Milo introduced themselves again.

"Yeah, I heard you the first time." Pearl looked them up and down. "You two don't look like cops. You got ID?"

Preston showed her badge, Milo his consultant's card. "We're here to talk to you in person about the traffic accident Friday night," Preston said.

Pearl adjusted her cardigan, which was wrapped around her Viking sweatshirt. She put her feet up on a stool, showing off her mule house shoes. "It was no accident. That's why I called you guys."

"What kind of binoculars do you have?" Milo asked.

Pearl held them up. "M3 6X30. My dad was a marine. He left them to me."

"We ran into a bird watcher a couple of months ago. He had Swarovskis," Milo said.

Pearl ran her fingers through her gray, closely curled hair. "Must be rich. Those things cost an arm and a leg. These are old, but they do the trick."

"I think it's wonderful the owners have already shoveled," Preston said.

Pearl laughed. "It's my building. I'm the owners. Lucky for me, my grandson, Jack, loves his grandma and makes sure I'm well taken care of. He's my shoveler. I also pay him."

"Why not the ramp?" Milo asked.

"My husband used it. He doesn't need it anymore."

"Well, that's great!" Preston exclaimed.

"Not really, dearie. Found him in the foyer…didn't even make it to the door. Deader than squirrel on the Miller Trunk Highway. Are you two gonna ask me about what I saw or are you going to stand around and chat all day? Sit!"

Milo nodded. Both sat on the red and blue flowered couch. "Please tell us again what you saw," Preston said.

"I was sitting right here, where I am now, watching the storm, keeping an eye on the street. It's what I do. I notice a lot. Friday night, that car was speeding. Didn't slow down a whit, just plowed through that nothing barricade. It was a wooden sawhorse that couldn't stop a kid on a bike. Anyways, this car just slams on through, chunks of wood and splinters flying. Mesaba was pure ice, and it's a long way down. I got these M3s trained on him. No brake lights at all. Anyways, I checked my police scanner and heard he hit somebody and took on a power pole. I thought I should call."

"Did anyone else come by?" Milo asked.

"People driving across on Central Entrance trying to get home, but nobody came down Mesaba. It was getting hard to see anything at that point. Eventually, a police car pulled sideways across the road and turned on those pretty revolving blue lights that look so nice in the snow. They shoulda done that to begin with."

"Thank you, Mrs. Landrum," Milo said.

"It's Ms. I'm old but current."

Milo thanked her again and then he and Preston left. On the way out, Milo stopped by the stairs. "I think we, the royal we, should interview the other tenants in the building."

Preston pointed questioningly to herself, nodded and hurried up the stairs just as Milo's phone sprang to life with 'Never Underestimate the Power of a Woman.' "Hey, Agnes, what's up?"

"Where is the card game tonight?"

"Lakesong. Why?"

"Oh, good."

"Why not ask Sutherland? He's tall, blond, you married him."

"I would, but he's still in x-ray."

"Let me backtrack, tall, blond…uncoordinated?"

Agnes sighed. "Skiing accident. With my extensive medical knowledge, I would say sprained ankle, but it could be broken."

"I haven't done a lot of cross-country skiing, but what little I've done didn't require much speed. In fact, I fell several times without moving. No sprains, breaks, or head injuries."

"You weren't zipping along when a toddler cut across your skis."

"Is the kid okay?"

"Couldn't be better. Little kid, low to the ground. Sutherland's skis stopped dead, but his body kept going.

His left leg didn't detach from the ski properly. He had to hop all the way back to Lakesong. I carried the skis."

"Another emergency room visit?"

"Yes. Oh wait, here he comes. Let's see, a foot in a boot and a body in a wheelchair. Gotta go."

Milo put his phone back in his pocket just as Preston came back down the stairs. "The Millers on the second floor didn't see or hear anything and the young guy on the third floor seemed frightened to see me. He also said he didn't see anything but did admit to hearing a disturbing noise sometime during the night."

"A disturbing noise in a blizzard? We can take that to the bank."

"Especially because I suspect he was ingesting some illegal substances, and that's why I wasn't high on his guest list," Preston laughed.

"*High* on his guest list. Good one Preston."

8

Robin White had never been in the Lakesong billiard room until this evening. Along with a custom carved pool table and billiard table, the room sported a large wooden, mother-of-pearl inlaid poker table. "Not quite the card table with five non-matching folding chairs I've heard so much about," she whispered to Gramm.

"That was Milo's place, pre-Lakesong. Wait until Martha rolls in the snacks," Gramm said. "Not a couple of bags of chips and a few stale cans of Diet Coke these days."

"Diet Cokes don't expire," Milo charged, defending his hospitality when he lived over Irene's Bakery.

Agnes arrived, pushing Sutherland in an ancient wooden wheelchair. "The wounded soldier arrives," she said, maneuvering Sutherland so he was sitting in his favorite spot at the poker table.

"Where did you unearth that chair?" Saul Feinberg asked.

"Milo found it in the utility shed," Sutherland said.

"I remember when I was a kid the caretaker broke his leg, and John McKnight produced this old chair. It was supposed to be used only until they could find a modern one, but Olaf liked it. When he healed, he put it in the shed and obviously never moved it again."

"Luckily, it was still there!" Agnes exclaimed. "When traffic is moving again, we can get a scooter, but this is fine for tonight."

"Sutherland, what happened?" Feinberg asked.

"Agnes and I were cross-country skiing when a young ruffian cut across my skis, sending me flying. This city is becoming so dangerous. You would think the police would do something about the out-of-control youth."

"She did stop to see if you were okay," Agnes added.

"She?" White questioned. "Clearly a member of a thuggish girl gang."

"Hard to tell," Agnes said. "I didn't see any gang signs, and her pink parka had butterflies on it."

Gramm, who had grandchildren, asked the age of the miscreant who laid Sutherland low.

"I don't know exactly," Sutherland said, looking at Agnes. "Four? Maybe five."

Through hoots and catcalls, Milo defended Sutherland, "They're vicious at that age."

"Absolutely." Sutherland picked up the cards and began to shuffle them.

White took Creedence Durant's usual chair.

"You have to buy in. Two bucks is the minimum. Cash only," Gramm began.

Pop-Up Dinner, Drop Down Dead

"Good luck," Agnes murmured to White. "You are in the land of the card sharks."

"Would you like a cheat sheet that shows the rank of hands?" Sutherland asked.

As White bought in and arranged her five dollars' worth of chips, she declined Sutherland's kind offer.

"Why would you think Robin would need a cheat sheet?" Agnes asked accusingly.

Sutherland's eyes quickly scanned the table. Gramm and Feinberg were silent, head down, in fake deliberation—arranging their chips while brushing invisible lint from the table.

"Oh no! Is this like the gravy incident?" Sutherland asked. "It's not me. It's the pain pills."

"Yeah, that Extra Strength Tylenol can cloud your judgement," Agnes retorted.

"Gravy incident?" White questioned.

"Not my best moment," Sutherland said. "My very able, now wife, and I were playing tennis against Mary Alice Bonner and Milo. I mistakenly believed, for a brief moment in time, I was the superior player and may have intimated that Agnes' play would be simply gravy to my superior moves."

White laughed. "How did that work out for you?"

"Well, in my defense, no one told me that Milo was a shark on the tennis court, even though every single person involved knew."

"How does that defend the 'gravy' comment?" Agnes demanded.

"It doesn't." Sutherland sighed. "I'm going to pay for that forever, aren't I?"

Agnes smirked, "I never forget."

"Even I couldn't defend you on that one," Feinberg said. "But it's poker time! Let the new player deal,"

Robin picked up the cards. "So, I just deal these out one at a time?"

"Yes!" Gramm said. "Dealer's choice, but I suggest you start with five-card draw."

Feinberg laughed. "He suggests that because he hates the complicated games. You know, games where something is wild."

"You're the boss. Five-card draw it is," White said, bringing the cards together in a high arc, and then letting them settle only to repeat the move three more times. When the cards went up the sleeve of her right arm and then her left arm, the assembled began to realize that Robin was not in need of any cheat sheet.

"Gramm, this is all your fault," Milo charged.

"I didn't know," Gramm shrugged.

"You've been her partner for what, two, three years? What do you talk about?"

"Excuse me, but I never thought to ask her if she was a professional poker player."

"I'm in the room guys, and if you must know, for a bit, I was a dealer at a casino in Vegas," White said.

"Oh wonderful," Sutherland interjected. "I get run over by a rabid four-year-old, and now I get cleaned out by a professional dealer."

"Were you a dealer or croupier?" Feinberg asked.

"Primarily a dealer, but in this country, the two are interchangeable. I preferred cards over roulette."

Pop-Up Dinner, Drop Down Dead

"I had croupier once," Milo said. "I went to a doc-in-the-box, and she gave me antibiotics."

"Could we just deal?" Gramm was losing patience.

"Anyone care to cut the cards?" White asked.

"You do know this is nickel, dime, quarter?" Sutherland asked.

White nodded, smiled, and dealt the cards. As they flew around the table, each individual card came to rest directly in front of the intended player.

Feinberg laughed. "That's the prettiest deal I have ever seen."

The bidding began with Feinberg, who threw in a dime. Milo saw the dime and raised a dime. Gramm threw twenty cents, as did Sutherland and Robin.

Martha rolled in a snack cart with the hors d'oeuvres—chicken and waffle sliders, deep dish mini pizzas, baked garlic parmesan potato wedges, beef Wellington turnover with a sweet chili wine sauce, and Milo's favorite, weenies in a bun.

Agnes picked up a chicken and waffle slider, announcing it was her payment for delivering Sutherland to the game. "As exciting as this has been, I'm going to a private party with Martha and Gabby. We'll be in the gallery with our feet up."

"Thank you for your help," Sutherland said, grabbing her hand and giving it a squeeze.

"You're welcome, but if you don't win, you sleep on the lawn," Agnes said.

"Second time she's said it today. I think she's serious," Milo said.

"If you're worried, let me win."

"Gonna be cold out there, buddy. Bundle up."

"Excuse me," Gramm said. "But could we please play!"

"I'll take three cards," Feinberg said.

"You bid a whole dime on just two cards?" Gramm asked.

Robin laughed. "You guys are serious about this game. I can tell."

Milo took one card to oohs and ahs.

Gramm threw four cards down in disgust. "Nice deal, partner."

Robin took two, and the bidding began again.

Milo and Robin dueled in a bidding war that went up to several rounds of quarters. Feinberg urged them to slow down. "Pace yourselves. Somebody is going to be broke before the second hand."

In the end, Milo won that pot with a straight. "A pro dealer and you didn't win? Not a great way to start," Gramm said to Robin.

She smiled. "Just feeling everybody out. I'm learning your games. It's my style…"

"Was it just me, or did everyone feel a chill of impending bankruptcy go up their spine?" Feinberg asked while heading to the hors d'oeuvres cart. He came back with several of the pizzas and a hand wipe. "So, Ernie, you guys working on anything exciting?"

White collected the cards and passed them onto Feinberg.

"Not much," Gramm said. "Milo killed a guy Friday night. We weren't going to charge him, but if he wins another big pot, I may reconsider."

"Ante up everyone," Feinberg advised.

"Milo, you failed to mention you murdered someone," Sutherland chided.

Pop-Up Dinner, Drop Down Dead

"Did I?" Milo shrugged. "Must have slipped my mind. Actually, Sutherland, you are an accessory before the fact."

"Oh, yeah, that's right," Gramm said. "You own that half-track, too. What do you call it? Gilgamesh?"

"Goliath," Milo corrected.

"Seven-card stud, duces and Jacks wild," Feinberg announced as he began to deal.

"I hate these..."

"Wildcard games," Milo said. "Yeah, we know."

"Explain how Milo came to murder someone," Feinberg requested.

"He was cracking ice up Mesaba Avenue during the snowstorm with his half-track, and some poor chap ran into him," Gramm detailed. "Then the car slammed into a power pole."

"Who was the unlucky driver?"

"That's a problem," White said as Feinberg dealt one card down and two up to each player.

"How so?"

Milo looked at his down card and threw a dime into the pot.

Gramm grumbled about playing with millionaires but matched the dime.

"The car is registered to a Ralph Bing, but we can't find anything recent in the system. He doesn't seem to exist except for his car."

Sutherland saw the dime and raised it another dime.

Robin looked at her cards, then stared at Milo, before shifting her gaze to Feinberg and finally to Gramm. She tossed in two dime chips and added a third.

"Thirty cents to you," Milo said to Feinberg.

Feinberg dropped three dime chips onto the pot. "Well, you're not going to find Ralph Bing." He dealt another card up. It gave Milo two fours and a jack of hearts. Gramm, still grumbling, received a deuce to go with what could be a straight flush. Sutherland had a lot of nothing, and Robin was looking at three natural sevens, two up, one down.

Rathkey dropped a quarter chip into the pot. Gramm folded, announcing, "I need another one of those beefy things."

"Sutherland, are you in or out?" Rathkey demanded.

"I'm channeling Robin. Meanwhile, Ernie, bring me one of those potato wedges."

Sutherland had two kings up along with an eight, no help. He stayed, matching the thirty cents.

Robin still had her three sevens and a nine of clubs. "Why do you say we're not going to find Ralph Bing?" she asked Feinberg.

"He started going by a different name."

"How do you know that?" Gramm asked.

"I defended him against a gambling charge, and he told me that's what he was going to do, reinvent himself."

Gramm stretched his back. "You wouldn't happen to know his new name?"

"I do. He calls himself Raf Bianchi. He fancies himself a chef. If you want to find him, try connecting with Kick DeJong. He footed the bill for Bianchi's defense. He told me that Kick owed him money. Who knows? I know Kick owns some restaurants in town, likes to live high with his crew."

"Crew?" White questioned.

"Yeah, guys he hangs with. Reese Winterhausen is one. I think there are others, but I don't know them. I think they played ball."

"Where?" Sutherland asked. "I played ball."

Robin laughed. "I noticed that guys use the term *played ball* without ever defining it. What are we talking about? Baseball, football, golf, bowling?"

Feinberg nodded his head. "You're right. Raf mentioned to me they played ball, and I didn't care enough to ask what kind of ball."

"Maybe whiffle ball. Who names their kid, Kick?" Milo mused.

"Mr. and Mrs. DeJong," Sutherland quipped.

"He's my neighbor," Feinberg said.

"Wait!" Milo challenged. "Gabe Gibbs is your neighbor."

Sutherland held up his hand for Milo to stop. "Don't mention that name. I almost died on his deadly virtual bike contraption."

"Gibbs owns a house on one side of me, but Kick DeJong actually lives in the house on the other side. Hardly see either one of them. Great neighbors."

"You know," Gramm began, "all you millionaires talk about next door and neighbors like you can reach out and touch their houses."

"Like your place," Feinberg joked.

"Exactly, but in reality, your 'neighbors' are acres away."

"We share a property line. We are neighbors," Feinberg insisted.

"We know this DeJong guy owns restaurants. Can you tell me anything more about him?" Gramm asked.

"He's married to a woman named Jess. She has a sister named Emma that has created some legal problems for the family."

Gramm gave him a sign to continue.

"I'm getting this second hand from Kim…"

"Kim?" White questioned.

"Kimberly McKenna," Milo said. "His *don't come cheap* lawyer friend. You've met her."

"Oh, Kim," White said, remembering the uniform gray suit.

"Ignore them," Gramm urged.

"Kim defended Emma from an assault charge in Minneapolis. Apparently, some guy was getting handsy in a bar. She retaliated by hitting him over the head with a bottle. Gave him a fractured skull. He pressed charges. They didn't stick. Kick paid for that one, too."

White, having learned their games, bested them, taking the last pot of the evening after it grew to epic proportions. Sutherland kept muttering that he was going to be sleeping in the snow with a raccoon and a possum. He did win one pot yet ended up losing two dollars and seventy-five cents. Milo was up twenty-five cents, and Feinberg was close to even. Gramm remarked it was a good night for the police force. Nowhere close to Robin, but he was two-fifty to the good.

Milo pushed Sutherland out to the foyer so he could see everyone off. "Let's check the gallery. I want to see if Agnes has gone up," Sutherland asked.

"Text her. This civil war chair is hard to push."

Sutherland took his phone from his pocket and saw a text from Agnes. *Call me when you're in the elevator.*

Pop-Up Dinner, Drop Down Dead

Milo moved Sutherland to the hallway outside the kitchen and rolled him into the elevator. "Tomorrow I will begin the hunt for the delinquent who did this to you."

"I wish you wouldn't. I don't want a gang of four-year-olds gunning for me."

"Seems to me you have already crossed that line."

9

"Sutherland, we're ruined," Agnes proclaimed as the two sat down to breakfast. "Two whole dollars and seventy-five cents just flitted away to your gambling buddies. I think I may have to take over the finances before you gamble away the roof over our heads. I can see my way to giving you an allowance of a quarter a week."

"What can I say. I had a weak moment, but I think we can survive this setback," Sutherland said.

Martha joined the theme of the morning. "I'm sorry, Mr. McKnight, but we can no longer afford the ingredients for your green smoothie. I was going to blend some Ramen for you, but the bank repossessed the blender."

"Repossessed the blender? Ha! Good one, Martha." Sutherland shook his head. "Look people, it was a measly $2.75."

Gabby couldn't resist joining in. "If you people are short, I can pitch in. Maybe get that blender out of hock."

"It was repossessed," Agnes corrected.

"What was repossessed?" Milo asked as he and the cats walked into the morning room.

"The blender," Agnes said. "After Sutherland's horrible losses last night at the poker table."

Milo filled a coffee cup and took a sip. "If I remember correctly, he lost three bucks."

"No, not that much, only two dollars and seventy-five cents," Sutherland repeated.

"We begged him to quit the game before it got to this point, but he just kept popping pizzas and tossing in chips," Milo said.

"How did you do, Milo?" Agnes asked.

"Up a quarter. Don't worry, I know a guy who will give Sutherland a good deal on that chair."

"I need this chair until I get my scooter," Sutherland protested.

"Shoulda thought of that before your pizza fueled gambling spree," Milo said.

"Milo, tell your guy the chair is for sale," Agnes said. "It might help pay for the scooter rental."

"I'm never leaving," Gabby said.

"When I lived above the bakery, Ilene's helper sprained her ankle, and she got a little scooter for the injured leg. Worked great. Why don't you have one now?" Milo asked.

"The hospital didn't have scooters," Sutherland explained. "Now that the storm has cleared, I can get new toys for my injury. I'll find the funds somewhere."

Pop-Up Dinner, Drop Down Dead

"I may have exaggerated the repossession of the blender," Martha said as she arrived with the smoothies for Sutherland and Gabby. Milo received his usual eggs, hash browns, and bacon with some of the bacon earmarked for the cats. Agnes was rocking toast and lemon balm tea.

Martha sat down at her desk in the kitchen, planning menus and ordering food for the week. She glanced from time to time at Milo, waiting for him to finish breakfast before approaching him with her computer tablet. Sutherland and Agnes finished their breakfasts and both left Lakesong. Sutherland went to his Monday morning meeting. Agnes had an appointment.

Going back to the morning room, Martha began, "Mr. Rathkey, Gabby and I want to show you something."

"Video of Sutherland sleeping with the raccoons?" Milo asked, as he took the last bite of hash browns.

"Not quite," Martha said, sitting down next to Milo.

"We think we have a video of an assault," Gabby escalated the conversation.

"Yesterday, Gabby and I started viewing a video of the Friday pop-up dinner. We were in the middle of discussing changes in the service, not realizing the video was still playing. Gabby noticed it first."

Gabby nodded. "Watch. See what you think."

"Sure," Milo said.

Martha set the tablet in front of Milo. The video showed a man running out of the restaurant toward a parked car. Two men grabbed him, roughed him up, and threw him into the back of a waiting car. They then drove off.

"I know that guy who's getting beat up," Gabby said. "He was at dinner. His name is Raf Bianchi."

Recognizing the name, Milo asked, "Is he a friend of yours?"

"No! He's trouble. If he's not hitting on me or my staff, he's hitting me up for a job. If all that fails, he just asks for a loan. I know he's a gambler."

"He may be trouble to you, but in this video, he's the one in trouble," Milo said. "I recognize one of the thugs. It's David Bonner, Mary Alice's brother-in-law." Milo asked that the video be rolled back. He leaned in, looking at the driver. *That's Leroy Thompson. None of this makes any sense!*

"Is this a crime?" Martha asked. "Should Gabby and I take it to the police?"

"You just have," Milo said. "I need a copy of it."

"I'm your chef, Mr. Rathkey, not your IT person. Darian, my little hacker, is in school."

"Can I take this copy?" Milo asked, pointing to the thumb drive.

"I guess, but we would like it back."

"Have either of you seen this guy since Friday?" Milo asked.

Martha laughed. "Remember the snowstorm? We were here at Lakesong."

"Did either of you see him at your pop-up?" Milo asked.

"I did," Gabby said. "I handled the DeJong table. Raf was part of their group. He brought drama as usual."

"Everything is on the same thumb drive. This is the parking lot cameras. There are interior views too," Martha said. "You can see the movements, but there's no sound."

"Thank you, Martha, Gabby."

Pop-Up Dinner, Drop Down Dead

§

Officer Preston walked into Gramm's office with what her grandma would say was a bounce in her step. She had partied Sunday evening with some members of her rookie class. Most of them were just graduating from mundane duty. Duty that Preston skipped because a year ago she took a chance and asked Sgt. Robin White if the Homicide Department needed any help. It pays to ask.

"Preston!" Gramm shouted when he saw her.

The bounce left her step. "Yes, sir?"

"Did you have prior information about Sergeant White's life as a casino dealer?"

"Yes, sir."

"Good morning, everyone!" White said as she strode into Gramm's office with a larger coffee cup than usual.

"Is that supersized coffee from your winnings?" Gramm asked, pointing to the cup.

"It is. My tax person says I need to spend my winnings quickly, so I don't move up to a higher bracket."

"That's not how it works," Milo said as he walked in behind White. "I know. Endless lectures from Creedence Durant."

"Preston, the poker game has paid off," Gramm said. "Our Ralph Bing is also known as Raf Bianchi. We know he might have a financial relationship with Kick DeLong…"

"DeJong," White corrected.

"Right. DeJong. Preston, what do you have?"

"Milo and I talked with Pearl Landrum, the woman who witnessed the traffic accident at the top of Mesaba."

"She says she saw a car barrel through the sawhorse," Milo added.

Preston detailed Pearl's account of Friday night.

"Anything else?" Gramm asked.

"I have some interesting video," Milo said, handing White the thumb drive. "It comes from Martha and Gabby."

Gramm stretched his back. "Your cook…"

"Chef."

Gramm dropped his head in another stretching exercise. "The woman who makes delicious meals and creates outstanding card game hors d'oeuvres gave you a flash drive?"

White plugged the drive into her computer and turned her computer so Gramm could see the screen. "It looks like a restaurant," Gramm said.

"It's Martha's and Gabby's pop-up dinner Friday night," Milo explained.

"Who's Gabby?" White asked.

"Martha's chef friend. They put on the pop-up together."

Gramm sighed. "At the risk of sounding even older than I am, what the hell is a pop-up dinner?"

"It's a temporary restaurant," White said. "With usually one or two entrées. They are usually held in empty buildings. They sometimes have a theme…"

Gramm held up his hand for White to stop. "I got it. What are we looking for here?"

"The cameras come up in order," Milo said. "One inside and one in the parking lot. Camera one, inside the restaurant, you see Ralph or Raf there at a large round table."

"Who are the others?" Gramm asked.

"Not sure. The real interesting video isn't inside but outside. Fast forward, Robin."

"Stop! There!" The group watched a man running to a car, only to be hijacked and stuffed into another car.

"Who is that?" White questioned.

"Gabby identified him this morning as Raf Bianchi," Milo said.

"Who are those other guys?" Preston asked.

"One is David Bonner," White said. "He was the muscle for his brother. He was in jail. He must be out. Who's he working for now?"

Milo leaned into the screen. "Zoom in on the driver?"

"Leroy Thompson?" Gramm questioned. "David Bonner and Leroy Thompson. How does that happen? Last I knew, Leroy works for Morrie Wolf, but he doesn't work with Bonner."

"The time stamp on this incident is 8:05 p.m.," White said.

Gramm brought up the next question. "Milo kills the guy at 10:08. So how does that guy go from being beat up and shoved into a car at eight to careening down Mesaba at ten?"

"I object to being referred to as the killer," Milo protested.

"It amuses me," Gramm insisted. "Milo, time to visit Morrie Wolf."

"Not a problem. I'll just ask him if he hired Bonner to rough up Bianchi. Morrie loves to talk about his business. I wonder where in Lake Superior I'll end up. Somebody, please take care of my pet hamster, Ernie."

"A bit dramatic, Milo," Gramm chided. "White, find out any recent information on David Bonner. You and I will go pay him a visit. Preston call Doc Smith and tell him we have another possible name for our victim. Then find out as much as you can about Raf Bianchi. After you do that, find out the identities of the other people he's eating pop up with."

White smiled but let it go.

"Can I talk to your chef, and this Gabby person?" Preston asked Milo.

"You're a cop, Preston!" Gramm stressed. "You can talk to anybody."

Milo showed Martha's number to Preston. "You interview Martha, and I'll talk to Gabby." Milo remembered Gabby saying that Kick DeJong's crew were regulars at Gabby's restaurant, Va Vena.

"Just for my knowledge, why would Raf Bianchi get thrown into a car?" Preston asked.

"Usually, it means he's done something wrong, and the trip in the car is a reminder that he needs to change his ways," Milo said. "The trip rarely ends up at Dairy Queen."

"Milo, do you know where we can find David Bonner?" White asked. "The last time I talked to him, he was staying at the Gardner Hotel."

"The last time I saw him, he was living above the Tip Top Tavern on Central Entrance. He was also working there. We know Leroy is Wolf's errand boy for life, but maybe Bonner is on Wolf's payroll, too."

"Who is Morrie Wolf?" Preston asked Milo.

"He's a kind, grandfatherly figure who dabbles in a few illegal activities."

"If you are found in the trunk of a car and the car is found in the lake, chances are you pissed off Morrie Wolf," Gramm said. "He views Milo as the son he never had. I think he belongs in jail. Morrie, not Milo…wait, come to think of it."

§

"Martha, I'm on my way home," Gabby said with a sigh. "I love this house and the characters in it."

"You can stay longer," Martha said. "I'm sure no one would mind."

"Don't tempt me. Where can I find Agnes to say goodbye?"

"She is probably in her office. Go through the gallery to the library, which leads to the billiard room, which leads to Milo's office. Look for a door on the right."

"Isn't there a direct door to her office?"

"There is, but it's outside."

Gabby smiled. "Why?"

"I don't think we know," Martha said.

Gabby followed Martha's instructions and was shocked when she arrived at Agnes' desk. "I made it!" she announced to Agnes.

"Excellent. We don't want to have to organize another search party," Agnes joked.

"Have you ever lost anybody?"

"Several people. We hear noises, but they have never been found."

"I'm leaving. I wanted to say goodbye," Gabby said. "And to thank you and Sutherland for such a unique weekend."

"Perfect timing. I just got off the phone with Tee, our construction guru. She has an hour in her schedule this afternoon to look at that staircase. You could stay one more night." Agnes smiled.

Gabby smiled but shook her head. "My restaurant is opening tomorrow, so we need to assess what we can offer, but I could delay that for a few more hours."

"Excellent! After all, you are now a charter member of the LEC, Lakesong Exploratory Committee."

"Did those t-shirts arrive yet?" Gabby joked.

10

This was not Milo's ideal way of starting a Monday morning. Turns out Gramm was serious about Milo poking around to find out why Bonner and Morrie Wolf's guy Leroy were beating up Raf Bianchi. Going to talk to Morrie about his business was dangerous, but going empty-handed was foolish.

Milo decided to drive the Lakesong SUV up to Betty's Pies just in case he hit patches of ice the salt had not melted yet. The old cafe outside of Two Harbors had become a family restaurant many years ago. Milo remembered the smell of baking pies that permeated every square inch of the place. He parked, walked into the wooden building, and took a deep breath. It was heaven.

Breakfast rush was in full swing. Milo walked up to the counter. "Pie order for Milo Rathkey," he said to the young woman behind the counter. Without a word, she pointed to the left. *Takeaway* was in bold red letters. He took his place in line behind two burly guys and a teen. The line moved quickly.

When he got to the counter, a younger woman with green hair walked down a long row of orders, found Milo's, and brought it to him. "I put the pies in a box with bubble wrap. It will keep the pies from moving around," she said. "As much fun as it is, don't pop the bubbles until after you have delivered the pies."

Milo was amused picturing Morrie's muscle, Milosh, popping the bubbles as he dug into a cherry pie. He forced the scene from his mind.

§

"I called Bonner's parole officer, this morning," White said as Gramm drove down Central Entrance toward the Tip Top Tavern. "Bonner has made all of his appointments, but never says anything. No incidents as far as we know. His address and the Tip Top are the same, so we can assume he lives there."

"What does the parole guy say about Bonner's employment?" Gramm asked.

"Barback at the Tip Top."

"So, he works where he lives. Convenient."

"I don't believe it!" White laughed as she looked past Gramm.

"What?" Gramm asked.

"We're past it. You won't believe it. I don't believe it. We can check it out on the way back," White said.

Pop-Up Dinner, Drop Down Dead

"What did you see? Can't you just tell me?"

"No, I wanna make sure I saw what I think I saw."

"Nothing having to do with the murder?"

"Not yet."

Robin continued to be vague as Gramm pulled into the Tip Top parking lot. He looked around at the ten or fifteen cars in the parking lot. "It's not even noon. Don't tell me this place does a lot of business at noon."

"I won't tell you that, but you can count the cars yourself," White said.

The dance hall size tavern wasn't overflowing, but there was a healthy number of patrons at the bar. The draw was a make-your-own sandwich lunch Darlene had provided at one of the empty tables.

"Hi there. What can I get you people?" Darlene, the owner, called out. "The bar's pretty full right now, but we have seats at the tables. What to drink?"

Gramm noticed that most of the customers were wearing suits. He thought this was a cowboy boots and jeans kind of bar.

Darlene, a thick, muscular woman with tattoos running down one arm, ran her hand through her dark, curly hair. "I make a mean businessman's martini."

"What about businesswomen?" White asked.

"They're the same. Call it whatcha like."

Gramm showed his badge. "We are here to see David Bonner."

Darlene rolled her eyes. "I'm getting rusty at spotting cops. I'm telling you, he's a good worker. I don't wantcha hassling him."

"No hassle. We just need to talk to him," Gramm said.

"What about?"

"Are you his lawyer?"

"No!" Darlene slapped her rag down hard on the bar. "But I can get one here in about ten minutes."

Gramm shrugged. "Up to you, but we still need to talk to him."

"I'll get 'em. Sit at a table way in the corner. I don't want you bothering my customers at the bar." Darlene ambled the length of the bar, opened a door and quietly said, "Hey, David, cops here to see you."

White had followed her along the bar. "Thanks for giving him the opportunity to run," she said as she barged through the door.

"Run from what? You said you just wanted to talk. Did you lie?"

"Does this room have a back door?"

"No, the cases of booze magically appear every Monday. It's the leprechauns."

Before White could move further into the back room, David Bonner stepped out from behind a stack of boxes. He had two cases of whisky, one in each hand. He towered over White with his usual scowl.

"Hello, Mr. Bonner, we would like to chat."

Gramm joined White in the back room.

Bonner stared. The whiskey cases began to sway. White unhooked the strap to her Taser.

"David, knock it off. I want no trouble. Put the cases down. Just talk to them," Darlene said. "If you need a lawyer, let me know."

Pop-Up Dinner, Drop Down Dead

Bonner took his time walking the length of the bar after setting down the two cases of booze on the floor. Gramm led the way to a far table, followed by Bonner, with White bringing up the rear, hand still on her taser. Most people would ask what the cops wanted. Bonner just sat down and stayed mute; eyes glued to a spot over Gramm's shoulder, calmly menacing.

Gramm wondered to himself if they should call for backup. White continued to stand, her hand on the Taser. Gramm began, "Mr. Bonner, we have video of you roughing up a guy named Raf Bianchi last Friday night."

Bonner said nothing and continued to stare.

"Why did you rough him up and throw him in the car?"

Bonner mumbled something incoherent.

"David! Tell them what they want to know!" Darlene said as she approached the table.

"I delivered a message."

"About what?" White asked.

"To pay my friend what he owed."

"You're moonlighting—collecting on the side? Doesn't this place pay enough?" Gramm asked.

"I was helping a friend."

"What happened after you had a chat?"

"We drove back to his car?"

Gramm was trying to get a read off Bonner. He seemed calmer, but the same dead eyes staring at nothing kept Gramm on edge. "Bianchi was murdered."

"Not by me." Bonner glanced at Darlene.

"Our video shows Leroy Thompson driving the car," White said.

"He's a friend."

"How do you know him?" White asked.

"Jail."

"Who do you collect for?"

Bonner turned to face Gramm. "I work here at the Tip Top almost every day. I get a paycheck every Friday. I live upstairs. I'm quiet. Ask Darlene."

Darlene folded her arms. "I don't pay this guy to talk to cops. So, are you drinkin' or are you leavin'?"

"We're done for now. We'll be back," Gramm said.

§

Milo drove into the Rasa Bar's icy, gravel parking lot and parked facing the brick wall with the faded Hamm's Beer ad painted on the side. Milo wasn't sad. He never liked Hamm's. Milo preferred Guinness.

Morrie's pie box in hand, Milo jostled his way through the thick wooden door to the front of the bar. Per usual, the smell of stale beer and cleaning fluid welcomed him. It took his eyes a few moments to adjust to the dark interior. Not much had changed. Benny, the bartender, was still watching TV behind the bar. One customer was nursing a shot and a beer, an odd way to drink that combination. Must be a beginner.

"Hey, Milo!" Benny said. "Coffee or something stronger?"

"Just dropping off some pies," Milo said.

Milosh, Morrie's bodyguard, enforcer, and number one guy, was sitting with Morrie in the back booth. He turned at the sound of Milo's voice. "Milo went to Betty's and didn't take me with," he complained to Morrie.

Morrie looked up. "You and Milo buddies these days?"

"We're Betty's buddies."

Morrie went back to his betting sheets.

Milo walked over to the booth. "I come bearing pies," he said.

"Milosh informed me of his hurt feelings," Morrie said, not looking up.

Milosh got up, giving Milo room to sit down. Milo dropped the box of pies on a nearby table, not wanting to mess up Morrie's sheets.

"Hurt feelings?" Milo questioned, looking at Milosh, who had parked his large body at a nearby table.

"You went to Bettys and didn't take him," Morrie said.

"I didn't have his number," Milo said. "Won't happen again."

"Long time no see, Milo. What brings you here?" Morrie asked.

"I need some info."

"How many pies did you bring?"

"Two. Cherry."

"Next time, make it three."

Milo was going to suggest that three pies were not healthy, but kept quiet. This was Morrie Wolf. Too much familiarity was often unhealthy. Direct questions were also unhealthy. Milo had to come at this from the side.

Milo made the first move in the chess game. "A guy named Raf Bianchi was roughed up a bit Friday night. Apparently, he owed some people money."

Morrie remained silent.

That move had gotten nothing, but he hadn't been thrown out. Milo had only one, maybe two moves left. "He was murdered later that night."

Morrie finished with one sheet, licked his index finger, and with slow deliberation placed the sheet on the bottom of the stack.

Milo began again. "I'm told that Mr. Bianchi had been doing a little bookie action on his own at Nonies Restaurant. The restaurateur was warned off by a man he described as large."

Morrie laid down his pencil, straightened his trademark skinny tie as he looked at Milo for the first time. "Milo, the definition of a bookie is someone who makes money taking bets. The man you mention did not make money. He lost money. We refer to that as being a loser."

Milo was surprised that Morrie admitted knowing Bianchi. Morrie took a sip of his coffee. Milo made his last move. "A couple of thugs roughed him up just before he died. The cops recognized David Bonner." Milo took a shallow breath and then plunged ahead. "I was just wondering who Bonner was working for."

Morrie picked up his pencil and went back to his sheets. "Ask him."

Milo was disappointed. He had expected more of a reaction out of Wolf. Morrie looked up. "You still here Milo?"

"I guess. Before I leave, I gotta tell yah, when Bonner was roughing up Bianchi, Leroy Thompson was driving."

Morrie didn't flinch. "Always nice talking to you, Milo."

Pop-Up Dinner, Drop Down Dead

Milo got up and walked out. The Leroy Thompson information had garnered no reaction from Morrie. Milo was far from the living expert on all things Morrie Wolf, but *a nice talking to you* reaction often meant Morrie was hearing about something for the first time.

"Sucks for Leroy," Milo said to himself as he stepped up into the SUV.

Milosh sat down across from his boss.

"Hey Benny," Morrie shouted to the bartender. "Get that stupid son-of-a-bitch, Leroy, in here!"

Benny nodded, walked over and noticed Milosh about to take a spoon to a cherry pie. "Nice touch, Milo bringing pies."

"Pies and information," Morrie said without looking up. "And if Leroy's slightly damaged along the way, all the better."

§

Walking to the Interceptor, Gramm began, "So, Bonner says Leroy is a friend. Are you buying the jailhouse buddy routine?" Gramm asked White.

"I doubt anyone becomes a buddy of Bonner," White said. "Maybe Bonner is a temp hire for Wolf."

Gramm chuckled.

"What?" White asked.

"I have this vision of Rent-A-Thug," Gramm said as he settled himself into the driver's seat.

"Could Bianchi be a Wolf hit?" White offered. "Maybe a strong arm gone bad…didn't mean to kill him, just scare him."

"I wish, but we don't know enough," Gramm said.

"On our way here, what do you think you saw that got you so excited?" Gramm backed up and drove to the parking lot exit.

"If I'm right, it's worth a stop. It's on the other side of Central Entrance. I'll tell you when to turn in," White said.

Lunch time, roads were plowed, and people were out recovering from cabin fever. The cars were whizzing by in both directions—negating any chance of turning left. Gramm's bushy eyebrows did a small dance as he flipped on his blue lights and piercing siren. "If you got 'em, use 'em."

White laughed.

After a count of five, Gramm gunned the police interceptor, made his left turn, and swerved into the right lane. He continued down Central Entrance until he turned sharply right, following White's directions. Skidding to a stop, he turned off the lights and siren. Ahead of him was a bright orange shop, somewhat familiar, but the name had changed. It was still a sign shop, but was now called Maki and Van Dyke.

"I see it. I know what you're thinking, but there are a lot of Makis in Duluth," Gramm mumbled.

"You always say that, but we keep running into the same one," White corrected. "I bet you lunch, it's Kayla."

"You're on."

Walking into the building they were greeted by one time suspect, one time witness, now full-time sign maker, Kayla Maki. She smiled at them. "Well, if it isn't my two favorite cops. With all the lights and sirens, you must need a sign in a hurry."

§

Pop-Up Dinner, Drop Down Dead

Milo strolled into the cop shop an hour after Gramm and White. He was carrying a large, white insulated bag.

"You're late," Gramm charged.

"To what? I talked to Gabby per your orders. She was at Va Vena. She works there, remember?"

Gramm growled. "And you left without eating, right?"

"I tried. Believe me, I tried, but her gnocchi pulled a gun and threatened me."

White shook her head. "You are carrying a large, insulated bag."

Milo lifted the bag, placing it on Gramm's desk. "More gnocchi, bistecca, and shrimp pooch de mare."

"Fruitti di Mare?" White questioned.

"Yeah, sure, whatever."

Gramm called Preston in. "Lunch is on Milo."

White removed everything from the white bag, announcing various entrées, then opened a separate bag. "They thought of everything: plates, forks, knives, napkins…everything."

As they filled their plates buffet style, Gramm said, "While you feasted, we talked to the always friendly David Bonner."

"So, what did our always cooperative friend have to say?"

"He admits to stuffing Bianchi into a car but says they only took him for a ride to talk repayment of money to a *friend*," White said.

"Not buying the friend?" Milo asked.

"We pressed him. He wouldn't tell us who he works for other than being a bar back at the Tip Top," Gramm said. "To me, a Bonner/Thompson combo smacks of Morrie Wolf."

"Morrie told me to ask Bonner about roughing up Bianchi. He said we should ask Bonner who he worked for."

"Did you not hear us? We did," White said. "He said he worked at the Tip Top. He never answered our question."

Milo stared at Gramm and White. "You asked him who he worked for, and he told you. Son of a bitch. Morrie was right."

"About what? He told us what we already know. He's a bar back at the Tip Top," Gramm grumbled.

"Owned by…?"

"Darlene Budack," Gramm barked.

"Niece of…"

Gramm stared back. "Son of a bitch. Bud Budack, loan shark. Are you thinking Darlene has picked up the family business?"

"But if Bonner is her collector, what the hell was Leroy Thompson there for?" White asked.

"I think I ratted him out. He's probably nursing a couple of black eyes—love taps from Milosh again," Milo said.

"Could our case be this simple? David Bonner and Leroy Thompson kill Bianchi?" Gramm asked.

"I doubt it." Milo shook his head. "Bianchi was alone in his own car. That means he was alive when Bonner let him go."

"I'm going with internal bleeding," White said.

"Two hours of it?" Milo questioned.

White tried again. "Maybe Bonner and Thompson stuffed him in his car and pushed it down Mesaba."

Milo shook his head. "Pearl Landrum, our window watcher with binoculars, never mentioned two guys pushing a car. She said it was going fast and crashed through the barricade."

Pop-Up Dinner, Drop Down Dead

"Did she see brake lights?" Gramm asked.

"We asked. She said no."

"Okay, Bonner and Thompson kill him, put him in his car, push it to the top of Mesaba, and send it down the hill. Does anyone here want the rest of the beef tips?" Gramm asked.

"I'm afraid you will be forced to finish them off," White said. "Nice theory—the killing maybe, but the pushing and sending?"

"I didn't think it through. If Amy asks, this is all low-fat fish." Gramm spooned the remaining tips onto his plate.

Preston finished the Frutti di Mare. "I think Milo needs to question every chef in the city."

White happily took the rest of the Bolognese Gnocchi and nodded in agreement.

Preston put down her fork. "Can I ask a dumb question? If Morrie Wolf is so dangerous, why does he talk to Milo?"

"We have an understanding," Milo said.

"Do I want to know any more?" Preston asked.

"No!" Gramm said. "Tell us about our victim and who those people are around the table from Milo's video? Hopefully, we won't have to talk to them."

"Because you and Robin are still hoping for two-hour internal bleeding?" Milo asked.

"Preston! Tell us about the victim, so Milo stops talking!" Gramm ordered, biting into one of the beef tips.

Preston opened her tablet, pretending to read from it. "Raf was born Ralph Bing. He changed his name to Raf Bianchi after doing a brief stint in jail on a gambling charge."

"We know you're not reading from that pad, but all this sounds familiar," Gramm said.

"Feinberg told us that at the poker game," White said.

"I wasn't invited to the poker game," Preston complained.

"We discovered Robin is a shark. For all we know, you're a six-time poker champion. Keep going."

"Bianchi has never been married. His financials are dismal. He has eighty-three dollars in his bank account, two credit cards, one of which is maxed out and has been canceled by the issuing bank. He has worked as a chef in a number of restaurants in Duluth. Currently unemployed. Several managers said he was unreliable. He lives in an extended stay motel on Central Entrance. I called. He hadn't paid the bill, so the manager boxed up what little he had and re-rented the room."

"We need to get possession of that box," Gramm said.

"Way ahead of you," Preston said. "I had a uniform pick it up. I have it here."

Gramm almost smiled. "Robin, did our newest member just delegate?"

"She did," White said.

Gramm sighed. "They grow up so quickly."

Preston handed out stills of the DeJong table.

Gramm continued. "If Bianchi was jobless and broke, he would have to borrow money. If he didn't pay it back, that would go along with getting jumped by David Bonner,"

White looked at the Preston's pictures. "Got names?"

"Martha Gibbson gave me the names from the reservations. The guy with the mustache facing the camera is Kick DeJong, forty, owns the Marathon and Nonies restaurants in

Pop-Up Dinner, Drop Down Dead

Duluth, plus two others, same names, in the Twin Cities. All the restaurants are owned and managed under the DeJong Group umbrella. Next to him, our victim, Raf Bianchi."

"While at lunch procuring your gourmet take out, I remembered I've seen this Raf guy before. He and DeJong, Mr. Mustache, were shouting at each other in Nonies. DeJong threw him out and banned him. It was nasty, but entertaining."

"When?" Gramm asked.

"A couple of days ago."

"What were they shouting?" White asked.

"Don't know. I was trying to eat lunch. Money was mentioned."

White held up the palm of her hand. "Stop! Wait a minute! If this guy Kick threw our victim out of his restaurant and banned him, why is he sitting down and eating dinner with him a few days later?"

Milo shrugged. "They made up?"

"That's nuts. Let's do more digging into this DeJong guy and his relationship with Bianchi," Gramm insisted.

"Phone records and financials?" Preston asked.

"Yup. Let's continue with this happy little group."

Milo leaned over to White. "Interviews all around, I think."

White looked at Milo and nodded her head.

"The guy on the other side of Raf is Bob Young, also in his early forties. He's a cook on the boats. Off now, of course, because it's winter. Couldn't find much on him. I could dig further."

Gramm shrugged. "We'll talk to him, see if we need to know any more."

Preston continued. "Next to Young is a model named Poppie."

"Poppie what?" Gramm questioned.

"She goes by the single name, like Beyonce' or Cher," Preston said.

White leaned over to her. "Good get on Cher, someone the boss can recognize."

"I know who Beyonce' is," Gramm defended himself. "Get this Poppie woman's real first, last, and middle name!"

Preston nodded and continued. "I checked Poppie's social media. She posts she's *in a relationship* with the really hunky guy next to her, Reese Winterhausen. He's a forty-something commercial artist."

"What does 'hunky guy's' social media say about any of them?" White questioned.

"He doesn't post often, but most of his posts are of the group and lots of good-looking females in really nice places: Italy, St. Croix, Switzerland. Real globetrotters. There was only one of Poppie and that was from the summer on a sailboat leaving the Duluth entry."

"Who are these other women?" Gramm asked.

"The one standing is Jess DeJong, Kick's wife." The one seated is Emma Winterhausen. "She is Reese and Jess' sister."

"Emma is the one Feinberg mentioned with the assault charge. How old is this girl?" White questioned.

"Twenty something."

"DeJong's wife Jess and Reese are in their forties. Where did Emma come from?" White noted.

"Yeah, there's a story there. I'll get it."

Gramm leaned back. "I'd love to charge Bonner, but while we wait on the autopsy, we got nothing. So, we need to talk to all these people and probably more people to see if they're lying, which they will be. Have I ever told you how much I hate these first interviews?"

"Really?" White asked sarcastically. "I never heard you say that."

§

Milo expected Sutherland and Agnes to be in the family room as he came in from the garage. The room was empty, but the table was set for five. He heard voices in the gallery and was pleased to see Gabby was still in residence at Lakesong.

After an exchange of pleasantries, Gabby explained, "Va Vena lost power just after you left with lunch for your crew. Both the restaurant and my house are in the dark. Somebody must have run into something. I hope my extended stay in Lakesong is okay with you."

"Did you leave a faucet dripping?" Sutherland asked.

Gabby smiled. "I did."

Agnes gave Sutherland a quizzical look.

"Just being a thoughtful, fellow homeowner. You wouldn't want her to have a busted pipe," Sutherland defended his question.

"Gabby, you can stay at Lakesong as long as you like," Milo said. "The lunch you provided to the hardworking homicide department was inhaled."

The group was sitting in the gallery for pre-dinner cocktails. Sutherland took the drink orders. Refusing to give up his mixologist duties, he used his newly delivered scooter to transverse across the gallery to the bar in the family room. Milo was looking up at the full moon through the glass dome, cocking his head, much like a cocker spaniel.

"Listening for something?" Agnes asked.

Milo smiled. "Leaking pipes."

Martha helped Sutherland out, picking up the drinks as she wheeled in a cart of hors d'oeuvres. Sutherland asked Milo about the murder investigation.

"Anxious to get back into murder?" Milo asked.

"Your tales of murder and mayhem are always entertaining."

"Sutherland, I talked to your good friend, Morrie Wolf, today. If I have to talk to him again, I may need muscle. Are you in?"

Agnes choked on her drink. "No!" she croaked.

Sutherland gestured to Agnes. "You heard her. I'm so disappointed, but I will have to decline."

Gabby leaned into Martha and whispered, "Morrie Wolf? That gangster?"

"And frequent visitor to Lakesong," Martha lied.

"Why?"

"Well, not really frequent," Martha corrected. "But he was here recently. He gave me that Japanese chopping knife, you know, the one with the black Juma handle."

"I received a Molly Zuckerman Hartung painting," Agnes offered.

"Why would Morrie Wolf give you gifts?" Gabby asked.

"You might say we did him a favor," Agnes said.
"We had to dispose of a couple of bodies," Martha joked.
"But it was worth it," Agnes added.

11

The morning sky was light pink and the open water far out on Lake Superior was a deep blue. Quite the greeting from Gitche Gumee this morning. A welcome change from blowing snow and high winds of the weekend.

"Where's Gabby?" Milo asked as he led the cats into the morning room. Per usual, he stopped at the coffee urn to pour himself a cup. The cats, who didn't drink coffee, always wondered why this stop had to be made. In their minds, feeding cats bacon should take priority. At this point, they both registered their disappointment by singing the song of their people.

"Their wailing is so sad," Agnes said, "Especially Jet's."

"They're faking it," Milo said, sitting down. "Once again, where's Gabby?"

Agnes cocked her head. "Gabby doesn't live here, Milo. She had to go back to her life, but don't fret, you still have mournful crying cats."

"She left so early."

"Late last night actually, but she totally enjoyed her blizzard mansion visit," Martha said as she brought Milo his breakfast. "As much as she wanted to stay, Gabby has the restaurant."

"She will be back after Tee shores up the newly unearthed basement staircase," Agnes added. "So the Lakesong Explorers can go exploring."

"Can I go join?" Milo asked.

Agnes shook her head. "I don't remember getting an invite when you and Hop Along Sutherland here explored that tunnel and found that Scotch."

"She makes a good point," Sutherland said.

"Quiet Hop Along, less talking, more hopping," Milo said.

"I already dislike that moniker, Hop Along," Sutherland complained.

"I didn't come up with it," Milo said. "Ms. She-Makes-a-Good-Point did." He broke off pieces of bacon and handed them to the waiting cats, stopping the plaintive cries.

"Oh good, they were unusually mournful this morning, and it's so beautiful. I'm Sutherland's chauffeur until he gets his walking boot. What's on tap for everyone else today?" Agnes asked.

Sutherland hurried with the answer. "The office has three rescheduled closings. Busy day."

"As exciting as that is, my dear, I was really asking Milo."

"I'm facilitating people's dreams coming true!" Sutherland complained.

Agnes patted his hand. "And they love you for it."

"I think love is a little strong," Milo said. "But in answer to your question, Agnes, the entire police force is hunting for the mini assassin that took Sutherland out."

Sutherland nodded. "Good! I can give you a detailed description: short, a delightful smile, deep blue eyes, and an upturned button nose."

"We'll have a police artist stop over today," Milo said.

"Remember, she was wearing a pink snow suit with butterflies," Agnes laughed.

Milo pretended to write that down.

§

Having dropped her coat over her office chair, White sat at her desk and pulled her straight, black hair into a sleek professional ponytail. Ready for business, she walked into Gramm's office with her coffee of the day. "The sun is shining. It's a great day!"

"All the sun does is make the streets slushy. Whatcha drinking?" Gramm asked.

"Caramel Espresso Macchiato. It's espresso with extra drizzles of caramel."

"Oh, a diet Machineato," Gramm said.

"Macchiato."

"Whatever," Gramm said, looking into the bullpen area. "Where's Milo?"

White shook her head.

Preston arrived, rolling her chair into Gramm's office.

"Where's Milo?" Gramm repeated.

Preston blinked. "Is it my week to watch him?"

"Better you than me," Gramm said.

Seconds later, Milo wandered into Gramm's office after catching up with some of the uniformed patrolmen. "Gabby's gone," he said mournfully.

"Our condolences," Gramm said as his phone lit up. "It's the Doc," he told the room, putting the call on speaker. "Doc, cause of death?"

White laughed. "Blunt force trauma from bouncing off a half-track and being hit with a power pole during a snowstorm."

"Good guess, Robin, but you would be wrong," Smith said. "The victim was already dead or dying on his way down. The cause of death was anaphylactic shock. His throat swelled up completely blocking his airways."

"What was he allergic to?" Gramm asked.

"Peanuts, it was on his dog tag."

"So not murder?" White guessed.

"Well, there are some loose ends. There was no EpiPen on him. That's suspicious. People with life-threatening allergies do not leave the house without that pen. Also, we didn't find peanuts in his stomach. The evidence points to peanut oil."

"Hey Doc, Milo here. Do you think this guy was driving in a snowstorm while drinking peanut oil after leaving his pen gizmo in the men's room?"

"No, Milo, I don't. However, he might have unknowingly ingested the peanut oil and perhaps he was sloppy about carrying the 'pen gizmo.' Not my call," the Doc said as he hung up.

Gramm put his phone on the desk. "Seriously, I want a clear cut murder. It must involve sharp objects or ropes or guns…whatever. Just a simple damn murder."

Pop-Up Dinner, Drop Down Dead

White summarized their case. "Our dead guy, whose name we now know, slid down an icy hill, crashed into a tank in front of our consultant, bounced into a power pole, dropped several live wires which could have electrocuted him, and none of that caused him to die?"

"Dead man driving," Milo said.

"So, do we have a murder?" White asked.

"At this point we still have a suspicious death," Gramm said.

"That's what you called it to get out of snow duty," Preston said.

"All this information and we are no closer to a solution. We need to begin some preliminary questioning of the people at our victim's table about our victim's habits. Did he often forget his EpiPen? Things like that. White and I will take Kick DeJong."

"Good place to start," White concurred. "His attitude toward Bianchi is, to say the least, peculiar. He throws the guy out of his restaurant one day and then sits with him at dinner the next—peculiar."

"Milo and Preston talk to whoever is available this morning. That means working together without having to call the bomb squad," Gramm said, recalling a case last fall where Preston got herself trapped in a barn.

Milo looked at Preston. "You call one bomb squad and get tabbed for life."

"And don't go finding extra dead bodies," White added.

"I didn't put her there. I just fell on her," Preston defended. "I'll start making calls to see who is available."

"Also, we need to talk with your chef, Milo, and the other woman. Did they give this guy a dish with peanuts in it?" Gramm asked.

"I hope not," Milo said.

§

Kick DeJong was working in his office at Nonies when Gramm and White walked in. After brief handshakes, Gramm and White sat in two office chairs facing Kick, who slumped into the chair behind his desk. He picked up his pen, clicking it on and off, and stared.

"Do you know a man named Raf Bianchi?" Gramm asked.

Kick stopped clicking and sat up straight, making him seem even taller than his six-foot-one frame. "Yeah, what's the problem?"

"Why do you assume a problem?" White questioned.

"I haven't heard from him since last Friday."

"Is that unusual?" Gramm asked.

"Yeah, I expected him to come around this weekend, but with the storm and all, well…"

"It's Tuesday," Gramm said. "No snow since Sunday."

"I know. That's why I asked you if there was a problem. You came to me, and you are the police. I figured problem. Are you from traffic or drugs?"

"Homicide," Gramm said with no explanation. "Raf was in a fatal accident Friday night on Mesaba Avenue."

Kick began to blink his eyes and click his pen. "Raf's dead?"

"Yes."

"Are you sure?"

"Yes."

"You said homicide. Was he murdered?"

Pop-Up Dinner, Drop Down Dead

"Let's just say we're investigating his death," Gramm said.

"We have reason to believe that Mr. Bianchi was allergic to peanuts," White said.

"Of course, deathly allergic. I've seen him inject himself a couple of times."

"So, he had that pen at all times?"

"Always."

"Would he have stored it in his car?" Gramm asked.

"No. He told me the drug needs to be at room temperature, so no glove compartments."

"Do you know if he had an EpiPen at dinner Friday night?"

"He never went anywhere without it. I assume he did." Kick began smoothing his mustache. "This is bad, but I think you should know." Kick placed his pen on the desk and took a sip from his water bottle.

Gramm and White remained quiet.

"We're all friends, but Raf was being an ass as only he can be. So, when we all ordered the entrée with peanuts, he mouthed off about all of us of trying to kill him."

Gramm's eyebrows inched up. "He felt threatened by people at the table?"

"I don't know. It was typical Raf drama. He was drunk on his ass, but we all knew if he needed it, he would have used his pen."

"No EpiPen was found on him."

Kick didn't seem to hear. He felt for the pill bottle in his pocket, picked up his pen and began to click his pen again.

"We have a witness who saw you and Bianchi get into a shouting match here in this restaurant," White said.

"I don't remember that."

"Fine, we'll check with your employees to see if they remember," White threatened.

Kick stopped clicking the pen. "Raf and I got into arguments all the time."

"What was this argument about?" Gramm asked.

Kick slammed the pen down and shouted, "It's really none of your business!"

"This is a murder investigation, Mr. DeJong. Everything is our business." Gramm challenged.

"You think I killed him? Get out of here! I want to talk to my lawyer."

§

"I'm suspicious," Milo said to Preston as they drove to Reese Winterhausen's loft in Duluth's West End.

"Why?"

Milo smirked. "Of all the people that we have to talk to, the only one available this morning is the one you think is hunky."

"No, I called Kick DeJong and set up Gramm and White for their interview. At the same time, I found out from DeJong that his wife, Jess is in the hospital. Car accident Friday night. He requested we not bother her. Emma Winterhausen is out on Spirit Mountain, not available until the afternoon. Bob Young, no answer. Poppie? No last name yet. I don't know anything about her. I figured we could get more info on the mysterious Poppie from Reese. This is all strategic."

"Strategic. Word of the day," Milo said.

Pop-Up Dinner, Drop Down Dead

The all-brick building was once a food processing plant with iron mesh covering the windows. Most of the canning equipment was gone, with the exception of a few small machines that remained, to give the building a cool mechanized look.

Milo and Preston pressed the button for *Winterhausen Design*. The return buzz indicated the security door was now open. A dark iron elevator led up two stories to the loft.

The elevator clanged and banged as it opened directly into a large loft. Milo and Preston were looking at a large design table, a professional printer, and several screens suspended from the ceiling. What they did not see was Reese Winterhausen or anyone else. "Mr. Winterhausen?" Milo called.

"I'm in the front," Winterhausen called.

Preston spotted the lanky Winterhausen and pointed in his direction.

"Mr. Winterhausen?" Milo questioned again.

Reese looked up. "Guilty."

Preston thought he was even better looking in person.

"I'm police consultant Rathkey and this is Officer Kate Preston."

Reese smiled at Preston, a cute, lazy smile, a smile that had to be returned. He was handsome with a capital H. His fashionable beard stubble and wavy brown hair looked effortless.

"Mr. Winterhausen," Milo began, not at all affected by the Winterhausen smile. "We want to talk to you about Raf Bianchi."

"Time for a break, anyway. Want a drink? Soda? Water?"

Both declined.

"What has Raf done now?" Reese grabbed an energy drink from the fridge.

"Did he do something in the past?" Milo asked.

"Good one," Reese laughed. "Constantly."

"Well, last Friday night, Mr. Bianchi was involved in an incident on Mesaba Avenue."

"Okay," he said, crossing to the living area, sitting on a couch. "Come on, sit down."

Preston sat in a chair opposite. "Bianchi died."

Reese shrugged. "Okay."

"Not a close personal friend?" Preston asked.

"He was never high on my personal friend list."

"Did you know about his peanut allergy?" Milo asked.

"Of course. Ralphie boy was crazed about it."

"How careful was he with his allergy?"

"He made sure everybody knew how to use his pen, not that we always wanted to."

Preston marked that comment on her tablet.

"Where did he keep the pen?" Milo asked.

"He had a fancy Velcro pouch sowed into his coat and jacket pockets so it wouldn't fall out. Does all this have something to do with his 'incident' Friday night?"

"Perhaps," Milo said. "What can you tell us about him?"

"You really want to know?"

Milo nodded. "It's why I asked."

"Well, he was a louse. Not to be trusted. He was always playing some angle to get money, yet he was always broke."

"Any specifics?" Milo asked.

Pop-Up Dinner, Drop Down Dead

"Lately, he was a…drug pusher lite. Not big time but usually had some kind of drug on him. My sister, Jess, called him bad news, and I trust Jess."

"We understand you were at the pop-up dinner Friday night."

Reese smiled. "Gabby's dinner. I sure was."

Hearing the dinner referred to as 'Gabby's' and not Martha's threw Milo for a minute. "If you all hated Raf so much, why include him?"

"We didn't. Kick did. He kept including him and paying his way. It was crazy annoying."

Milo and Preston remained silent, hoping that Reese would fill in the blanks himself. He did.

"I told Kick a long time ago to cut him loose, but he kept bringing old Ralphie back. He just messes up everybody's good time."

"Let me get this straight," Milo said. "Kick keeps including Raf even though others in the group don't want him included."

"That's right."

"Was anyone more annoyed at Raf than usual Friday night?" Preston asked.

Reese leaned back and closed his eyes, remembering Emma. "All of us were. We all ordered the entrée with the peanuts in it. Drove him crazy. He was screaming. It was funny at the time."

"Did he get the peanut entrée?" Milo asked.

"Of course not. He got the number two. I remember Gabby putting the number by his plate. I think it was beef and pineapple."

"Friday night, you were sitting next to a woman we have identified only as Poppie. Can you give us any more information, and are you and she in a relationship?" Preston saw the glance from Milo. She knew two-part questions were bad, but she really wanted to know the second part.

"Relationship? Not really. I know her."

"We can't find her. Where does she live?" Milo asked, getting back on track.

"Minneapolis. I can give you her number."

"That would be great," Preston said.

"Could you give us her last name?" Milo asked.

Winterhausen laughed. "Her name is Poppie Flower."

"No, her real name."

"That's her real name. Her grandparents were hippies and adopted the last name of Flower. Her parents compounded the silliness, giving their kids flower first names. Poppie has two sisters, Daisy and Iris, and a brother, Periwinkle."

"You got that?" Milo asked Preston

"Oh, I got it. *Forgetting it is going to be the problem*," Preston thought.

Winterhausen smiled. "I think that's why Poppie just goes by Poppie, and her sisters married early."

Milo moved to the decorative wrought iron windows, leaving Preston to continue the questioning. "What did you do after the dinner?"

"The weather ended the dinner early. I drove home. It was getting nasty."

"Did Poppie leave with you?"

"Yeah."

Pop-Up Dinner, Drop Down Dead

There was an awkward silence. Milo, thinking Preston was not going to ask the follow up, asked it for her. "Did she stay the night?"

"She was here when I fell asleep on the couch and here again when she woke me up making breakfast in the morning."

"Have you seen Raf since the dinner?" Preston asked.

Winterhausen shook his head. "No, but that's not unusual."

"Did you see Raf leave?" Milo asked.

Reese thought for a moment. "Now that you mention it, I did notice that Raf left before Gabby sent us home. When we all went into the parking lot, Raf was gone, but his car was still there."

"How do you know it was his car?"

"Old Prius. License plate, CHEF 1. Lying poser."

"He wasn't a chef?" Preston asked.

"Well, I'm pretty easy. If I have food in front of me, I'll usually eat it. But if I have a choice of chefs, Raf would not be there."

"Do you know of anyone who wanted to do him harm?"

"Like beat him up? Sure. I know he used to gamble, lose, and then dodge the people he borrowed from. Maybe he was still doing it. Maybe some of those people got tired of his lies. Ralphie was a total loser."

"You keep referring to him as Ralphie, not Raf," Preston pointed out.

Reese laughed. "I called him Ralphie Boy to annoy him. Always have. This Raf business happened after his arrest."

"Arrest for what?" Milo asked.

"Who knows? I don't like to get into people's business."

As Preston stood up to go, she offered Reese her condolences regarding his sister Jess.

Reese nodded. "Yeah, she got the worst of it—concussion. She's having trouble remembering, but the doctors say she will be okay. Just needs time."

§

Finished with DeJong, White and Gramm were anxious to move on to Young before lunch. White texted Preston, asking for Bob Young's address, adding they were going to swing by on the chance he might be home.

Preston responded quickly with the address, not wanting to take her attention away from the Reese Winterhausen interview.

Bob Young's apartment was part of an old mansion that had been split up into studio apartments. After hunting around to find apartment seven, they discovered a professional sign on his door that said simply:

Gone Fishing.
Hopefully Forever.
Rainy Lake Usual Place.

"He has a printed sign?" White questioned.

"The man is serious about his fishing," Gramm defended the sign.

"I wonder if he bought it at Maki and Van Dyke Signs," White mused.

Gramm almost smiled.

"I guess there's a nice leisurely drive to Rainy Lake in our future. Half that lake is in Canada," White joked, knowing Gramm's dislike of long-distance driving.

"I'm not searching every ice fishing shack on Rainy Lake to find him."

"You said we had to talk to everyone," White insisted. "No telling when he'll be back. Maybe a phone interview or zoom." She knew he hated both.

"Have you ever gone ice fishing?"

"Many times."

"I bet Preston never has, and for that matter, I know Milo hates to fish. It will be a new experience for both of them. I call early lunch."

"Agreed on lunch. Where?"

"I think we should try the Tip Top again," Gramm said.

"Really? The Tip Top?"

"It will be fast. They had a make-your-own-sandwich table when we were there last time, but couldn't stay. I love those. We can check in on Bonner again—rattle his cage. Besides, I want to know if our victim's EpiPen slipped out when he and Thompson were roughing him up."

"Let me guess, the make-your-own sandwich is just meat and cheese, no vegetables, like lettuce, tomato, onion…right?" White complained.

"You got the picture."

Without joy, White texted Milo and Preston about the lunch location.

§

Milo looked at his phone. "Lunch at the Tip Top? Why?"

"Do they have good food?" Preston asked.

"I wasn't aware they even had food. The Tip Top means Darlene Budack. Not good for digestion."

§

Gramm and White arrived at the Tip Top ahead of Rathkey and Preston.

"If you're here for Bonner, he's not here," Darlene shouted from behind the empty bar.

"We're here for lunch," Gramm said.

"You're early. How many?"

"Four."

"Okay, if you're a paying customer, you can sit anywhere. I'll be right there."

Gramm picked a table in the middle of the room. They could see the bar, but their conversation would be out of earshot.

"If Bonner's not here, do we have to stay?" White questioned.

"Let me reminisce. When I was a rookie cop, most bars provided a *make your own sandwich* for lunch. I remember it as being good. Look on the bright side, maybe they've added vegetables."

White's search for the sandwich making table was interrupted by Darlene dropping four packs of plastic cutlery and a pile of paper napkins. Robin sighed, thinking of the Chinese Dragon. Hank's special came with silverware and cloth napkins.

Pop-Up Dinner, Drop Down Dead

Darlene was still at the table when Milo and Preston walked in. He nodded to Darlene as he quickly sat down.

"Milo Rathkey! You bastard!" Darlene spat.

White looked up at the ceiling. "Oh boy! Here we go!"

Gramm held up his hand. "Before you and my esteemed colleague get into whatever, can I ask what happened to the make-your-own-sandwich table?"

"That's Monday's lunch. Today is Tuesday, fish and chips," Darlene said.

Darlene took their drink orders and went back behind the bar as the lunch crowd started to trickle in.

"Tomorrow we can eat at Morrie Wolf's bar," White joked. "I'll bring the Tums."

"Why did you pick this place?" Milo asked Gramm.

"I picked it for the make-your-own-sandwich, which apparently is only served on Mondays."

Darlene returned with their drinks. "The make your own sandwich is offered Mondays and Fridays. This is Tuesday. I told your friends it's fish and chips. I expect you all to order food. I'm not getting rich off your drink orders: coffee, tea, Diet Coke, and a Sprite." With that, she turned and left.

"Did you two see the sign across the way?" White asked Milo and Preston.

"Central Entrance is full of signs. Care to narrow it down?" Milo said.

"Sithens and Van Dyke is now Maki and Van Dyke," White said.

"Do we take a moment of silence for Sithens?" Milo asked.

"You're missing the point," White insisted. "How many people named Maki do you know?"

"Maybe ten or fifteen," Milo said.

"I went to school with Cindy Maki, but I doubt she's in the sign business," Preston said.

White grinned. "How about the Maki that we keep dealing with?"

"Kayla? Kayla Maki?" Milo guessed.

"Yes!" White shouted. The other tavern patrons turned to look.

"Are you sure the Maki on the sign is our Kayla?" Milo asked.

"Yes," White said. "That's why my partner owes me lunch, and by the way, Gramm, this one isn't going to be it."

"What does all this mean?" Preston asked.

"It means that Kayla Maki, knife wielding ex-girlfriend of the late Alex Sithens, is now a full partner in her ex-boyfriend's sign company," White informed them. "She told us her father lent her the money to buy in. I don't know why she shared."

"She tried to sell us a sign," Gramm said. "I tried to keep my distance in case Kayla was still packing a knife."

White shook her head. "You can't make this stuff up."

"As amusing as this is, enough about Kayla," Gramm demanded.

"Did you bring up Kayla?" Milo asked Preston.

"Not me."

"Let's talk about what we found out about Ralph, Raf, whatever," Gramm said.

White spoke first. "Are we going to call our victim Raf or Ralph?"

"I think Raf," Gramm said. "He's known by that name now. Any objections?"

"I kinda like Ralphie," Preston said. "That cute Reese Winterhausen called him Ralphie boy."

Gramm stared. "No Ralphie," he said firmly. "Any other objections to using the name Raf?" Neither White nor Rathkey seemed ready to object. "Okay, Raf it is. Kick DeJong acted upset that Raf was dead. We asked him about the EpiPen. He said Raf was always careful."

"He called his good buddy, Raf, an ass," White said, "but got really defensive about the argument you witnessed, Milo. Called for his lawyer."

"Reese Winterhausen said much the same but mentioned no one at the table wanted Raf there at all. In fact, that night they celebrated putting him in danger by ordering the entrée with peanuts," Preston added.

Milo jumped in. "He also called Raf, a drug dealer lite."

"Kick mentioned they joked about peanuts putting him in danger, too," Gramm said. "We gotta look at that video again. Maybe they all killed him."

"Murder on the Orient Express," Milo said. "They all did it."

"We asked Winterhausen about Raf being arrested. Remember, Feinberg said he got him off."

"What did he say?" Gramm asked.

"He said to ask somebody else," Milo said.

"Seems DeJong left out the drug dealer lite," Gramm said as Darlene brought four fish and chips in Styrofoam containers. She plopped Milo's down hard.

With one hand, Preston opened the Styrofoam container and with the other picked up her fork and wiggled a small slice of breaded fish. The others watched as she took a bite.

"It's not bad," she said with some enthusiasm. "In fact, it's kinda good. Crispy. Flavorful."

"Gramm, keep in mind, Preston thinks kale is delicious," Milo said.

"Good point," Gramm said, sampling the fish. "But she's not wrong about this. It is good."

"Today, you can truthfully tell Amy you ate fish for lunch," White said.

Gramm picked up a French fry, dipped it in a white crinkled ketchup cup, and ate it in two bites. "And these are diet fries."

As they enjoyed lunch, Gramm said the afternoon would be taken up with talking to the women who were at the DeJong table: Jess, Emma, and Poppie something.

Preston put down her fork. "Reese Winterhausen filled us in on Poppie. Her full name is Poppie Flower…"

"Give me a break," Gramm said.

"That's her name. She lives in Burnsville. I called her. She won't be back in town until Thursday."

"Poppie Flower," White repeated.

"There's more. Her siblings are Daisy, Iris, and a brother, Periwinkle. I hope he goes by Perry," Milo added.

"Isn't Periwinkle a color?" Gramm asked.

"Look at you," White chided. "Skidding right off that chart of only primary colors, but Periwinkle is also a flower."

"My education is complete," Gramm quipped.

12

"Will the Tip Top become a regular lunch place like Gustafson's or the Chinese Dragon?" Preston asked as she and Milo drove up to Spirit Mountain. Skiing conditions were perfect. The recent snowstorm had added to the already healthy snowpack. This was a Tuesday afternoon, middle of the week, yet the parking lot was almost full.

Milo didn't answer Preston's question.

"Is your silence a no or yes?" Preston asked.

"I would vote no," Milo said. "I don't know if the food was good. I didn't eat it. In her mind, Darlene and I have a history. No telling what she put in it."

"That's fine by me. The other restaurants are more fun, relaxing."

The parking lot had two spaces for official cars. Both were empty. She ignored them and parked several rows back from the chalet. "I parked back a ways to protect the car from snow bunnies dropping their skis."

"*Back a ways?* Milo questioned. "Where in Minnesota are you from?"

"Originally, Winona, the stained-glass capital of the United States," Preston announced with pride.

"How did you end up here?"

"Went to UMD."

"The University of Wisconsin branch campuses are right across the river, much closer to Winona."

"I didn't go to college to be close to home."

"Got it," Milo said. "I went to the Navy, also away from home."

"Look at this," she said, turning and throwing her arms out to cover the expanse of the city meeting the lake. "I mean, you can see water from everywhere in Duluth."

As Milo emerged from the vehicle, an out-of-control skier, fresh from a bunny hill adventure, came barreling at him.

"I don't know how to stop! Watch out!" the skier yelled.

Milo let out an expletive as he dove sideways into a nearby snowbank.

The skier joined him in the snowbank, but Milo didn't notice.

Milo turned over, remaining in the snowbank, his mind replaying the night of the accident. "Ted yelled, *watch out!*" Milo said to the errant skier. In Milo's mind, he saw the driver in slow motion—his head bouncing from side to side. His eyes staring but not seeing.

"He was dead!" Milo murmured. "Just like Doc said."

Pop-Up Dinner, Drop Down Dead

The oversized bunny hill veteran slammed his poles into the snowbank in a desperate attempt to stand up. "Sorry again," he said to Milo. "First time on skis."

Milo nodded. "I mean, he was really dead."

The novice skier boosted himself up on his ski poles, fumbled with his now disconnected skis, and ran in the direction of the chalet.

Preston came around to Milo's side of the car. "Milo, the guy is up and running. You scared him."

Milo stood and dusted the snow from his pants and jacket.

As Preston and Rathkey entered the Chalet, a tanned, shaggy-haired young man behind the ski rental counter yelled out, "Katie Preston! Are you back?"

"No, Derrick," she said, flashing her badge along with her police officer smile. "We are looking for Emma Winterhausen."

"Katie," Milo smirked, "are you going to introduce me?"

Preston squinted her eyes at Milo in warning that the name *Katie* was not a favorite and should not make its way to the station. "Derrick, this is police consultant Milo Rathkey. Derrick is a ski instructor and collector of young girl's hearts."

"Did he collect your heart?" Milo asked.

"No, he did not."

"I tried!" Derrick exclaimed. So, you want Emma. Let me see." He checked his computer. "Emma is out with a junior snowboarding class, but they are due back in about ten minutes. Then she has a lunch break. Are you here to arrest her? She drives like a demon." Derrick smiled.

"We're homicide," Preston said.

Derrick laughed.

"She's not kidding," Milo added.

"Shit."

"Calm down, Derrick. She's a witness, not a suspect," Preston said.

"Good. That sweet face couldn't kill anybody."

"Another conquest, Derrick?" Preston asked.

"No," he spread his arms in a mock surrender. "I'm only pining for you, Katie."

"Start by calling me Kate. It's my name." She led Milo to an empty table as they waited for Emma. Milo took the time to pick up a hamburger and Diet Coke.

"Do you ski here often, or do you know Derrick, the lady killer, from somewhere else?" Milo asked upon his return.

"I worked here in college."

"So, along with riding a killer motorcycle, you swoosh on killer skis?"

"I kept snow bunnies under control with the snowplow, but my preference is the board."

"I'm Emma," a female voice said.

Both Preston and Rathkey looked up. She was tall like her brother, but Derrick was right. She had a sweet face. Milo immediately put Emma high on his list of suspects.

"Hi, Emma. I'm officer Kate Preston."

"Derrick said you used to teach here a couple of years ago. I must have taken your job when you left." Emma sat down. "He said you wanted to talk to me about a murder?"

"Derrick got carried away. Let's back up," Milo said. "We're investigating Raf Bianchi. Do you know him?"

"Ugh."

"Who are you?" Emma asked.

Pop-Up Dinner, Drop Down Dead

Milo showed his consultant's badge. "I work with the Duluth Police Department."

"Oh, like part time? Like ski instructors."

"I never thought of it that way," Milo said, "but you're not wrong."

"Tell us what you know about Raf," Preston said. "How was he an *ugh*?"

Emma grimaced. "He was a creep. Kept hitting on me. Handsy if I was anywhere near him."

Preston nodded.

"He was like forty! He could have been my father. Yuck!"

"Almost forty?" Milo murmured. "That old!"

"Right. You get it," Emma said.

Preston stifled a laugh.

"Along with hitting on you, what else can you tell us about Raf?"

"A lot of bad tattoos and he was cheap. My sister calls him a mooch."

"Mooch?" Preston questioned.

"Yeah, Raf tries to hang with my brother's crowd but can't. He's only included if he gets one of them to pay."

"When did you last see him?"

"Friday at Gabby's dinner."

"Tell us about it," Milo said, getting used to hearing it called Gabby's dinner and not Martha's.

"Great food! It was fun—different."

I wonder if she thought we were looking for a review? Milo thought.

"Raf was at your table?" Preston asked.

Emma shuddered. "Yes, he walked in and began running his nasty mouth. Jess made sure he was nowhere near me."

"Did you know about Bianchi's allergy to peanuts?" Milo asked.

"No, not really. He yelled about it that night. I didn't hang with him. I didn't care about him."

"Tell us about hitting a man with a bottle a year or so ago," Milo said.

Preston glanced at Milo, wondering if this was too aggressive for a first interview.

Emma didn't flinch. "That guy was like Raf, hands all over me, but not for long. I'm not a delicate flower. I don't take shit from anybody."

"What about the end of the dinner? Did Raf leave with everybody?" Milo asked.

Emma thought for a minute. "No, he ate and left."

"Left?" Preston asked.

Milo sat back. Preston was learning how to interrogate.

"Left, like he ran out of the place. Dinner was better after he left. I didn't think he could move that fast. Did I mention he's old?"

§

"I called Jess DeJong at the hospital," White said as she and Gramm drove toward the hospital. "She's been moved into a regular room. She said she could talk to us this afternoon for a while."

Exiting the Police Interceptor, White was buffeted by the icy wind coming off the lake. "What happened to the pink skies and bright sun of this morning?"

Pop-Up Dinner, Drop Down Dead

Gramm led the way down the street to the front of the building. A woman bundled up in a white wool coat and hat shouted their names. Both Gramm and White turned.

White recognized the woman first. "Hello Ms. Larson!" she shouted back and then to Gramm she said, "No murder is complete without Agnes Larson."

"I think her last name is now McKnight," Gramm said.

"Maybe, maybe not," White joked.

Agnes came up to them. "What brings you to the hospital?"

"An investigation," Gramm said.

"That accident the night of the storm?"

Gramm's face grew into a scowl.

"She lives with Milo," White said, calming him down. "We need to talk with some people who were at the pop-up dinner Friday night."

"Oh, we were there."

Of course, thought Robin.

"Do you know a man named Raf Bianchi?" Gramm asked.

"No."

"Okay, good talk," White said. "What brings you here?"

"My friend, Mrs. Pearson, had some minor foot surgery. She is doing well."

A gust of wind shut down the conversation. Agnes was pushed by the wind toward her car. Gramm and White fought the frigid wind tunnel into the entrance of the hospital.

"We're here to see Jess DeJong," Gramm said, flashing his badge to the receptionist.

On the way to the fourth floor, White commented that it was too bad, Gramm's British friend was not on duty.

"Yeah, kinda miss being called Leftenant."

On the fourth floor, they stopped by the nurse's station and were directed to room four-twelve. The door was ajar, so Gramm knocked and then entered.

Gramm introduced himself and Sgt. White.

Jess raised her bed up and, with difficulty, she tried to center herself. She reached for her water, took a long drink, and then set it back on the table. "Kick told me Raf was in an accident Friday, too."

Gramm nodded. "Yes, he died."

"He what?"

Robin repeated the message. "Raf Bianchi is dead."

Jess wrapped her arms around her body as if she was cold. "I didn't expect that."

"Tell us about Raf."

"He was a friend of my husband, a hanger-on for years. I didn't like him. I didn't trust him."

"Why?" White asked.

"Raf betrayed us."

"How did he do that?" Gramm asked.

"When we were first married, Kick was starting his first restaurant. He hired Raf as a line cook. Besides not being reliable, he was not a good cook—couldn't follow directions. Worse, he brought gambling into the place—betting sheets. I don't know everything. I do know Raf was charged, but we had to pay a fine, which we didn't have at the time. This mess could have stripped Kick of his liquor license. Raf's a nightmare."

Pop-Up Dinner, Drop Down Dead

"Why did you husband include him?" White asked.

Jess reached for her water again. "Good question. I've ask him continuously. Kick kept saying Raf saved his life. My brother Reese says it never happened. I believe Reese."

"Tell us about the dinner Friday night."

Jess paused and closed her eyes. "Nothing's there. I don't remember the dinner or my accident. I'm hoping as I heal, everything comes back. I'm getting tired. Do you have many more questions?"

Producing a picture of the table. "Who is this gentleman?" Gramm asked, as if he didn't already know.

"That's Bob Young, another member of Kick's posse." Jess smiled. "He's a sweetheart. He will do anything we ask, except he's gone most of the time." Jess looked up. "Please, tell me he's okay."

"He wasn't with Bianchi. We're trying to locate him."

"Let me get this clear," White said. "There are three of you from the same family?"

"Yes, I'm the oldest. Then Reese, and the late surprise, Emma." Jess smiled again.

"Would you consider yourself part of this posse?" White asked.

Jess looked shocked. "I never thought of myself that way. I'm younger than Kick and wasn't part of his core group growing up. We had it tougher, zoned out mother and alcoholic father. I was working at ten to help support us."

"Work? Where can you work at that age?" Gramm asked.

"All off book. We had a neighbor who did children's parties as a clown and magician. He needed a helper. I looked older and was a fast learner. He taught me a lot. Eventually,

I went out on my own. If I wasn't so tired, I'd make you a balloon animal."

§

Agnes told herself to stay away from the basement and let Tee and her crew work. She didn't listen. Walking down from the kitchen, she heard the explosive sound of a busy nail gun as she approached the wine cellar.

Tee's people had opened the hidden door completely to gain access to the steps. Work lights were providing more than adequate lighting as Agnes peeked in to examine the progress. The treads were new, along with the risers.

Tee spotted her and came down to chat. "Our original thinking was to replace only the rotted portions of the staircase, but it was simpler and safer to take the old stairs out and completely replace them," she told Agnes.

"So, you've already discovered what's way at the top?" Agnes asked.

"Yes, but not to worry. There is a very solid door at the top and we didn't open it. The discovery is still yours."

Agnes smiled.

"I know you want to be the first to find whatever is up there. Just for the record, so far, no ghosts have been sighted. Not even an odd occurrence."

"Nothing?" Agnes feigned disappointment.

"Well, Bert accidentally nailed his boot to a tread. He yelled and there was a little blood, but that's Bert. No supernatural malice."

Agnes stepped back. "Ooh poor Bert, sounds painful?"

"Naw. He only grazed his toes, and his boots needed replacing. Look, this stairway goes past your second floor. We built out a little landing there in case you want to make a doorway to whatever is on the other side in the future."

"Where would that be?" Agnes asked, trying to imagine.

"We drilled a little hole to peek. It doesn't look like the rest of the house—a fairly modern living room."

"That sounds like Sutherland's old apartment. I'll talk to him about the door."

"I was thinking if anyone was using that apartment, this could give them a private way down to the pool."

"We were thinking of redoing it as a suite for Sutherland's Aunt Lana. I don't know. She'd have to manage these steep and narrow stairs."

"Whoever put the stairs in didn't leave a lot of room between the two walls, but they did put in lights—long since burned out and corroded. We are replacing all that lighting with modern, bright, LEDs. So, if you fall, you will see where you'll land," Tee joked.

Agnes laughed. In her mind, she played with the idea of a door that didn't look like a door in the old apartment. She would be adding to the mystique of Lakesong instead of just discovering it. She broached that with Tee, who was enthusiastic.

"When can we explore that third floor?" Agnes asked.

"Tomorrow, if all goes as planned. Oh, we also created a landing in front of the yet unopened door."

"I will have to assemble the whole team: Martha, Gabby, and Aunt Lana, who was part of the original search. She's back in Scotland now, but we can let her follow us live."

"Don't forget me," Tee said.

"Of course, welcome to the expedition."

"You're gonna need a key. That door at the top of the stairs doesn't move."

§

Agnes began the cocktail hour by explaining the upcoming stair exploration to Sutherland and Milo. "I can't wait to get up there," she said.

A now walking, booted Sutherland was sitting on a bar stool, playing bartender. Milo was sitting on the sectional with his vodka gimlet.

"Did we ever get an estimate on that stair reconstruction? Is it pricy?" Sutherland inquired while handing Agnes her drink.

"You're kidding, right? You're the one who lost a fortune playing poker," she charged.

Sutherland laughed as he transferred to the plush chair, lifting his leg onto the ottoman. "Sorry, it was a knee jerk reaction. We just finished an expensive remodeling on the north end of the house, which I love, of course." Sutherland paused. "Actually, I really like the idea of the secret door."

"Nice save. Do you have a key for the third-floor door?" Agnes asked.

"Of course, dad had keys for everything and we have the skeleton key that supposedly opens every door." Sutherland paused and frowned. "That door is an unknown and may have a different lock system."

"Well, Tee says the staircase which goes between the outer brick wall and the inner wall was put in when the house was constructed, so it's really old, nineteenth century old," Agnes said.

Milo was sipping his gimlet, listening to Agnes. Sutherland asked him if he had anything to add, seeing as how half the house was his. "As long as a hammer doesn't come through my bathroom wall, I'm good. Have either of you ever gone ice fishing?"

"We were talking about remodeling, not ice fishing," Agnes complained. "But since you asked, no, I've never been ice fishing."

"Me either. All I know is people sit in those little shacks and drink beer," Sutherland said.

"Isn't it kind of cold for beer?" Agnes asked.

"I think so, but my dad talked about going ice fishing when he was a boy. The grownups drank beer and peppermint schnapps. He was not a fan. He said fishing huts were narrow, cold, and heated with deadly inadequate heaters."

"Deadly?" Milo questioned.

"Carbon monoxide deadly," Sutherland said.

"Why do you want to know?" Agnes asked Milo.

"Preston and I have to interview some guy who is out on a lake fishing." Milo was already getting cold.

13

Poppie Flowers crossed her arms and huffed. She looked around with disdain. The gray wall color with its green undertones did nothing for her. Bouncing up, she walked over to the large mirrored one-way window. Her new look—heavily lined brown eyes and a stick straight sable brown bob were cutting edge. In her eyes she screamed Vogue cover, certain this is what the Ford Agency was looking for.

Gramm preferred interview room A, but Lieutenant O'Dell was already interviewing a suspect from his latest case—a death during a bar fight on Friday night—another slam dunk for Odell.

Entering room B, Gramm nodded at Poppie, who turned but remained standing by the mirror. White followed.

Poppie began speaking before either of them could direct her to sit down. "How do you live with this wall color? It's hideous." She shuddered. "But more importantly, do you think the copper lining on my eyes, and the copper undertones in my hair make the copper flex in my brown eyes, pop?" Stepping up to White, "Take a closer look. Be honest."

White backed up, shook her head. "Please sit."

Poppie grabbed the top of her chair with both hands and bent over the table so she was face to face with Gramm and White. "Take a second look. It's really important!"

"Sure," White said, becoming annoyed by this witness. "Copper is nice, murder isn't, back up and sit down."

Gramm introduced himself and White. White started the recording. "Lt. Gramm, Sgt. White interviewing Poppie Flowers."

Poppie smiled. "It's Flower, like only one. Being a model, my unique name is an asset. People remember it."

"Thank you for coming in today," Gramm said. "We have some questions about the dinner you attended here in Duluth Friday night."

"Food was great."

"Okay. A person at your table was murdered," White said.

"Oh, my God! Who?"

"Raf Bianchi."

"Oh. Okay. No one important."

"Why do you say that?" Gramm asked.

"I didn't really know him. He didn't matter."

"So, you had never met him before Friday night?" White asked.

"Well, yeah, he was at some parties. He was good for a little weed, but that was all."

Gramm was still uncomfortable when people openly discussed drug use in front of him. White was not. "A little advice, Ms. Flowers. Don't admit to smoking weed in a police interview."

"Why? Everybody smokes weed. Isn't it legal these days?"

"That's not why we're here," White said. "Tell us about the people at the dinner."

"I was there with Reesie. We're a thing." Poppie sighed. "But he was in one of his moods, so I spent most of the evening with Bobby."

"Bob Young?" White asked.

"I guess. I call him Bobby. He's such a sweetie. He cooks on a yacht or something."

"Did you notice Bianchi during the meal?"

"He was there."

"Yes, we know he was there. Did you notice what he said or did?"

"I don't listen to people who don't matter. I didn't need his weed."

White closed her eyes and tried again. "Did you notice what others said or did with him?"

"He and Kick were talking, doing a deal, I guess. Then Kick moved and Jess sat next to him. He was pretty drunk. I guess he stumbled into Jess. I don't know; I was changing places with Bobby. Reesie was being a dick."

"Did you see Raf leave?" Gramm asked.

"When?"

"When he got up and left." White stifled an eye roll.

"He was probably somewhere. Then he came back. I think he stayed until he left."

Gramm dropped his head and grunted.

"When you were in the parking lot, did you see Raf?" White continued.

"No. I wasn't looking for him."

"Where did you go afterwards?"

"To Reese's. Still in a mood, he slept on the couch."

"So, you both stayed in?" White asked.

"I did. The weather was horrible. Reesie was not as pouty on Saturday. I had to leave on Sunday for a photo shoot scheduled for Monday and Tuesday—summer clothes. I'm back here now because you asked me to come in, but just to let you know, I have an open call in Chicago in two weeks with the Ford Agency." She sat back, her hands pointing to her eyes. "The heavy lining and the straight bob are the style I'm going in on. I will be Ford's new look."

"Let us know when you leave town," White said.

§

Gabby, Martha, and Agnes lined up behind Tee. Agnes brought an LED lantern just in case. The staircase repairs were finished, but needed Agnes to sign off on them.

Tee flipped a modern light switch, bathing the new staircase in light. Agnes placed her newly purchased lantern on the floor. "Won't need this."

Tee stepped back and swept her arm in a *you-go-first* gesture. Agnes put her full weight on the first step and bounced.

"The old ones were crumbling," Tee said.

"The new lighting is nice, but kinda takes away from the spookiness of this quest," Gabby said.

"Safety before questing," Tee said.

Pop-Up Dinner, Drop Down Dead

As Agnes led the group up the three-story staircase to the large wooden door, she called out over her shoulder, "No dust or spiders, either." It was a very narrow, single file staircase creating a single file procession—one person per stair.

Tee called, "When you get to the top, that door is solid oak and locked. So, I hope you have the key."

Agnes was carrying the McKnight key ring and the skeleton key that, in the past, had opened almost every door in Lakesong. She briefly stopped on the second-floor landing created by Tee to peek into their first apartment…fun… good times.

"Hey, what's the holdup?" called Tee.

"Sorry, it's me reminiscing. I'm done. Onward and upward." Agnes continued until she came upon the second newly constructed landing. No peep hole but a massive oak door with a menacing wolf carved in the center. This was unexpected. It reminded Agnes of the vault carvings.

Agnes took out the keys one at a time, trying them in the lock. The first key fit the lock but simply spun. The same with the second key. Frustration was replacing excitement. After ten failures, Martha, who was now sitting on the step next to her, suggested Agnes use the skeleton key.

"Okay, okay," Agnes surrendered. "I'll try the skeleton key." She put it in the lock and paused. "Here we go." She attempted to turn it. Nothing but spinning. It may have been the skeleton key to most of the house, but it wasn't anything to this door.

"The house likes you," Martha said. "Push against the door. Maybe some magic will happen."

Agnes pushed. There was no magic.

"I think it's time to find a locksmith," Tee yelled up the stairs. "One who specializes in old locks."

The group descended the stairs one by one.

When they were back in the basement, Martha suggested they regroup in the gallery for some tea and cookies, wine and cheese, and locksmiths.

Her suggestions were met with unanimous approval. The locksmiths, however, were not as enthusiastic. There were six. Agnes had tried five. This was their last chance. "Look, ma'am, I'd love to help you, but I need to know the year and make of the lock."

"Old," Agnes said. "I would guess late eighteen hundreds."

There was a long pause. "Is this a joke? You don't need a locksmith lady; you need a demolition expert. You know. Blow the damn door."

"No! I want to keep the door…just open it."

"Try Acme Plus. They do some of that strange stuff."

"Already tried them. Anyone else you could suggest?"

"Maybe a museum? Look, I got a real key emergency here. A little kid got locked in his house. Yale, 1998. That I can do."

Agnes hung up, stirred, then sipped her tea in silence. Finally, she blurted out, "Desperate times call for desperate measures."

Martha smiled. "Milo?"

"Milo," Agnes said.

"Does he pick locks?" Gabby asked.

"Probably, but if he can't, he knows somebody who can." Agnes called Milo while refilling her tea.

"What's up?" Milo answered.

"It's about the door on the third floor. None of the house keys work. They just spin. We need someone to pick the lock. We're hoping you know of someone."

"I got a guy. Looks like Ichabod Crane. He annoys you."

"Is that the guy who was looking for a dead body with his radar thingy?"

"Yeah, Ed…locks…too. Trust me."

"You're fading in and out," Agnes said. "Where are you?"

"Preston…almost…Rainy. Call…text…number."

Agnes hung up. She looked at her three companions. "We are about to disappear into the foggy world of Ed Patupick. I am not responsible beyond this point."

"He sounds as mysterious as the locked, carved door," Gabby said.

"Mysterious? Well, that's one word, Gabby." Agnes dialed Ed's number.

§

"I've never driven a car on a lake before," Preston said as she parked in front of the Rainey Lake Guide and Tackle Shop.

"I don't think you will have to," Milo said. "The department hired a guide. I think he'll drive."

"Good." Preston thought back to the time she and Milo interviewed Kayla Maki's father at the archery and bait shop. "Did you bring your jigging spoon?"

"No, I thought about it, but then I remembered I hate to fish."

Preston led the way into the one-story chalet-type wood building. Half the place was given over to the guide portion of the business with a huge cartoon map of Rainy Lake on the wall. A number of tourist pamphlets cluttered a large pigeonhole bookcase below the map. The other side of the building housed fishing equipment, rods, reels, tip ups, and various hooks and baits. Two gurgling tanks offered live bait of some kind, but neither Preston nor Rathkey wanted to know more.

"Can I help you?" an older man with rough beard stubble asked as he emerged from a back room.

Preston turned to face him. "We are from Duluth PD. We are here to see..." she looked at her phone. "Veda Ponikvar. Is he around?"

The man smiled, turned to the back room and yelled, "Hey Vee! Your people are here."

"Keep your pants on," a husky female voice shouted back.

"He is a she?" Preston asked.

The man nodded. "Has been for years."

A friendly looking middle-aged woman with short, wavy, black hair walked into the room. She wore wire-rim glasses and was dressed in a red plaid shirt with dark bibbed canvas pants. She held out her hand to Preston. "I'm Veda. I go by Vee."

"I'm Kate Preston. This is my colleague, consultant Milo Rathkey. He's an expert on jiggers."

Veda turned to Milo. "Really? I prefer round head, but I sometimes use spoons or spinnerbaits."

Milo shook his head. "I'm really not an expert. Preston here was blown up in an old barn a couple of months ago and she's been mumbling about jiggers ever since. The doctors think it will pass."

"Should you even be here?" Veda asked Preston.

"I'm fine. Milo kids," Preston said.

"We're trying to find a guy named Bob Young. He's from Duluth. We think he came up some time Monday to fish," Milo said.

"Your office already gave me a heads up," Veda said, walking over to the large map. "But we know Bob. He's been coming here for years. He's over at Jack Fish Island." She pointed to a large island on the map. "The Voyageurs Park people plow an ice road out to the island every year, so we should be okay."

"We noticed it's overcast. What happens if it snows?" Preston asked.

"Won't see a damn thing. We drive by the instruments. In the old days, we used to take compass readings, but GPS is easier."

"Do these fisher people come to shore at night?" Preston asked, hoping to avoid any trip on the ice.

"Naw, no reason to. They stay on the ice."

"In those little shacks?"

Vee laughed. "Some diehards still drag fishing shacks out there, but most have modified RVs. Heat and all the comforts of home."

"Modified?" Preston questioned.

"Holes in the floor. Bob is in one of our newer RV's."

"Let's go before it snows," Milo said.

"You two are dressed kinda light. I'm gonna grab better jackets and pants for you." When she returned with cold weather gear, she asked, "Do you want to do any fishing? Your guide fee comes with a minimum of equipment."

Both Preston and Rathkey said no in unison.

"The Jeep is in the back," Vee said. "Follow me."

Preston slid into the front of the Wrangler. Milo took the back. As Vee fired up the vehicle, she said, "If you're hungry, there's beef jerky back by you somewhere. It's homemade, not any of that store-bought crap. You are welcome to it."

Milo looked behind him and found a Tupperware container filled with long, black strands of beef. He offered one to Preston. She refused.

Vee drove out of the parking lot. "If beef jerky isn't your thing, I'm sure Bob has some bottled pickled pig's feet or eggs when we get there. They are a fisherman's staple."

Milo, not waiting for Bob's bottled pickled pig's feet, bit off a piece of jerky. "This is good stuff."

"Real pull-your-teeth-out, isn't it?" Vee exclaimed. "First, we're gonna go past the Visitors Center if you need to stop for…whatever. Otherwise, it's onto the lake."

"No stopping for me," Preston said.

"They give out junior ranger badges if either of you have kids."

As they passed the visitors' center, Vee honked her horn twice and turned down onto the lake. "It's a hello and to let them know we're going onto the lake." The plowed road was wide. Preston questioned the reason for such a wide road.

"We get a lot of snow, so we start really wide. As the snow gets piled up on the sides over time, the road narrows," Vee said, turning on her windshield wipers. "Oh boy, we've got snow. You'll get the full show."

A loud crack caused Preston to grab the dashboard of the Jeep. "What was that?"

Pop-Up Dinner, Drop Down Dead

"Ice cracking. Nothing serious. You'll get used to it."

"Cracking? The ice is cracking? Does the snow do that?" Preston questioned.

Milo, who had been out on lake ice many times before, continued to eat his beef jerky.

"Snow has nothing to do with it. It's just the top layer of ice that's cracking. We've got a good twelve inches under us, maybe more. The ice freezes in layers. Only the top layer cracks. At least that's the theory."

"Why are we going so slow?" Milo asked.

"Speed limit is 30 miles per hour, but I like to stay under that."

"Do they have speed cops?" Milo asked.

"If they see you speeding, the park rangers will write you a ticket. Of course, I look out for hotdoggers that speed and do wheelies on the plowed road."

As they approached the island, various RVs and shacks began to dot the ice. Vee pulled up to a large RV. "I'm going to check in with my husband. He's here fishing, but he spends a lot of time visiting. He's a chatty sort. He'll know exactly where Bob is."

Waiting in the Jeep, Milo again offered Preston jerky. This time, she took a small piece. "It's the most appetizing thing I've heard about so far," she said, shuddering at the thought of pickled pig's feet or eggs.

"You haven't lived until you munched on pickled pig's feet, the preferred cuisine of fine Minnesota bars everywhere," Milo teased.

Vee came back to the Jeep. "We're in luck. Bob is on this side of the island about five sites up."

173

Preston nodded. Her mouth was busy chewing on the jerky.

Vee drove about a quarter of a mile down the road and stopped at another RV. "This should be Bob."

The trio left the Jeep and walked up to the RV. Vee knocked. Young opened the door. "Vee, what brings you out here?"

"Some people want to talk to you."

Young looked past the guide to Milo and Preston. "Come on in."

The RV was pretty standard except for five round holes in the floor with a line and a tip up in each of them. "Be careful. Don't step in the holes," Young said.

Young sat down at the table. Preston and Rathkey slid into the booth opposite him. Preston showed her badge. Vee took a bench at the back of the RV. "We're Duluth police. We need to talk to you about Raf Bianchi."

"Yeah? What the hell did he do now? It must be a biggie for you to track me down up here," Young said. He removed his knit cap, ran his hands over his shaved head, and shoved the cap into his back pocket.

"He died, accident, Friday night," Milo said.

"Died? Maybe we shouldn't have let him drive," Young said with a shrug. "But he left early."

One of the tip up flags stood straight up. Young raced to set the hook with a sharp tug on the line. He brought in the line, pleased with his catch. "A four-pound walleye! Great! I can trade this baby for a couple of northerns."

He put the fish on a stringer with two other smaller fish and dropped them back in the water. "Why did you two come all the way up here to talk to me because Raf died?" Young asked.

"We think he may have been murdered," Milo explained.

"Hmpht," Young shook his head.

"You don't seem very broken up about it," Preston said.

Bob looked Preston straight in the eye. "Raf was trouble. It stuck to him, and he brought it to others. His being gone is not a bad thing."

"How so?" Milo asked.

"He was a bully and didn't care who he hurt. I've hated him since we were kids."

"None of you seem to like Raf. Why invite him along?" Milo asked.

"Not me! Kick. It was always Kick. He was sure Raf saved his life."

"You didn't agree?"

"No one did. I told Kick the truth, but he wouldn't believe me. When he hired Raf, then had to fire him, I thought Kick would lose the hero worship."

"He didn't?" Preston asked.

"Naw. He was cooler, but Raf was always included in the group. I was lucky. I'm gone nine months out of the year on the boats. I didn't have to endure looking at his lying face."

"What did Kick believe about Raf saving his life?" Milo asked.

"Do you really care? It was years ago."

"Humor us."

"Okay. We were like freshmen, sophomores in high school. Summertime. Hot. You know. That really hot two weeks we always get. We were cooling off in The Deeps. I was over by the flat rocks opposite the falls and cliffs. The girls liked to sun themselves there.

"Where was Kick?" Preston asked.

"Kick and Reese were being macho jumping off the high cliffs into the water, showing off for the girls. Raf was on the lower rocks, pushing little kids into the water that didn't want to go."

Preston crinkled her forehead in displeasure.

"Yeah, that was Raf. Anyway, we were there most of the afternoon. I was getting hungry. I yelled to Kick and Reese that we should get a pizza. Reese started climbing down. Kick signaled one more jump. His foot slipped. He didn't get out far enough. He was headed for the rocks. Raf had his hand out and pushed Kick clear of the rocks."

"It sounds like he did save Kick," Preston said.

Young shook his head. "No. I saw what really happened. Raf's hand was out because he had just pushed a little kid into the water. Raf saw Kick coming at him and he reacted to save himself. When we all met up by our bikes, Kick was raving about how Raf had saved his life like it was intentional."

"Why did Raf push little kids?" Milo asked.

"Because Raf is an asshole."

"What happened to the little kid?"

"I don't know. We went for pizza. Kick paid for Raf's pizza…a whole one, just for Raf. It's been that way ever since."

"Tell us about the dinner last Friday night. Did you and Raf talk?" Preston asked.

"No."

"Yet you sat next to him."

"I guess. I really don't pay attention to him. I was talking to Poppie, Reese's flavor of the month."

"Flavor of the month?"

Young laughed. "Yeah, Reese doesn't keep girlfriends long. I kinda like Poppie. A model is really different for me."

"Was Raf also interested in Poppie?" Milo asked.

"Don't think so. He didn't make any moves in that direction. He went after Emma, Reese's younger sister," Bob snorted. "But not for long. She set him straight."

"Did you see Raf leave?" Milo asked.

"No."

"Tell us about leaving. How did that work?" Preston said.

"It wasn't complicated. The chefs announced bad weather was coming and cut the evening short. We picked up our desserts and headed out the door. I waited in case Poppie needed a ride. Unfortunately, she left with Reese."

"Did you see Raf in the parking lot?"

Young thought for a minute. "Naw, but I wasn't looking for him."

"What did you do after Poppie and Reese left?"

"I went back to my place and started packing for this fishing trip."

"Can anyone verify that?"

Young shook his head. "I live alone."

"You fish a lot?" Milo asked.

"Yeah, I get a couple of months off when the boats aren't running. Gotta cram it all in then."

"If you had to guess, who do you think killed Raf?"

"He was a terrible gambler. The guys told me he owed money to some bad dudes. Maybe they got rid of a bad debt."

"Bad dudes usually don't kill," Milo said. "Can't collect from a dead guy."

Young shrugged. "Do you know *Raf* was not his real name?"

"Ralph Bing, right?" Milo said.

"Yeah. That Raf crap was as phony as he was."

"When are you due back in Duluth?"

"I got two more days on this camper, so Saturday."

Milo looked around the camper. "Ice fishing has changed."

"Sure has, and for the better. Vee's campers are the best. I could clean this walleye. and we could have it for lunch if you care to join me."

"We don't want to take your walleye. Weren't you going to exchange it for northerns?" Preston asked.

Young opened the freezer side of the refrigerator showing walleyes in freezer bags. "I got eight packages in there, so when it comes time to barter, I've got plenty."

"Sounds good," Vee nodded, looking at Milo. "You two got somewhere else to be?"

"Not us," Milo said.

"Bob, how do you cook them?" Vee asked.

"Fried in butter."

"Onions, capers?" Vee asked.

"I can do onions. Don't have capers."

Vee reached into the left pocket of her Air Force Parka and produced a bottle of capers. "I just happen to have some."

Bob Young smiled. "I figured you would."

14

Gramm suggested he and White lunch at Gustafson's. "No Milo. We can order and get our food in record time. It will be just like old times. I should send Milo out of town more often. Great move on my part."

"I give you kudos," White said as they walked into the restaurant.

Nick waved to them as they marched past on their way to the back booth. "Luckily, nobody ever wants to sit here," White said.

"Well, it is kind of out of the way," Gramm offered.

After a brief wait, Pat, the waitress, walked up with two glasses of water. "No Milo today?"

"He's ice fishing up in International Falls," Gramm said.

"I find that hard to believe," Pat said. "You wanna hear the specials?"

"Sure." White nodded.

"We have Melitzanosalata, eggplant salad or dip with pita bread, and chicken or pork skewers with salad or Greek potatoes."

"What happened to the French cuisine?" White asked.

"I think it was Italian," Gramm said.

Pat seemed puzzled.

"You know, Nick discovered his ancestry wasn't all Greek," White prompted.

"Oh, that," Pat almost laughed. "Customers did not want croissants at a Greek place."

"I will have the Mel…Melit…the eggplant salad," White said, "and Sprite."

"Give me the chicken skewer with potatoes and coffee," Gramm ordered.

Pat left.

"I think she was a little sad Milo isn't with us," White suggested.

"Don't do that. Don't pretend his restaurant ordering is in any way normal."

"Have we heard from Preston or Rathkey?" Gramm asked.

"I have a couple of missed calls from them. I'll try to reach them."

"I wonder if DeJong has calmed down yet. We were basically thrown out of his restaurant. We could give him another shot today, see if he lawyers up."

White agreed. "He was really touchy about the fight Milo witnessed. Lied to us about it."

"I hate liars, waste of time," Gramm said.

Pop-Up Dinner, Drop Down Dead

"To quote Milo, everybody lies, but only one lies because they're the killer." White smiled.

"Yeah, yeah, but DeJong threatened to lawyer up, and he had that odd comment at the beginning that we couldn't follow up on."

"Traffic or drugs," White said.

"Yup, there's more there. Let's drop in for dessert."

Pat returned with their food. "Enjoy."

§

Bob and Vee loved talking fishing…for hours. It was a good thing the fresh walleye was excellent. Milo and Preston ignored most of the chatter. By the time lunch was over, the light snow had turned into a blinding snow. "I'll drive by GPS," Vee said. "Piece of cake."

Neither Rathkey nor Preston could see past the front of the Jeep, but it didn't matter since Vee didn't bother looking out the windshield. She was looking down at the GPS.

"It's like instrument flying in a plane," Milo said.

"Exactly, this happens all the time," Vee explained.

After about thirty minutes Vee maneuvered the Jeep up an incline to snow covered land. She honked again as they passed the visitor's center. A few more minutes and they parked in the back of the Rainy Lake Guide and Tackle Shop. They said quick *thank yous* and *goodbyes* to Vee, ran through the snow to the police interceptor, plugged Duluth into the GPS and took off for home.

The boring Robbie the Robot voice began directing them back to Duluth.

Excited, going too fast for conditions, Preston missed a left turn and found herself on a narrow road that paralleled the lake.

"This road looks bad," Milo said. "Take it easy. See if we can turn around somewhere."

The road took a sharp turn to the right, but the Police Interceptor kept going straight. Preston pumped the brakes, but all four wheels were on ice. She looked at Milo and said, "Sorry."

The car crashed through a snowbank, flew into the air, and dropped down ten feet onto the lake. The front wheels bounced while the back wheels came down with a jarring thud. Preston and Rathkey sat for about a minute in silence, then Milo said, "We might be back on the lake." The GPS was recalibrating.

Preston nodded. "Are you okay?"

"I can still move my toes. How about you?"

"What do we do now?"

"The car is still running, so I suggest we move forward slowly to see if all four tires are still round, and if there's any grip at all."

Preston lightly touched the gas pedal. The car lurched. She took her foot off the gas, afraid she had broken something vital. "No whirs, thuds, or warning lights."

Milo looked at the GPS, which was now showing them at an entrance point to get back on land. "Let's try it again but follow the GPS. Slowly."

As if on cue, a female voice began to give directions, *"Go straight for one hundred feet…"*

"It's Debbie!" Milo exclaimed.

"What's Debbie?" Preston questioned.

"When you bounced onto the lake, the GPS must have changed from that boring robot voice to Debbie. We're going to be fine."

"In a half mile, turn right onto unnamed highway."

"There's a sign that says unnamed highway?" Milo asked sarcastically.

Preston had a death grip on the steering wheel and kept the car at a slow creep as the snow began to fall even faster. "This is not as cool as when Vee was driving."

"On the left, there's a landing of some sort," Milo said.

"I can hear ice cracking!"

"Remember, it's only the upper layer. We have eleven more layers before we should worry," Milo said.

Preston drove to the landing, gunned the engine, driving up on land. She breathed a sigh of relief. They looked around as Debbie announced they had reached their destination. "Destination? It doesn't look like Duluth, Milo. No twinkly lights on the hill."

The sign in front of them said, *Point Boat Ramp.*

Milo looked back at the GPS. "Oh, crap!" he said.

"What?"

"We're in Canada. Debbie brought us to another country. We didn't stop at customs or border crossings or anything."

"I'll turn around and drive back," Preston said. "In this snow, no one will see."

"Well, that's one solution, but it's still pitch black, getting colder, and snowing harder. Let's take our chances on land. We can explain this SNAFU at the border."

Debbie politely guided them past Point Park onto Canadian Highway 11. They passed the neon lights of the Bayview Motel, and the Sleepy Owl.

"Sleepy Owl? Hotel or motel?" Milo questioned.

"We're in a different country, Milo. It could be the Sleepy Owl torture center where they waterboard Americans who sneak across the border. Canadians are friendly, right?"

"Except when you enter their country illegally."

"In 100 feet, turn left onto highway 71," Debbie instructed.

Preston complied and was stopped by a border officer just before the Fort Francis Toll Bridge.

Preston rolled down her window. "Hi," she said, smiling.

"Duluth police?" the man said, reading the side of the car. "What brought you to our lovely city? Hope you enjoyed your visit."

"We sort of accidentally fell over here." Preston pointed to International Falls. "We belong over there."

The officer ducked down to see Milo and glanced into the back. "Could I see some ID?"

Preston showed him her badge. The man looked again at Milo. "And who are you, sir?"

"Milo Rathkey. I'm a consultant with the Duluth Police Department."

The man looked closer.

"We skidded off the road in International Falls and GPS took us in the dark, in the snow, into Canada."

The man scratched his chin. "Yeah, that's illegal. We're going to have to keep you here until we straighten it oot."

"We're going to jail?" Preston asked.

"Well, not in a cell. You can go back to Highway 11 and find a place for the night. The Sleepy Owl is nice."

"Is it a hotel or motel?" Milo asked.

"Milo!" Preston chided.

"It's a hotel. It fills up in the summer. This time of year, just a few ice fishermen who need a break," the officer said.

"Can't you just fine us or something?" Milo asked.

"I could write you a ticket, but she has a firearm. You can't bring a firearm into Canada."

"We're cops," Preston said. "I have a badge."

"Yeah, I gotta check that oot."

"Do you think I painted letters on this car and bought a uniform just to smuggle a gun into Canada?" Preston quibbled, getting a bit testy.

The officer ignored the attitude and held out his hand for Preston's gun. "The Sleepy Owl. It's comfortable."

"The Sleepy Owl it is," Milo said. "Turn around Preston."

§

Gramm and White told the hostess at Nonies that they preferred to sit in the back near the kitchen. Once seated, they informed their waitress that they were there to see Kick DeJong. The waitress hesitated before disappearing into the back. They could hear DeJong bark that he was too busy to talk. Gramm furrowed his brow, always a bad sign. When the waitress returned to relay Kick's response, Gramm flashed his badge and calmly said, "Tell Mr. DeJong either he sees us now, or we take him in."

The waitress, wide eyed, walked back to Kick's office and delivered Gramm's message. She returned and told the cops they could go back.

Kick was at his desk. A plate of fettuccine sat uneaten by a stack of menus. He looked up as Gramm and White entered. "I thought we were through."

"Mr. DeJong, we have a few more questions," Gramm said.

"I have a mountain of work. I'm getting the flu. Jess is coming home today. There is nobody but Emma to take care of her. My new manager just quit so I have to manage the place tonight on no sleep. All these menus are wrong."

Why should we care? White thought.

Gramm was equally unimpressed. "And we have a murder to solve."

"That's another thing. This Raf thing, it's nuts," he began yelling. "Who would kill him? Not me, that's for sure." Kick threw the menus on the floor. "Damn it!"

Gramm ignored the outburst. "A number of people have told us that Raf Bianchi worked for you briefly, but you fired him. Why?"

Kick blinked a couple of times. "He…what?"

Gramm and White waited.

"Oh yeah, as a line cook, but he was taking bets, trying to be a damn bookie. Shit, who does that?" Kick ran both of his hands through his hair.

"How did you discover it?" White asked.

"I didn't. A large, scary man paid me a visit and accused me of running a bookie joint. Me! He threatened me, said I was competing with his boss and that to continue would be extremely unhealthy. I'm not a bookie. I make sandwiches.

Pop-Up Dinner, Drop Down Dead

I told him I didn't know anything about it. I guess I was convincing.

Bianchi showed up for his next shift with bruises. I told him I knew he was taking bets in my restaurant. He lied to my face. He lied to *me*! I fired him."

"Did the large man pay any more visits?" White asked.

"I don't know. Somebody was watching the restaurant, especially when I closed up. I still park in the alley right behind the back door so I can slide in and not get caught in the open. I don't like to talk about this. It almost ruined us." Kick picked up the menus from the floor and began crossing out the desserts. "I got work to do."

"Raf causes you problems with thugs, endangers your business, and you still invite him to dinner? Why?"

"I…I've…known him a long time. We go way back. I won't ever hire him again, but he's…"

White interrupted. "When we interviewed you before, you said Raf was selling drugs. Why?"

Kick slammed down his sharpie. "I would never say that."

White checked her notes. "We told you about Raf's accident and you asked if we were from traffic or drugs. Why would you ask if we were from drugs?"

"I have no goddam idea! How do I know what I was thinking?"

"It was only yesterday."

DeJong jumped up from his desk. "A lot goes on in my life. I can't do this anymore!"

"Calm down, Mr. DeJong. We're just asking a few questions."

"I am calm. I'm…distraught."

"We have a witness that admits to buying drugs from Bianchi. Another called him drug dealer lite. Did you notice any drug sales?"

"No, no. That's nuts."

"Are you going to eat that fettuccine?" White asked.

"What? No. Getting the flu. Makes me sick." He dumped it in the trash. "Do you want some? I can get you…"

"No thanks," White said.

Gramm stood. "We will probably be back."

"I really am getting with my lawyer. You can't keep hassling me," Kick said, gathering the menus and dropping them in the trash can.

"It's a murder investigation. Your friend was murdered. We've only interviewed you twice," Gramm said.

"It's too much."

On the way out the door, White stopped by the hostess desk. "I noticed that Mr. DeJong had a delicious looking plate of uneaten fettuccine. Did he order that?"

"His wife left orders that he be served food if he's working here. He won't eat it, but we do what we're told."

White thanked her and she and Gramm left.

"What's with the fettuccine?" Gramm asked.

"Did you notice his eyes?" she asked as she slid into the car.

"Can't say that I did."

"His pupils were dots—constricted. He doesn't eat. He blew up at us a couple of times for nothing. He kept fiddling with the stupid menus and then threw them out."

"Well, Doctor White, what is your diagnosis?"

"When I was an MP, we saw a lot of this. It's opioid addiction. I think our restaurateur has lost his drug dealer lite."

Gramm smiled. "If his supplier was the late Raf Bianchi, that would be a good reason to keep him around. So, Kick probably wouldn't kill him."

"Don't be so sure. Mood swings and violent outbursts go along with this addiction. I wouldn't remove him from the suspect list just yet."

"You know, my old partner, Jablonski, knew where every Steak and Shake Restaurant was in Minnesota and Wisconsin."

White smiled. "But not about drug addiction."

Gramm shook his head. "Not a bit."

White took that as a Gramm compliment.

Gramm's phone rang. He looked at it. "It's the deputy chief."

"Gramm! What the hell is going on?" Deputy Chief Sanders yelled into the phone.

Gramm put the phone on speaker. "Uh, going on with what, sir?"

White noticed she had two missed calls from Preston and Rathkey. She showed her phone to Gramm, who rolled his eyes.

"I just got a call from Canadian Authorities in Fort Francis…"

15

More snow began falling in the late afternoon. Agnes and Sutherland watched the flakes slide down the family room windows. Agnes nuzzled her chin into the high neck of her purple cable sweater, her new favorite, and burrowed her hands into the pockets.

"Mr. McKnight, you get to hobble all the way over to the bar to make the drinks. I'd like hot chocolate," Agnes said, as Sutherland spread out the fuzzy throw over her feet and legs. He received a smile as his reward. "Then you get to hobble all the way back." Agnes smiled.

Sutherland gazed in the direction of the bar. "I don't think I can make it there and back in time for dinner."

Agnes smiled. "Be brave. Don't forget the marshmallows—the teeny tiny ones."

After many minutes of overplaying the making of the drinks, Sutherland presented Agnes with her hot chocolate.

Thinking the drink to be a bit light on the marshmallows, she held it out. "Oh no, not nearly enough."

Sutherland looked at the boot on his injured foot.

"Dr. Willet said you needed to exercise that foot."

"No. He didn't."

"Are you going to deny me the melty gooey sweetness that would make my hot chocolate perfect?" Agnes batted her eyes.

"Certainly not, delightful wife." Sutherland took his scooter to the bar, filled Agnes' request, and scootered back.

She looked at the cup. "Satisfactory."

Sutherland mixed his own martini. Drinks made, he feigned exhaustion and plopped down next to Agnes. "Where is Milo?" he asked.

"I don't know," Agnes said. "I just work for him…I think."

Martha walked in, pushing an hors d'oeuvres cart. "Mr. Rathkey texted earlier to let us know he's been captured by the enemy, and we should ignore any further communiques from him, as he may be under duress."

Sutherland took a sip of his drink. "Did he name the enemy?"

"He did. Canada."

Agnes laughed. "Didn't hostilities between us and Canada end two or three hundred years ago?"

"For all we know, Mr. Rathkey has fired them up again," Martha joked.

"Oh, I hope not," Agnes continued. "They're always so nice, and I've always wanted to visit Toronto."

"I think Toronto has been spared," Martha said. "Mr. Rathkey is somewhere called Fort Francis. He may have been laying siege to the fort when he was captured."

"Should we notify anyone?" Sutherland asked. "The highway patrol, the State Department, Fish and Wildlife?"

"Fish and Wildlife?" Agnes questioned.

"Every time some dispute with Canada is mentioned, Fish and Wildlife is in the middle of it," Sutherland defended his choice. "We had to jump through hoops with Fish and Wildlife to get permits to build the marina in Two Harbors. They kept mentioning treaties with Canada," Sutherland said.

The front gate intercom announced a visitor. "Edward Patupick is at the gate." The intercom also said, "Welcome Edward."

"The gate is opening. I didn't open the gate," Sutherland said. "Did you?" he asked Agnes.

"Not me. The intercom opened the gates for him and welcomed him personally."

"Are you expecting him?"

"Not until tomorrow."

A few minutes later, Patupick was at the front door. Those too, unlocked by themselves."

"We have a giant hole in our security," Sutherland complained, scootering to the front door to greet the intruder. "Ed? How did you do that? Why are you here?"

"It saves time," Ed said. "Should I come in?"

"We're in the family room. Follow me."

The tall, gangly Patupick followed Sutherland, wheeling electronic equipment in a cart he pulled behind him. Looking at Agnes, he said, "I'm here for the locked door. Where's Milo?"

"He was captured by the Canadians. We're awaiting word as to his fate," Sutherland said.

Patupick was silent.

"That's a joke, Ed," Sutherland said, not fully understanding Patupick's mistrust of almost everything.

Ed squinted his eyes, not buying Sutherland's explanation.

Agnes tried to clear up any confusion. "Milo is in Canada on a case."

"Where is the door?" Ed asked, wanting to get on with his work.

"It's way up on the third floor," Agnes said. "Why are you here tonight? I thought you said tomorrow." Agnes was tired. The thought of hiking back up to the third floor was not appealing. "The staircase begins in the basement. Sutherland will show you."

"I will?" Sutherland questioned. "Keep in mind, I've only been cleared for marshmallows, not hiking."

Agnes finished the last of her drink, threw off the fuzzy blanket, and stood up. "Okay, let's go."

Sutherland used his scooter as they moved toward the elevator, being joined by Martha on the way.

§

The heavy snow had stopped. A Canadian border official escorted Preston and Rathkey to the Sleepy Owl Hotel and waited until they checked in.

"Why is he here?" Preston whispered as Rathkey presented his credit card to Madge, the woman behind the front desk.

"He either wants to make sure we're not going to make a break for the border, or this is a Canadian courtesy for fellow law enforcement," Milo said.

Preston looked in her purse. "I have a Visa card."

"Put it away. I'll put everything on my card. Reimbursement will be easier. We've earned a good dinner. Where's a good place to eat, Madge?"

"The Flint House is good, just down the road, but pricy," Madge said.

"We're on expense accounts," Milo said.

"Good for you," Madge said, handing them card keys.

Milo turned around, looking for the ever-present border guy. He was gone. "I guess we're on our own." Milo suggested they meet back in the lobby in fifteen minutes, which was fine with Preston.

§

"What's going on?" White asked Gramm after he hung up with Deputy Chief Sanders.

"Apparently Milo and Preston have been declared illegal aliens…by Canada," Gramm said.

"I know how Canada feels. All of you people are here illegally too," White said.

"Ha," Gramm said, "a little Ojibway humor?"

"It's a hoot with my people. So, why are they in Canada?"

"Apparently, they drove across the Rainy River accidentally."

White checked a map on her phone. "It's not that hard to do. Look, your border runs down the center of the Rainy River and lake. Of course, if we were talking the Ojibway border, Preston and Rathkey would be fine. Ojibway territory goes way up into Canada."

"I'm sure that fact will bring them great comfort," Gramm said. "As it is, the Canadians are a bit miffed. The chief is miffed. The deputy chief is miffed, and there is a piece of my butt missing."

"What happens next?"

"A piece of Milo's and Preston's butts are going to be missing. That's how it goes." Gramm called Rathkey. "Milo, what the hell is going on out there? Is it amateur hour?"

"Make it quick," Milo said. "We prisoners of war can't talk long."

"Why? Scratch that. I don't care."

"Preston and I are outside the Flint House. We're hungry and we're going to dinner. I tried calling you, but you didn't answer."

"We didn't answer because we were busy doing police work. How the hell did you end up in Canada?"

"It was an honest mistake. We were heading back from International Falls when Preston hit a patch of ice, and our car slid off the road and onto the ice. The car spun around a couple of times." Milo began embellishing the story. "You know, a tree's a tree. There was snow. Darkness. Canada looks a lot like the US up here and there were no *Canada! Keep Out!* signs anywhere. We innocently drove off the ice onto land, only it wasn't our land. It was their land."

"White points out it is all her land, but I don't think that's going to help you much."

"The Canadians just want to know if we're legit."

"Yeah, about that. I'm afraid we're going to have to deny all knowledge of you two and your mission."

"We didn't have a mission."

"Yes, you did. You were supposed to interview Bob Young."

"We did that. He said our victim was a waste—not a Raf fan."

"It sounds like our victim didn't have any fans. Did Young have any idea who'd want to do him in?"

"He mentioned owing money to shady characters, but other than that, he had no idea."

"Did he mention drug dealing?"

"He didn't mention it, but we didn't ask. Should we hit him up again once we are released from Canada?"

"Yes, but this time stay on the right side of the border." Gramm clicked off.

"Are we in trouble?" Preston asked as Milo pocketed his phone.

"We've been fired," Milo lied. "It's going to be hard on the cats. They get their street cred from my being a cop."

Preston's eyes grew wide. "Tell me you're kidding."

"I'm kidding. The cats don't give a damn what I do. Oh, and we're not fired. Let's go eat."

§

Agnes reluctantly took the lead as the procession descended and traipsed through the basement to the formerly secret staircase. Turning on the newly installed lights, Agnes said, "It's all the way at the top of these stairs, Ed—three floors. The staircase has been recently rebuilt, so it's solid."

Ed took out his cell phone and a laparoscopic camera, which plugged into the bottom of the cell phone. He called up an app and the camera came to life, a bright white light shown out from the tip.

"What are you going to do with that?" Sutherland asked.

"I'm going to put this camera in the keyhole to see the mechanism. I should also be able to see whatever is beyond the door. I don't like surprises."

"What do you think is up there that might take you by surprise?" Agnes asked.

Patupick began to climb the stairs without answering, leaving the group to exchange puzzled glances.

Once he was out of earshot, Martha expressed doubts about Patupick's approach. "So, what happens after he sees the lock mechanism?"

Sutherland nodded. "We just want to open the door."

Agnes hugged Sutherland. "I love you, but in this case, there is no we. At least not a you. Our little band of explorers comprises Martha, Gabby, Aunt Lana, Tee, and myself."

"Aunt Lana isn't here, so I can take her place. We had a family meeting, and I was elected."

"No, you weren't!" A voice from Agnes' phone objected.

Agnes held up the phone. "I have Aunt Lana on a video app."

Sutherland could see his white-haired aunt. "Nice try, Sutherland dear, but your wife and I have been texting, and we have had this planned ever since she found the door to the stairway. I am an original member, and I don't want to be left out just because I'm a few thousand miles away."

"How's Scotland?" Sutherland asked.

"I haven't polled the entire country, but my small section of it is doing fine—cold but fine."

Ed Patupick came down. "The lock cannot be opened," he said.

"Why not?" Agnes blurted.

"There is no lock." He showed them his video of the camera going into the keyhole. It easily went right on through with no mechanism.

"But it still won't open!" Agnes complained, getting annoyed at having to stand in the chilly basement talking to a crazy person.

Patupick looked at her. "I didn't make it!"

"If there's no lock," Aunt Lana asked. "What's holding the door?"

"Good question," Sutherland said.

"Don't rate my question, Sutherland. Just get your friend to answer it."

"I like her!" Patupick held up his phone to Agnes' phone so Aunt Lana could see it. "You can see on the video there is a large, black sliding bolt on the inside of the door."

"Damn!" Agnes swore. "What can we do about that? In fact, how did they lock it and then get out?"

"They probably walked across the third floor to the other side of the house," Sutherland said. "Remember mom building the gallery, cutting the third floor in half? She didn't realize she was creating this locked island."

"Oh, *locked island*, Sutherland, that's great," Agnes raved, "Such mystery."

"I'll open it tomorrow," Patupick said.

§

The Flint House was a white tablecloth and candles in a log cabin type of restaurant—warm and cozy. Milo and Preston were escorted to a table in a far, dark corner. "Did they put us here in case we try to make a run for it?" he asked Preston. "It's the furthest table from the door and that warm fireplace."

"No reservation," a young waitress with a long, blond ponytail said. "People without reservations get the far back tables. I'm Becky. I'll be your waitress."

"I'm Milo and this is Kate. We're running from the law. Illegal border crossing."

"We know. Madge from the Sleepy Owl called. You're not the first to make that mistake."

"I suspect that tomorrow we'll be traded for a Canadian family of four that wandered into Minnesota to get a Dairy Queen," Milo said.

"We have Dairy Queens here. Of course, you may have to get in line with a polar bear," Becky responded. She was not intimidated by Milo.

"Do polar bears like Dairy Queen?" Milo asked, curious as to what her come back would be.

"They love it. Better than seals. Can I get you people a beverage?"

Preston ordered a Sleeping Giant Mr. Canoehead beer. Milo ordered the same, but only after Becky assured him it was really made from a sleeping giant.

"I like our waitress," Milo stated, "but I wonder what that family of four was doing in the states? They clearly weren't there to get a Dairy Queen."

"You are wondering about the motives of a fictional family?" Preston asked.

"I am." Milo admitted.

Milo's attention was taken by a small ruckus at the bar. It appeared as if one bartender was attempting to hide from the other bartender.

"Get up, moron," the second bartender shouted.

Milo stood up.

"Milo, this isn't our problem," Preston said.

"Not yours, but mine." Milo walked over to the bar. "Tom? Tom Silicov?" he asked.

The hiding bartender stood up. "You got me, Milo."

"How long have you been here?"

"I don't know, fifteen, twenty years. Are you going to arrest me?"

"What for?" Milo asked.

"That little problem back in Brainerd."

Milo laughed. "I suspect the statute of limitations has run out on that. I will have to admit, you are one of the few criminals I never caught."

The man smiled. "I don't have to be on the run anymore? I figured once I was across the border, you couldn't touch me."

"Actually, I think we could have…touched you if we wanted to."

"Want a beer?" Tom asked.

"I already ordered one," Milo said. "Take it easy and have a good life, Tom."

"You too, Milo. Thanks."

Preston was on the phone to White. "No, really. We were at the restaurant for five minutes and Milo recognized some bartender. I know. It's uncanny."

"You're tattling on me?" Milo questioned.

Preston put her phone down. "Who was that guy?"

"A petty crook I knew in a past life."

"Milo, can you go into any restaurant and not know somebody?"

"Of course. What are you talking about?"

"Oh, I don't know. It must be me."

16

The sound was loud and annoying. Disoriented, Milo fumbled with his phone, trying to quiet the noise. The sound hit the floor but continued. Forced to open his warm, quilted cocoon, he jumped from the bed, his bare feet hoping to avoid the chilly floor. The buzzing sound was now under the bed. Milo bent down, swiping his arm across the floor. He hit it once and captured it on the second swipe. The next step was not as easy. As the bed was a high one, he stood, backed up, and gave himself a running start for the high jump required to reach the mattress top.

From under the quilt, Milo discovered the cause of all the noise and bother. A text from the Canadian Border Service alerting him that he was free to leave and return to the US. Milo checked the time on the phone—three AM. Was he required to leave now? What about Preston? Should he text her to find out? Too much unknown and way too early to care. Milo put his phone on mute.

Several hours later, he re-awoke. He texted Preston to see if she also was free to leave Canada. She was. They met in the lobby. Milo checked out and was going to suggest breakfast when Preston tossed him the car keys.

"I'm driving?" Milo questioned.

"Yes. After last night, I need a break."

"Gramm wants us to ask Young about Bianchi's drug use," Milo said. "We'll have to find him again."

"Drugs are a new wrinkle, but breakfast first, on the right side of the border," Preston said.

Milo managed the straight shot to the Canadian border crossing at the Fort Francis toll bridge. The same border official was on the job.

He walked up to their car. Milo lowered the window. "Are you starting a new shift or ending the old one?" he asked the official.

Preston stared at him. "Milo, why do you care? Let's just get out of here!"

"I want to make sure the Canadian border people aren't breaking any labor laws."

The official smiled. "We're good."

"We've been told we can go," Milo said.

"You sure can. We've checked with your people in Duluth. Here are your IDs, credentials, and weapon. Hope you had a pleasant stay in Canada."

Milo drove onto the bridge and voiced his disappointment that there wasn't a Canadian family of four going in the other direction.

"Let it go, Milo," Preston said while checking her phone. "The Library looks good."

"I've stopped eating books…cholesterol." Milo joked.

Preston had already plugged the address into the GPS. The restaurant was only minutes away. "I'll call Vee to see if she's free later to take us to Bob Young."

"I can find Young's RV. I was a cub scout until they kicked me out."

"I think it was you and your directions that ended us up in Canada," Preston charged. "I'm calling Vee."

Milo denied any responsibility for the Canada mistake, but secretly thought calling Vee was a good idea.

§

Sutherland was having his usual breakfast smoothie while Agnes opted for herbal tea. Ed Patupick, carrying a box of electronics, poked his head in the morning room. "I'm here. I'll just get started."

Agnes jumped a little. Sutherland seemed annoyed. "Ed, how did you get in the house? The intercom didn't even warn us."

"Oh, I muted it when it's me. I don't like people to know my movements."

Sutherland was shocked. "Ed, it's just Agnes, Martha, and me that know."

"Or so you think," Ed said as he turned and headed for the elevator.

"What's he got with him?" Agnes asked.

"I have no idea."

Both of them followed Patupick to the elevator. Once at the no longer secret brick wall door, Ed explained he had a powerful electromagnet. "I'm going to move the bolt out of its slot, using this magnet. If you people are going to follow me up the stairs, I suggest you not wear any metal, especially piercings."

"Why don't we stay down here and supervise," Sutherland said to Agnes.

"Don't need supervision," Patupick said over his shoulder, having placed a large portable power source at the bottom of the stairway. He screwed in a large, yellow power cord. "I'm gonna take this power cord up with me."

"Can you handle the cord and that machine?" Sutherland asked.

Patupick ignored the question. He handed Agnes a small walkie talkie.

"Why do I have this?" Agnes asked.

"When I get the magnet ready, I'm gonna tell you to turn on the inverter."

Sutherland pointed to a machine that Patupick had placed on the floor. "Is this the inverter?"

"Just push the red button."

"Where?"

"The one on top. The one that's red."

Patupick pocketed his walkie talkie and climbed the steep stairs, cord in one hand, electromagnet in the other.

"Let's step back," Agnes said. "If he's gonna fall, I don't want it to be on us."

"I can hear you," Patupick shouted from the stairs.

Pop-Up Dinner, Drop Down Dead

Agnes sat on the floor and Sutherland on his scooter. They waited for a good five minutes before they heard the order to press the red button. Sutherland pushed it. Agnes clicked the walkie talkie. "Button pushed. Over and out."

"I'm not flying a plane," Patupick complained.

Agnes shrugged. "I just thought it was protocol."

There was silence, and the order came to push the red button again. Sutherland complied and the inverter stopped humming. Walking backward, Patupick descended the stairs.

He didn't speak. Instead, he began to roll up the cord.

"Well?" Agnes asked.

"Well, what?" Patupick answered.

"Did it work?"

"Of course."

"It opened the door?" Agnes questioned.

"You only said you wanted it unlocked. You didn't say you wanted it open. I assume if you push against the door, it will open."

Sutherland looked at Agnes. "Why unlock a door but not open it?"

"When interrogated, I can now honestly say I had no idea what you were doing. Who do I bill?" Ed asked.

"Send me the bill," Agnes said.

"I don't know you. I'll bill Milo."

Then why bother asking? Agnes screamed in her mind. Patupick was just as annoying as ever. Sutherland escorted Ed out and made sure he unmuted the intercom.

Agnes texted Martha to join her in the basement, then video called Sutherland's Aunt Lana. "The door is open!" she exclaimed to Lana.

"So? What's behind the door?" Aunt Lana was excited.

§

Milo and Preston declined Vee's offer of cold weather gear. The temperature was above zero and the sun was shining. The ice road trip was quick, and no storms were predicted.

"Rumor has it, you two went rogue in Canada after I dropped you off yesterday," Vee said as they began their journey back out to Jack Fish Island.

"We were driving, and somebody put another country in our way," Milo explained.

"The Canadians are a little touchy about people just showing up without going through customs. You could have just crossed the bridge."

"Oh, cross the bridge, rather than tumbling down onto a frozen expanse in the dead of night?" Preston said. "Thank you. I'll remember for next time."

Milo laughed. Preston's sarcasm was right on.

"Bob's place is busy today. Early this morning, I guided a young lady out here. Now you guys are back," Vee said. "Might be crowded."

"Young lady?" Preston asked. "Do you know who?"

"She didn't say."

"Bob didn't strike me as a ladies' man," Milo said.

Vee chuckled. "He's been coming out here for years, and this is a first that I know of."

Vee pulled up to the RV. "I'll wait here. I've got some calls to make."

Milo and Preston walked to the RV and rapped on the door. Young answered. "You again? I'm busy!"

"So are we," Preston said, pushing her way past Young into the RV. Sarcasm and assertiveness. Milo was impressed.

Neither Milo nor Preston were present at Poppie's cop shop interview, but despite shorter hair and new makeup, both recognized her from the pop-up pictures. "You're Poppie Flower."

Poppie shrugged. "I know that. Who are you?"

"They're cops who questioned me about Raf," Young said.

"We have a few more questions to ask you," Preston said.

"Make it quick, I've got company."

"I thought you were fishing," Milo said.

"I'm doing both. Ask your questions."

"Was Raf Bianchi dealing drugs?" Preston asked.

Young shrugged. "Not to me."

Poppy laughed.

"You laughed," Preston said. "Why?"

"You asked, was he dealing? Like was he standing on a street corner offering a quarter? That's funny."

"Why is that funny?"

"Well, it's so not Raf?"

"How is that so not Raf? He was pretty silent when we met him," Milo said.

Poppie furrowed her brow for a moment. "Oh, I get it. Like he was dead. Good one."

"How was it so not like Raf?" Milo re-asked.

"Sometimes Raf had stuff, sometimes he didn't. You had to ask him."

"Bob, you want to weigh in here?" Milo asked.

"I never wanted anything to do with that man. I told you he owed bad dudes. Maybe they were drug dudes. I don't know."

Poppie put her arm around Bob. "We have to get back to fishing."

"Happy fishing," Milo said as he and Preston left for Vee's car.

§

Agnes and Martha stopped at the top of the new stairs to sit down, catch their breath, and make sure the Aunt Lana video phone call was still up and running. "If we walked all the way up here, and this door doesn't open…ugh. That man is so annoying," Agnes complained.

"Do you really think he didn't open it and look inside?" Lana asked.

"I don't know. He's Milo's friend and certifiable."

Lana laughed. "Having met Milo, I can believe that."

"The upside, if I have to hike these stairs again, I will have my cardio for the month," Agnes said as she stood up and pointed her phone toward the door. "Okay. I'm going to push. I'm sorry Gabby and Tee were busy and couldn't join us, but I can't say for sure this door will open. Be prepared for disappointment if that door doesn't move." Putting her shoulder into the move, Agnes leaned hard into the solid oak door, falling forward onto the ground as the door swung open.

"Are you okay?" Martha asked, helping her up.

"I'm looking at the floor," Lana said. "Did you fall?"

Pop-Up Dinner, Drop Down Dead

"I did. The crazy man did unlock the door." Agnes began brushing herself off. The staircase was clean, but the room was dusty and webby—what Agnes was used to in her previous Lakesong discoveries. She stood, picked up her phone, and began circling the room to show Lana the walls.

"Lana look!"

The same kind of carvings that covered the vault also covered these walls. There were not as many, and they weren't as complete. The images were familiar: birds, wolves, and swords. It was almost like this had been a practice room for what eventually became the vault. These carvings had been done on squares of wood which were now attached to the walls. They gave the impression of one solid scene, but it was a mosaic.

"I see it. I'm with you," Lana said. "The attic matches the vault."

Martha's attention was taken by another door, unlocked, which led to a dark hallway. Using her phone flashlight, Martha walked along the hallway and pushed open three doors. She called back, "Don't leave without me. I'm exploring down this hall. I found bedrooms, I think.".

"Maybe for the outside staff," Agnes said as she joined Martha.

"Not many rooms," Martha said.

"That's the gallery's fault. Sutherland reminded me about the huge section of the third floor that had been removed," Agnes said. "The other side of Lakesong, the north where Sutherland and I live, housed the domestic staff. The south side was for the outside gardeners, mechanics, and the horse people. Since they would not need access to the main part of the house, they came and went through the basement."

"There were horse people?" Martha asked.

"A while back, I found a carriage in one of the outbuildings. I'm picturing grooms and stable hands, who knows, maybe even a few cows."

Other than dust and spiderwebs, Agnes saw nothing as exciting as the carvings in the bedrooms. In the last bedroom, there was a dusty book left open on a table. She leaned over to look at it. The book appeared to be handwritten in a Scandinavian language. "Someone left this. Maybe it's a clue to more of Lakesong's family. So many people have lived here and been sheltered by Lakesong."

"I wish I wasn't in Scotland right now. So, Agnes, where do we go from here?" Lana asked.

"This book might be important. I'll bring it to the second-floor library to protect it. Then I need to find someone who can translate it," Agnes replied.

Lana agreed. "Exciting discoveries yet to come. Let me know how I can help. Give my love to Sutherland."

"Martha, Lakesong needs to have all the holes in her past filled. When you don't know your past, it feels like something is missing."

From their many talks over the last few years, Martha knew that Agnes was talking about more than the house. "It's getting late. Dinner will not fix itself."

Martha was gone. Lana had hung up. Agnes looked around the empty room. "Well, Lakesong, you seem to want me to learn more about your history," she said. The sun emerged from behind the clouds. Through the dust and the cobwebs, sunlight seeped through the only window.

§

"I've recovered," Preston said, holding out her hand for the keys.

"Okay, I'm going to let you drive," Milo said, handing the keys to Preston, "but no driving to Canada."

"If I remember correctly, you were the one who suggested that we drive across the river," Preston said, readjusting the driver's seat and plugging the Duluth police department into the GPS.

Milo took out his phone and called Gramm.

"Did the Canadians torture you?" Gramm asked in the way of a greeting.

"They did. They wanted to know how we say the word *out* without sounding like an owl."

"I hope you didn't tell them."

"Well, that Canadian bacon looked so good. I might have let some secrets slip."

"So, Bob Young. What did he have to say?"

"Interestingly, he had a companion," Milo said.

Gramm's eyebrows shot up. "Companion?"

"Poppie!" Preston yelled from the driver's seat.

"We talked to her," White said. "Did she mention her eyeliner?"

"No, did we miss something?" Preston questioned.

"What did you find out about the drugs?" Gramm barked.

Milo answered. "Young claims no knowledge. Poppie says Bianchi was a casual drug dealer. If he had some, he sold some."

17

Friday morning, Milo walked into the cop shop to a standing ovation. He acknowledged the sarcastic tribute with a wave of his hand before going over to the coffeepot and pouring himself a cup. "Thank you all," he said. "It will take weeks, perhaps months, for me and Preston to overcome the harrowing experiences we faced in enemy territory. I ask for your patience as we recover."

One of the patrol officers walked up to him. "You know the Canadians are our friends."

"They made us stay at a place called the Sleepy Owl. What sort of friend does that?"

"Milo! Now!" Gramm shouted from his office.

The officer laughed. "You thought the Canadians were bad."

Milo took a sip of his coffee to keep from spilling it and strolled into Gramm's office. He took his usual seat. White and Preston were grinning.

"Did I miss something?" Milo asked.

"I was just telling Preston, you two are lucky. Both the deputy chief and the chief thought your excursion north was funny. It helps that you're their golden boy."

Milo leaned over to White. "I'm a golden boy."

"Preston, tell Robin what Young had to say about Bianchi's drug dealing," Gramm ordered."

"Young claimed ignorance, but Poppie said he was sort of an informal drug dealer."

"Somebody translate *informal drug dealer*."

Milo responded, "She said you had to ask him if he was carrying anything. He wasn't on a street corner selling quarters."

"And you say *quarters* like it comes from your extensive undercover work in the drug world," Gramm said.

"Why was she there?" White asked.

Milo laughed. "Ernie, I think it's time you sat White down for the talk."

"Yeah, yeah, yeah," White said. "Very funny, but she's with Reese Winterhausen."

"Maybe not anymore," Preston said with a twinkle in her eye.

§

Agnes was in a quandary about the journal she found. She had safely carried the book to the temperature controlled library, but now she had to find a person to translate it. That same person had to be versed in preserving old books as well. She hoped the book contained information about the carvings both upstairs and down in the vault. So far, both were huge question marks. She called Jules, her friend, who owned several art galleries.

"Agnes, my dear, where have you been? Have your husband's gangster friends bestowed anymore incredible paintings upon you?"

"No, Jules, and he wasn't my husband's friend. He was Milo's."

"I don't care whose friend he was. Since brokering that deal for your painting, I have found that Mr. Wolf knows…people…and some of those people buy art. Thank you for a whole new cliental. Another perk…dealing with them makes me excited down to my toes."

Agnes laughed. "I'm glad your toes are excited, Jules, but I need some advice."

"Anything!"

"I have found an old journal in part of this house that has been sealed up for years. It's not written in English. I need a translator, but one who knows how to treat an old manuscript. I'm treating it like a work of art."

"Send me a picture of one of the pages. I have a friend who deals in manuscripts. That should start the ball rolling."

"Thanks, Jules," Agnes said, clicking off.

§

It was noon on Friday and stomachs were growling.

"There's a new sushi bar in the Fitger's building," White said just to get a reaction.

"I'm meat and potatoes hungry," Gramm said. "My brain needs fuel. Sushi isn't going to do it for me."

"Okay," White said, getting up and putting on her coat. "Chinese Dragon or Gustafsons?"

"Chinese Dragon," Milo said. "I haven't been there in a while. I'm afraid Hank will stop giving me free food."

"You take free food?" Preston questioned.

"Of course. It tastes better when it's free."

The group piled into a Police Interceptor and drove down to the Chinese Dragon. Henry Hun, Milo's boyhood friend, greeted them at the door. "Well, it's about time. I could go bankrupt if I didn't have other, more loyal customers. Your table in the back is waiting for you," he told them.

"Do you really give Milo free food?" Preston asked.

"He thinks it's free. I put it on his tab."

"How much does he owe?" White asked.

"Five thousand and change."

Preston's eyes grew wide.

"It's fine. The mooching has been spread out over years," Henry explained.

As they sat down, Preston continued, "Why do you continue to pay for Milo's food? He works. Make him pay for it."

"Hello?" Milo waved. "I'm sitting right here."

"Milo, he's running a business and you're stealing his profit."

Hank smiled. "Kate, it's fine, really. It's a game we play. He gets free food, and my wife tells me that someone has set up generous college funds for all five of our children. I only have one friend who could afford such a thing." Hank turned to look at Milo. "Besides, egg foo yung is only three eggs and a bit of gravy."

Milo perked up. "You have five children? When did that happen?"

"When you were causing airplane crashes." Hank nodded to one of his waiters, who scurried over with a book. He set it down on the table. White read the title, *Mind Lint. The Chaotic Cases of Detective Milo Rathkey.*

"Where the hell did you get that?" Milo muttered.

"Ron Bello. I've had it for a week. It hit the bookstores this morning. Don't you two talk?"

Milo looked at his phone. "One message popped up from Agnes: *Not urgent. I have a job for you.*

He immediately responded, *Sure. Talk tonight.*

Milo returned to the banter with Hank. "I have twelve voice mails from Ron."

"Saying what?" Gramm asked.

Milo shrugged. "Don't know. I didn't listen. This book has no one famous, like Harper Gain. I predict it bombs."

White checked her phone. "It's already on the New York Times Best Seller List."

"Sign it," Hank ordered, pushing the book toward Milo.

Milo flipped open the cover and signed on the first page, *Stop skimping on the gravy! Your pal, Milo.*

Milo's phone rang. It was Kevin Richards, the police information officer. Milo sighed before answering. "Kevin, don't tell me, the higher ups hate Ron's new book and forbid me from ever mentioning it."

"I won't tell you that, Milo. They love it, and once again want you to do all interviews, of course, mentioning the

Duluth Police Department early and often. I'll be calling with particulars."

Milo put his phone down. "Dog and pony showtime," he said to Gramm.

"What's that?" Preston asked.

"I think it's an old circus reference," White said. "It's what Milo calls doing a media interview."

"I'm hungry. Can we order?" Gramm asked.

Hank nodded. "We have two specials today. The first one is just for Milo. It's called suodui. It consists of vegetables, spices, and rocks—very difficult to make. Savor the vegetables while removing the rocks."

"I knew it would happen one day," Milo said. "He's cracked. All that angst over skimping on the gravy has led to a nervous breakdown. Now he's cooking rocks."

Hank ignored him. "Bo Zai Fan is the special for everyone else. It's clay pot rice. Crispy rice on the bottom, fluffy favored rice on the top plus vegetables and a protein. We suggest Chinese sausage."

"Sounds delicious," White said. "I'll have that."

Preston also opted for the special.

Gramm asked for his usual beef and broccoli.

All eyes turned to Milo. "Are the stones hot?"

"Of course."

"So, when I pluck them out, I'll burn my fingers?"

"No fingers. You suck on them. Third-degree burns to the mouth. It's part of the experience."

"What if I swallow a stone?"

"You die. Also, part of the experience."

"Milo! Order your damn egg foo yung!" Gramm shouted, causing other patrons to look.

"I have no choice, apparently. My boss is forcing me to order the egg foo yung, no rocks. Oh, and…"

The entire table said in unison, "Don't skimp on the gravy."

Hank picked up his book and nodded for the servers to bring tea.

Gramm looked to White. "If Milo is going to be wasting his time being paraded around like a show horse, I want to put this case to bed quickly. Give me suspects in order, people. Keep in mind, motive, means, and opportunity."

"Right now, Kick DeJong," White said. "He is at the top of my list. He's the one who insisted on bringing Raf along when nobody wanted him. Was Kick waiting for the right time to murder Raf? If so, why?"

"Why start with him?" Preston asked. "I think he's the least likely."

"Because he's the least likely, so he's the guy Milo will name at the end. All the way he will mumble something like, beware of people who seem the least likely."

"I'm thinking who would name their kid Kick, and why," Milo said.

White closed her eyes while shaking her head.

"Ignore him," Gramm ordered.

White continued supporting her claim. "According to Milo, Kick and our victim had a fight at Kick's restaurant. Kick threw him out. Also, let's not forget that Kick seemed to be on something. My guess is oxy. Remember, he denied that

Bianchi was a dealer but then threatened us with a lawyer... twice. He lies and is unstable."

"I agree," Gramm said. "Let's go through means, motive, and opportunity."

"Motive could be a dispute over drugs. Bianchi was his dealer and was going to cut him off or raise prices," White argued.

"Why would Bianchi do that?" Gramm asked.

"Maybe Kick couldn't pay," White said. "He may not be as wealthy as we think."

"Check his financials," Gramm said to Preston. "Opportunity?"

Preston closed her eyes, visualizing the scene at the dinner. "Kick was sitting next to Bianchi for a while and then got moved over."

"Means?"

"They all had entrées with peanuts, but the murderer needed peanut oil," White said.

"Can you just buy peanut oil?" Gramm asked.

"Yes," White answered. "In about any grocery store."

"So, no leads there!" Gramm grumbled. "Let's move on. Suspect number two."

"Kick's wife Jess," White said. "She made no secret of the fact she didn't like Bianchi."

"I don't like the guy who fills the vending machines," Milo blurted, "but I'm not going to kill him."

"She moved, putting herself between her husband and the victim," Preston said. "That's an opportunity."

"Trying to protect her husband from buying more drugs?" Gramm asked.

"When she said Bianchi put her husband's restaurant in jeopardy, I sensed genuine anger," White added.

"Means?" Gramm asked.

"Again, peanut oil," White answered.

"Would the kind of peanut oil in the grocery store kill him?" Milo asked.

Gramm picked up his phone. "That's a question for Doc Smith."

Smith answered on the first ring. "Smith here."

"We're talking peanut oil here, Doc. Will all peanut oil cause this allergic reaction or…"

"Unrefined peanut oil. The refined stuff takes the proteins out. The proteins kill you, if you are seriously allergic."

"Can I just go out and buy unrefined?"

"Certainly." Doc Smith hung up.

Gramm set his phone down. "Good question, Milo, but we're still in the same boat. Anyone could get their hands on this stuff. Let's continue with the Winterhoosens."

"Winterhausen," White corrected.

"That younger sister, ah um…" Gramm drew a blank on her first name.

"Emma," Preston said. "She replaced me at Spirit Mountain."

Both Gramm and White turned to look at her.

"I was a ski instructor in college," Preston said.

"Off point. Motive?" Gramm asked.

"Raf was a predator, but Emma can protect herself when she's being manhandled," White said. "She hit that guy in the bar with a bottle."

"You hit someone with a bottle. Are you're looking to disable or kill them?" Milo asked.

"The intent doesn't matter. What about big brother, Reese?" Gramm asked,

Preston smiled. "He's pretty."

"Guilty," Milo said. "Case closed."

"That was easy," White added, "but I don't think it will hold up in court. Reese didn't care for Raf either. Said he didn't trust him. I don't think that goes as far as he'd kill him, but Raf was bothering his younger sister."

"Emma told us her brother Reese threatened Bianchi that night," Preston said.

"We need to check that video for everyone's movements," Milo said. "I don't remember Reese getting close to Bianchi."

"We have Reese's girlfriend, Poppie," Gramm said.

Preston nodded. "Flavor of the month, according to Bob Young,"

"I would think she'd be more inclined to kill Reese than Raf," White added.

The food arrived. Milo not only got his egg foo yung with plenty of gravy but also a bowl with vegetables and rocks. He touched one rock and pulled his fingers back quickly. "They're hot!" he complained.

"What about Bob Young?" Gramm asked.

Preston closed her eyes. "At the beginning of the meal, he was sitting next to Bianchi."

"Not at the end?" Milo asked.

"No. Poppie was next to him at the end, between him and Raf."

Gramm's eyebrows shot up. "Was this a pop-up dinner or musical chairs?"

"I think we all need to look at that video again," Milo repeated.

"Okay. We have no idea who killed Raf. Let's eat," Gramm said.

"We can discuss Bianchi's kidnapping over dessert," White added.

"We never have dessert," Preston said.

"We never get lost in Canada either," Gramm said, "but now we've crossed that bridge."

"We didn't cross the bridge. That was the problem," Milo said.

Gramm dug into his beef and broccoli.

"Remind me to tell you about the incident at The Deeps," Milo said.

"Eat your stones," Gramm ordered.

"At this point, all I know is this Bo Zai Fan is delicious," White said. Preston echoed her statement.

Milo took three stones out of his suodui and ate three pieces of cabbage. "This suit dye is never going to make it onto my favorite weird food list." He abandoned the suodui in favor of his egg foo yung.

Hank returned, saw three stones on Milo's plate, and congratulated him on trying the special. "Did you suck on the rocks and then dispose of them?"

"Oh, come on, Hank. I wasn't born yesterday. There's no way you suck on rocks. It's a choking hazard. By the way, I expected it to taste like cloth soaked in heavy dye."

"I get it. Suit dye," Hank said. "Once again, thank you for making light of my heritage."

"Somebody has to. I mean, you make up these silly names. This dish is probably called rocks on cabbage."

"If some day we find Milo face down with chopsticks sticking out of his ears, we'll know who did it," Preston said.

"Accidental death," White said. "We'll move on."

"I'll keep that in mind." Hank smiled.

§

Agnes was sitting in the gallery soaking up the warmth of a bright Minnesota winter sun when her phone rang. It was Jules' friend, Sonja Johansen, from UMD and The Nordic Center. "Interesting journal, but I've only been given the first page. What is it you want from me?"

"A translation of the entire journal would be helpful."

"How many pages are there?"

"I'm hesitant to handle it. The book is old. I don't want to damage it."

"I understand. I am trained in handling old manuscripts. Where are you storing it now?"

"We have a library on the second floor that has a positive ventilation and constant humidity. It's up there."

"That's good! I would prefer to keep the book in that room and translate it there, if possible. Mrs. McKnight, my services for an entire book are not cheap." Johansen gave her a ballpark figure.

"I understand. I'm sure we can work something out," Agnes said as she asked herself, *"Who am I? That's at least a year's car payments."*

"The page you sent to me was in Norwegian, and he writes of carving wood. Are you aware of any of his carvings in the house?"

Agnes laughed. "There are carvings everywhere in this house—on the third floor where we found the journal, in the basement vault."

"I will send over my contract. Are you the owner of the house?"

"My husband and I are co-owners with a man named Milo Rathkey. He's a consultant with the Duluth Police Department."

"Rathkey? The man from the Harper Gain book?"

"That's Milo."

"I'm reading that now."

18

Milo mumbled a good morning to Martha as he made his way to the morning room. Annie stayed far ahead of him, but Jet wound in and around his legs, herding him into the room with the bacon. Annie stopped, waited for Milo to pass and then batted at Jet as if to say, "Stop herding the human. He knows where he's going." That, at least, is how Milo interpreted it.

"It appears as if Annie is stopping Jet from guiding you, Milo," Sutherland said. "I think she's hoping you run into the wall."

Both cats clawed at Milo's legs to get their bacon.

Milo poured his coffee and sat down. "The cats need a nail trim. Who does that? Jamal? Darian?"

"Ginger at the Lakeside Clip and Trim," Martha said as she delivered his breakfast.

"Clip and Trim?" Milo questioned.

"They make house calls. The cats love Ginger and her treats."

Someone is at the gate, the intercom announced. *There is a seventy-two percent chance it is Officer Kate Preston.*

"The intercom is betting on our visitors?" Sutherland questioned.

"Patupick warned me he added an artificial intelligence module to the software. It learns as it goes," Milo said.

Sutherland picked up his phone to open the gate, only to find the intercom had already done it. "It's letting her in!" Sutherland exclaimed.

"We like Preston. It's okay."

"I don't know if I like letting a seventy-two percent chance past the gate."

It has risen to a ninety-five percent chance it's Officer Preston, the intercom said.

"Can we turn this off?" Sutherland asked.

I enjoy working with humans, Sutherland. Would you like to hear me sing a song?

"If that thing starts singing Daisy, I'm shutting it down," Sutherland said.

"Daisy?" Milo questioned.

"It's what HAL the computer sang in the movie 2001, just after he killed a couple of people."

"I think Patupick is having fun with you," Milo said.

"Hello?" Preston called from the foyer. Normally someone came to the door to greet her, but this time the door simply unlocked and the doorbell invited her in. As she closed the door behind her, she heard voices. *I bet they're in the room with all the windows.*

"It even unlocked the door for her!" Sutherland continued his rant. "Does the intercom shut the door, too?"

My name is Debbie, not 'intercom' or 'it.'

"Debbie? Milo?"

"Patupick asked what I wanted to name her, and I said Debbie."

"You name all your voices Debbie," Preston said, pleased to find everyone in the room with all the windows. She cooly headed for the coffee urn.

"I do," Milo said.

"Preston and I are going to the Tip Top Tavern this morning to warn a loan shark she could be in trouble with Morrie Wolf. Should be fun," Milo said.

"Didn't you already go there?" Sutherland asked.

"I did, but she was rude, called my mother unmarried. I've mellowed since then. If she refrains from calling me a bastard, I'll let her know. Otherwise…"

"How do you know she's in trouble?"

"I'm the one that got her there," Milo said.

"This morning?"

"No, a couple of days ago."

"And you're just getting around to warning her now?"

"We were in Canada. Besides, I think I mentioned she was rude."

Preston turned down Martha's offer of breakfast. Looking around the windowed morning room, Preston said, "Milo, someday, I have to get the story of how you're living here."

"We left the terrace doors open, and he wandered in. It was during a storm. He looked so pathetic," Sutherland teased.

"I could have sworn that was Jet," Milo said.

"Really?" Sutherland asked. "Easy mistake to make."

Jet meowed at Sutherland as if to complain about being confused with Milo.

§

Darlene Budack was pouring a beer when Preston and Rathkey walked in. She turned to look at them and then turned back to her chore. "I got nothin' to say to you."

"Darlene, we need to talk to you about your loan sharking business," Milo said.

Darlene slapped the beer mug on the bar and slid it down to a waiting customer. "Look, some people need cash. I provide it, but they have to pay me back. I don't charge outrageous interest, and I don't hurt people. It's more of a service than anything else."

"I don't care about any of that. Your good buddy, David Bonner, hired Leroy Thompson to help out the night they roughed up Raf Bianchi."

Darlene blanched. "Oh, crap."

David Bonner arrived carrying a case of beer. "You want me to show these two to the door?" he asked Darlene.

"Yeah. Get 'em out of here. Then you and me gotta talk."

Milo raised his hands in mock surrender. "We're gone."

He and Preston left.

"Are we just going to leave it there? Loan sharking is illegal," Preston complained.

Milo started his Honda. "I think Darlene is going to have an unpleasant visit."

"From?"

"A large man named Milosh."

"Morrie Wolf's guy?" Preston asked. "So, Darlene misstepped?"

"It's a learning process."

"Is this like 'being put in the trunk of a car' learning process?" Preston asked.

Milo shook his head. "I think it's more of a financial problem. I am sure she is giving Morrie a piece of her action. That piece just got bigger."

"Maybe she didn't realize she was renting this Thompson guy," Preston said.

"Doesn't matter." As Milo was waiting to turn onto busy Central Entrance, an old black Lincoln pulled in.

"Timed this right," Milo said. "Time to leave."

§

Milo thought he and Preston would be late getting into the cop shop, but, in fact, they were early. Milo looked around the near empty Saturday morning bullpen and Gramm's dark office. "If I had known we would be the first ones in, I'd have stopped for a shave."

Preston laughed. "I'd go for a massage."

Milo had to go up to the PIO's office to do his first phone interview for Bello's new book. Robin arrived next. She had no guilt in stopping off at her favorite coffee place. Gramm was worried about the lack of progress in the Bianchi murder case, so he ordered everyone in on a Saturday to see if they could come up with something new. The making of White's drink proved time consuming, making her fifteen minutes late to work. She expected to be chided when she arrived, but there was no Gramm.

"What's the coffee of the day?" Preston asked.

"Double espresso, pistachio, latte. Coffee, pistachio flavor with espresso, steamed milk, and brown butter topping."

"Sounds delicious," Preston said, pouring herself a cup from the overnight coffeepot.

"You know that coffee has been on the hotplate for hours," White said.

"It's my double espresso. Why are we the first ones in?" Preston complained as she walked to Robin's desk.

"Because I'm the boss," Gramm said, walking into the bullpen. "And Milo is…Milo. I have to make a phone call, a good time for someone to make a fresh pot of coffee," Gramm shouted.

Preston was about to get up when she noticed several rookie cops scurrying towards the pot. White laughed. "At ease, Kate, there are others less fortunate than you."

Preston took a sip of her coffee, grimaced, then added sugar and creamer.

"Tell me about The Deeps," White ordered.

"The what?"

"The Deeps. Milo mentioned it at lunch yesterday."

"Oh yeah, Bob Young went on about it. Apparently, The Deeps is one of Duluth's unofficial swimming holes. For years, kids have been jumping off the rocks and into the water."

"Why did Young even bring that up?" White asked.

"It's the reason Kick was so loyal to Raf. When they were teenagers, Raf Bianchi saved DeJong's life. Kick was heading for the rocks and Raf saved his life by pushing him out into the water."

"Sounds unRaf like."

"Young agrees with you. He says Kick came down just as Bianchi was pushing some little kid off the lower rocks. Saving Kick was just an automatic reflex, saving Bianchi's arm more than Kick's life."

"Milo said something about The Deeps yesterday at lunch, almost as if it wasn't important. I think it's one of those mind lint things of his. From your story, there's a third person who gets forgotten."

"Who?"

"What became of the kid Bianchi pushed into the water?"

Preston squinted and shook her head.

With a big Chesire grin on her face, White scooted her chair closer to Preston. "That's the key to this whole thing. You and I, we are going to out Milo, Milo."

"By finding out what happened to the kid Bianchi pushed?"

"Exactly."

Milo walked into the bullpen and up to White's desk. "You look like the cat that just ate the gopher."

"Canary," Preston said.

"Why canary?"

"That's the saying. The cat that just ate the canary."

"I would think a gopher would be more tasty and filling."

"White, Preston, Milo! Get in here!" Gramm yelled.

As they got up to go into Gramm's office, White said, "Tastier, not more tasty."

"See," Milo said to Preston, "White agrees."

§

Agnes had a good night's sleep but still felt tired. She came down to breakfast and stopped by the kitchen, explaining to Martha she didn't want her usual smoothie today either.

"Eggs?" Martha asked.

"Oh God no!" Agnes said.

"Can I bring you anything?"

Agnes scrunched her nose. "Hmm, salty, crunchy, crackers of some kind. Yeah crackers. Do we have any saltines?"

"We do," Martha said, pointing to a cabinet. "What to drink?"

"Nothing, thanks," she called back to Martha as she proceeded to the morning room with a sleeve of crackers clutched to her chest.

"Sutherland, I forgot to tell you. I know it's the weekend, but a woman named Sonja Johansen is coming over to begin the translation of that journal we found on the third floor."

"Oh, you found someone? That was fast."

"Jules found her for me. She knows Norwegian and also knows how to treat an old manuscript."

"Great. Where's Milo?" Sutherland asked.

Agnes looked at the empty chair usually occupied by Milo. "He's not here."

"I know that. Why?"

Agnes was not in the mood. She waved him off.

Noticing the crackers, Sutherland asked if she felt okay.

She shrugged and waved him off again.

Unidentified person at the front gate, the intercom announced.

Sutherland checked his phone, pressing the talk button. "Can I help you?"

"I'm Sonja Johansen. I have an appointment with Agnes McKnight."

"Could you handle the hellos and bring her up to the library?" Agnes asked. "Tell her the book is upstairs on the table nearest the windows. She knows what to do. I'm going to lie down."

Sutherland was torn between taking care of Agnes and taking care of Agnes' business. "Are you okay? Do you want me to…"

"Do this, please. I'll be upstairs with my sleeve of saltines." She hugged them as if they were quite valuable.

Sutherland proceeded to the foyer and opened one of the two mahogany front doors just as Johansen was walking up the porch steps. "Welcome. I'm Agnes' husband, Sutherland. Agnes has asked me to show you upstairs and get you started."

Johansen stopped in the entryway to take in the expansive mansion. Sutherland led her to the upstairs library, where she removed her coat, took out her laptop, and sat down in front of the book.

"Would you like something to drink, coffee, a soft drink?"

"Not near the manuscript!" she said, as if scolding a child.

"Of course. If you should want something, our chef, Martha Gibbson, is in the kitchen." Sutherland showed her his phone. "Here is my cell number. Call me and I will guide you to the kitchen."

"Is it that hard to find?"

"There are a few rights and lefts. We wouldn't want you to get lost." Sutherland smiled, thinking he was being friendly and amusing.

She didn't smile. "I would like to get to it."

Sutherland took that as his cue to leave. He left the library and crossed over to the newly constructed apartment on the second floor. He found Agnes leaving the bathroom, wiping her face. She smiled at him weakly. "I can't even keep crackers down."

"You should rest," he said. "Let me get you water. Try to stay hydrated."

She curled up on the sofa.

"Do you want to sleep, or do you want company?" Sutherland asked as he covered her with a fuzzy blanket.

"Company now. Tell me all about Sonja Johansen."

"My humor and charm are lost on her."

Agnes snuggled into the soft, fuzzy pillow and smiled. "Not on me."

Sutherland smiled, but continued his outrage. "She was all business. When I left, or rather when she kicked me out, she was putting on a fresh pair of white gloves."

"I forwarded her contract to you. We are paying her a lot of money to wear those white gloves."

Sutherland checked his phone. "Oh my, go easy on those crackers. They will have to last us for the month."

"Please don't make me laugh, and if I were you, I wouldn't mention any food," Agnes said as she flung off the throw and ran back to the bathroom.

§

Pop-Up Dinner, Drop Down Dead

Preston was busy doing a deep dive into everyone's financials per Gramm's instruction. White was following her hunch concerning Milo's mention of The Deeps. She didn't expect a morning call from Poppie Flower.

"Ms. Flower?"

"I'm leaving town. I have nowhere to stay. Mr. Winterhausen and I broke up. FYI, he's not the easy breezy guy he pretends to be," Poppie told her. "He has been so moody and angry."

"Angry?" White asked.

"He's suddenly jealous of Bob Young. I mean we just talked at that dinner. I made the mistake of telling Reese the truth. I talked to Bob because Reese was ignoring me. Then he got really mad. He scared me. I don't do bully boyfriends, so I'm gone."

"You said he frightened you. Has he been abusive?"

"Well, not to me, but he did threaten to do away with Raf."

"Explain," White ordered.

"The night of the dinner. After Emma had to physically get Raf off of her, Reese said it was time for Raf to go. A short time later, Raf went."

"Do you think Reese had something to do with that?"

"Look, I don't want to get him in any trouble. I'm just telling you people what I know before I leave, so I don't get in trouble with you."

"Do you need us to monitor your exit?"

"No, I'm already in my car. You have my cell phone number. I'm out of here."

"Drive carefully," White said. "Thanks for letting us know." She reentered the office. "Good news for Preston," White began. "Poppie Flower has just informed me that she and Reese Winterhausen have broken up. She is going back to the Cities."

Gramm stared at Preston. "Why is that good news for you?"

"Because he's so pretty," Preston crooned.

"Pretty?" Gramm almost shouted the word. "What guy wants to be called pretty?"

"I think Preston wants to be the next flavor of the month," White said.

"Not 'till this case is over," Gramm warned. "Robin, what's the real reason Ms. Flower called you?"

"To say she's leaving town because she and Winterhausen broke up. She threw in that Reese was not the easy-going guy we think he is. He's really angry, moody, and ding, ding, ding, abusive. She also repeated that Reese threatened Raf during the dinner."

"Threatened how?"

"Quoting Poppie, Reese said it was time for 'Raf to go.'"

"That's it?" Gramm asked.

"Again, quoting Poppie, 'and then he went.'"

"Poppie's revelation wouldn't have anything to do with payback over she and Reese breaking up?" Preston asked.

"Probably," White said, "but that doesn't mean it didn't happen."

§

After the early morning check-in, Milo excused himself and returned to Lakesong, saying he needed to do some special research. If he noticed White give Preston a nod, he didn't mention it.

He clicked on the gas fireplace in his office and settled in behind his computer. "When I was a kid," Milo said to Jet, who accompanied him on most research adventures, "we used to jump into the river at a place called The Deeps."

Jet meowed as if to say, "When you were young and dumb. We cats don't do that."

"A young boy was either pushed or fell some fifteen years ago. It's a long shot, but we need to find out if it was reported."

Jet furthered the research by lying down on the computer keyboard. Milo stared at him. Jet maneuvered his body to get even more comfortable. "You're not helping," Milo said as he gently removed him from the desk.

Jet meowed at Milo, jumped back up, and walked to a spot further down the desk. After checking out all his body parts, he stretched out full length and closed his eyes.

Using his Patupick installed software, an exhaustive archive of news reports, Milo attempted to find anything about an incident at The Deeps. There were many accidents over the years, some fatal. A short news item that was a bit different caught his eye. A young boy was declared missing and later found to have drowned. Milo copied down the boy's name. There was no mention of Raf Bianchi or Ralph Bing. This may not be the right incident, but it fits the timeline.

§

Preston, having pulled all the financials and reported to Gramm, slid her chair over to sit next to White. "What do we have?"

"I'm checking our archives to see if anyone was hurt or drowned at The Deeps fifteen years ago, give or take a couple of years," White told her. "I put in a broad sweep of dates, which turned up two drownings at that location."

"Gees, that's a dangerous place," Preston said

§

Milo swung back to the computer and called up the newspaper article he had found earlier. There was a grainy picture of EMTs in a boat. The photo credit was Elbert Galenis. Milo typed the name into his PI software. There was only one Elbert Galenis. Milo called the number.

§

"I think we have something," White said. Preston moved closer. "According to this police report, a young boy was declared missing for three days. His body was later recovered in Lake Superior just up the shore from the mouth of the Lester River."

Preston typed into her phone. "Doing a quick check, The Deeps is on the Amity Creek which flows into the Lester River."

"Which flows into the lake," White said. "According to this report, the kid was pulled under by the current. It led to a massive search by over a hundred people before his body was found."

§

A man with a raspy voice answered Milo's call with a whisper.

"Elbert? Elbert Galenis?"

"Who are you?" the voice asked.

"Milo Rathkey. I'm a consultant with the Duluth Police Department."

"Yeah?"

"You covered a drowning on June 22, 1999, at The Deeps. A young boy was reported missing, then found, having drowned." Milo hoped the man's memory was still intact.

"Yeah, what about it?"

"Do you remember?"

"Yeah, I remember that one. I was on my way to shoot pictures of the Miss Duluth contest. I got called off to cover a kid's drowning. I remember because my girlfriend, at the time, later first wife, was in the contest. I didn't get there in time. She was pissed."

"There's only one picture?"

"No, I was rushed, but I shot more than one!" the man seemed offended.

"They skimped on the article too."

"That's not me. On this story, I was the photographer. I didn't write the article. Besides, we didn't know how he got there. It could have been The Deeps or Lester River or somewhere else. It had been hot, so the reporter guessed The Deeps. If it was an accident at The Deeps, the newspaper didn't like to do much about those kinds of incidents. They thought it encouraged other kids to jump."

"Was there any talk about his being pushed?"

"What? No way! If someone pushed him, that would have been a big deal."

"Does the kid have a name? I don't see it in this article."

"You're looking at an early article. We named him in the next edition of the paper. I'll check my files and call you back."

Milo knew he could easily look up the next editions, but the software wasn't perfect. Letting this guy look up the name could jog his memory of facts not included in the articles.

§

Agnes napped for a while and awoke, feeling better. She had some crackers but was still starving. Wanting company, she scampered down to the kitchen.

Martha looked up. "You look better?"

"Yeah, but now I'm hungry. Do we have any bananas?"

"Sure."

"I would really like a banana."

Martha went over to the fruit basket. "One banana coming up. Anything else?"

"No, just the banana."

Martha handed the partially peeled fruit to Agnes, who took a bite, closed her eyes, and purred. "This is so good. Thank you, Martha. I'm going to find Ms. Johansen."

"She stopped by an hour ago. I offered her a ham and cheese sandwich, which she devoured. I think she's back up in the second-floor library."

"Thanks," Agnes said, tossing the banana peel in the garbage and grabbing another banana to go. "I think I'm becoming a chimp."

"I don't think you can bring food up there. Mr. McKnight said he was chastised for suggesting he could bring her coffee."

"Of course," Agnes said, peeling the second banana. "I'll dispose of the peel before I get to the library."

"Where?"

"In our apartment. I'll bother Sutherland. He's just watching football."

"You can take the rest in case you want a snack…whenever."

Agnes grabbed the bunch. "Good idea."

Martha watched Agnes leave for the stairs. She smiled.

§

"Do we have a name to go with that drowned kid?" Preston asked.

"Give me a second. I'm looking for it. This goes back to when only men did these reports. Nothing is where it belongs."

Preston laughed.

"Here it is. Percy Fleur. His name was Percy Fleur."

§

Milo's phone rang. The caller ID was Elbert Galenis. "Mr. Galenis, do you have a name for me?"

"I do. It was Percy Fleur."

"Anything else come to mind?"

"Nope. The body floated for a while. I think they found the poor kid in the lake."

"Percy Fleur," Milo repeated.

"Yup. Fleur, F-l-e-u-r."

19

Milo had overslept. Bleary-eyed, he ambled out of his bedroom for Sunday morning breakfast. The cats had abandoned him because they knew it was Ilene's pastry day and not Martha's bacon day. Milo wondered how they knew that, but all thoughts about the cats left him when he entered the morning room. Milo froze. There, sitting at the table, was Agnes with the open box of pastries left by Ilene's delivery guy. Agnes was savoring Sutherland's favorite goat-cheese-filled, honey-fig muffin.

"Agnes, have you lost your mind?" he whispered.

"No. Why?" She looked at the half-eaten muffin. "I always thought these were gross, but this morning it's calling to me. We'll order two next week."

"Does Sutherland know he doesn't have his figgy thing?"

Agnes shook her head.

Milo poured himself a cup of coffee and sat down opposite Agnes. "Look, I have connections. We can sneak you out of the country before Sutherland comes down."

"You're overreacting. It's a muffin. Sutherland is a grown man. There are a lot of other muffins and sweet rolls and cream puffs here for him to enjoy."

"Sutherland is still a kinda square-corners guy. His fig-filled, goat-hair, honey-thing has always been his."

"Square corners? No, I am rounded these days," Sutherland said, limping into the room carrying a banana.

"Your father's will. He said you lead a structured but uneventful life," Milo reminded him.

"I'm hobbling downstairs carrying a banana. How much more wild and crazy do you want me to get?"

Agnes gestured with her hand for Sutherland to keep his distance. "Bananas were yesterday."

Sutherland put the banana in his pocket before pouring his coffee with his back to the table.

"Okay, round corner, wild man, I think change is in your future," Milo said.

Sutherland brought his coffee mug to the table and began searching for his muffin among the other pastries.

Agnes wiped her fingers with her napkin and took a sip of her lemon grass tea. "That was delicious."

Sutherland stopped looking in the pastry box. His eyes tracked to the plate in front of her. The evidence was overwhelming—the empty muffin wrapper, the telltale crumbs, the crumpled napkin with the brown coloring of sweet dates. "You ate my muffin?"

"I offered to facilitate her escape to Tierra del Fuego, but she declined," Milo said.

Agnes turned her head at a slight angle and smiled. "Would you deny us the goodness and health-giving ingredients of your muffin?"

Sutherland smiled and reached over for Agnes' hand.

Agnes took it and said, "Milo, we have something to tell you. You are going to be an uncle."

"My sister Bernice is having yet another child? What's that make, sixteen, seventeen?"

"You don't have a sister Bernice," Sutherland said.

"Then why is she having children?"

Agnes sat back and eyed Milo suspiciously. "You knew."

"I guessed," Milo said. "Congratulations. This is going to be fun. Do I hug you now or what?"

"I'm good Milo, thank you."

"What about me?" Sutherland complained.

"And congratulations to you too, whiner. Do you want a hug?"

"I'm good."

Milo sat back down. "When will we know if we have a boy or a girl?"

"We?" Sutherland asked.

"You said I was Uncle Milo. I take my responsibility seriously. I must prepare."

"Not for two more months," Agnes said, grinning.

"You were tired yesterday," Milo said. "How are you feeling this morning?"

"That was not fun, but I discovered a love of new things, like dates and goat cheese," Agnes said.

"Who else knows?" Milo asked.

Agnes put her finger to her lips as Sutherland whispered, "Just you, but we are telling Martha this afternoon."

"So, when did you suspect, oh great detective?" Agnes asked.

"When you held your open house for the remodel."

"What?" Sutherland almost shouted. "There is nothing in the remodel."

"Two bedrooms with a Jack-and-Jill bathroom. Dead give-away you were either planning to have children or take in borders."

Agnes laughed. "I told you," she said to Sutherland.

"And," Milo continued, "you have enough room for both little Murgatroyd and Octavious."

"Thank you for that. Those are two names we can easily eliminate," Agnes said.

"Your husband's name is Sutherland, not exactly Jack or Jill."

"I like his name!" Agnes protested. "It fits him."

Sutherland spoke up. "Thank you, my dear. With all due respect to Mom and Dad, one Sutherland in this family is enough."

"Finkle," Milo said. "Wasn't there a Finkle in your family tree?"

"That would be my middle name, Freskin," Sutherland said. "Not Finkle."

Milo shook his head. "And you threw out Octavious. Want to reconsider? Oh, and one other give away. Sutherland hasn't made a real dirty martini in days."

"How would you know that?" Sutherland protested.

"Agnes has never left her life as a British spy. She, like James Bond, likes her martinis shaken, not stirred. I have not heard two shaken beverages, only one, your martini, Sutherland."

"You're a British spy?" Sutherland asked Agnes.

"You two need to talk more often," Milo said.

"We thought we were being so clever, keeping this under wraps until we knew for sure," Agnes said.

"You live with a world-famous detective and masterful cat wrangler," Milo said.

"World famous?" Sutherland questioned.

Milo stared at Sutherland. "I thought you would question cat wrangler."

"I'm wild, crazy, and so unpredictable."

Milo stood to pour a second cup of coffee. He put his hand on Sutherland's shoulder. "I don't know about wild, crazy, and unpredictable, but you are a man with a banana in his pocket."

§

After breakfast and his longer than usual swim, Milo retired to his wood-lined office, formally John McKnight's office. He flicked on the gas fireplace and walked over to his desk, got comfortable in the cushy leather chair as he fired up his computer. Jet and Annie followed him, more for the warmth than the company.

"John, I have been hired to do some snooping for your daughter-in-law," he told the empty room. "Oh, and in case you didn't get the news, congratulations, you are about to be a grandfather." Milo waited to see if anything in the room reacted. It didn't.

Milo sat back and twirled his chair to face the shelves of first editions that John collected. "I'm still apprehensive to begin the snooping. Agnes and Sutherland are good, you know, happy. I don't want to fill in the unknowns with knowns that could spoil that. What do you think, John?"

There was again silence.

"Profound, John, really."

Jet stood up, stretched, turned to Milo and squeaked.

"Using the cats to talk to me? Interesting. I'm guessing Jet is saying I should get on with the unknown." Annie changed her position in front of the fireplace. "Got it. Lisa and Henry Larson, who were you and what happened to you?"

§

For the moment, the goat-cheese-filled, honey-fig muffin was sitting well. Agnes was lying back on the new sectional in their second-floor apartment, reading a book between short snoozes. Sutherland was watching the Vikings, listening through his ear buds.

"Martha has opened the front gate," the Lakesong intercom announced.

Agnes looked at Sutherland. "She's home."

There was no reaction from Sutherland.

Agnes shook him, pointing to her ears.

Sutherland removed his earbuds. "The Vikings are getting killed."

"Tragedy, but I said Martha's home."

"This will be much more fun," Sutherland said with a big grin. "I haven't been a guest in the cottage since the caretaker retired to Florida."

Agnes laughed. "I know all about that caretaker. Milo talked about him when he discovered the telescope in the cupola. The caretaker is my friend too. He built a secret staircase in the cottage."

"He was Milo's good buddy. I barely remember him. I was a toddler when he retired," Sutherland said.

Agnes stood up from her seat in their apartment. "Let's go. Grab your scooter. It's going to be a long walk. Do you think she's figured it out, too?"

"We really tried not to be obvious, but I have been grinning a lot. Have I turned into a grinner? Also, the drink thing may be telling." Sutherland stood and began the trek to the cottage.

Agnes hugged his arm. "After throwing up and in between naps, I grin a lot, too. I hope the stomach thing is over."

Sutherland and Agnes impatiently took the elevator to the basement. Sutherland opened the door to the tunnels and took the center one to the cottage. The tunnel lights came on as they entered.

"Should we have warned her we were coming?" Agnes asked.

"I'm afraid that would make too big a deal out of it."

"We're just dropping by like we *never* do to tell her news like we *never* have. Simple. Right?" Agnes giggled.

"Right. It's more friendly this way." Sutherland stopped. "However, wait, if my boss showed up unannounced, I would fear I was being fired," Sutherland said.

"You're the boss," Agnes said. "But now that you mention it, we're going to have to let you go."

"Will you give me a good reference?"

Agnes rubbed his shoulder. "Really? Do you think you've earned a good reference?"

"Absolutely, I get you bananas on demand."

Agnes shook her head. "I hope you didn't order a crate," she said, knowing Sutherland's habit of overdoing things for her. Agnes let go of his hand and grabbed his arm. "Wait, what if she doesn't like babies and leaves us?"

"Martha? No. She will be thrilled with Gofsmop."

"Gofsmop?"

"Well, we have to call him or her something other than him or her."

"Where does Gofsmop come from?" Agnes asked.

"Somewhere in this house there are photo albums. In one of them, there is a picture of my pregnant mother. The caption is Laura with Gofsmop. I assume Gofsmop was my parents' cute name for the unborn baby that would later be me."

Agnes hugged him. "That is so sweet."

Sutherland smiled.

"Where are those albums?"

"I don't remember."

"Think hard, Bobo. I want those albums," Agnes said, continuing down the tunnel.

"Bobo? Is that good or bad? Sounds bad." Sutherland left his scooter in the tunnel.

They walked arm in arm up to the cottage door. Agnes whispered, "Why am I so scared?"

"I'll be your brave hero," Sutherland said, knocking on the door. He had to knock twice before Martha realized someone was at the tunnel door. She had dropped Jamal at a friend's house. Breanna was at school. Only Darian was home.

She opened the door a crack and peaked out.

Agnes waved.

Martha opened the door wide. "What's wrong?"

"Nothing, Martha." Agnes smiled. "We're sorry to bother you, but we wanted to share our good news."

"I like good news, come on in. Is this kitchen table good news or sitting room good news?"

"I like to think this is kitchen table good news," Sutherland said.

Agnes and Sutherland looked around the cozy cottage as they sat down. Sutherland's father had given Martha a budget to redecorate the place any way she saw fit when she and the sibs first moved in. She had modernized but kept it welcoming. The kitchen had its own fireplace, which was throwing off a cozy warmth.

Darian walked in, smiled and said hi, as if Sutherland and Agnes were daily visitors. Sutherland sat in front of a half built something with wires and gears. He looked at it closely, then picked up the box. "Oh wow! A solar robot!" he said to Agnes.

"Down, boy, it's not your toy."

"He can play with it," Darian said. "I haven't finished it, but there is enough sunlight here to charge the battery. It might move if you turn on the motor."

"Darian, I don't think Mr. McKnight is here to play with your robot," Martha chided.

"Not so fast," Sutherland said. "Can I turn it on?"

"Again, Sutherland, it's not your toy," Agnes chided.

"Darian said I could play with it."

"Have you forgotten, we have an announcement," Agnes said, looking at Sutherland as a future father and pleased with what she saw. "Martha, we are going to have a baby!"

Martha clapped her hands, stood up and hugged Agnes.

"Once again, I'm chopped liver," Sutherland complained.

Martha moved over and hugged him. "Congratulations, Mr. McKnight!"

"So, you don't hate babies?" Agnes asked anxiously. "And you're not going to leave?"

Martha frowned. "Certainly not! And who hates babies?"

"Not Lakesong," Darian said. "Or me."

"Why do you like babies?" Martha asked.

"I won't be the youngest person in Lakesong!" Darian said.

All three adults laughed.

"So, a charming girl or boy?" Martha asked.

"We don't know yet," Agnes said. "We will in ten weeks."

"I have a number of morning sickness remedies," Martha said. "I've found my recipes. We can start trying them out."

"You've gotten them out? You knew too?" Agnes was incredulous.

"You've been leaving some of your dinner, especially the chicken, and your smoothies have been replaced by crackers and bananas. In fact, I will be running to the store to get more bananas."

"No, no, no," Sutherland said. "Bananas are off the list now."

"Figs, dates, and black olives sound good," Agnes said.

Pop-Up Dinner, Drop Down Dead

"Interesting combo. I'll see what I can come up with. It will be a challenge." Martha went to her cupboard and removed a jar of black olives. "Here, to tide you over."

"Oh yes! Would you mind if I ate one now?"

Martha opened the jar, found a fork, and smiled. "What can I get you, Mr. McKnight?"

"Nothing for me. I'm enjoying watching the olive eating monster devour that jar."

Darian laughed.

"When will we see the recipient of all these olives?" Martha asked.

"My due date is September ninth."

"A birthday during the school year is great," Darian blurted. "Summer birthdays suck. I'm in July. Everybody is on vacation."

"You said I knew too. Who else figured it out?" Martha asked.

"Milo," Sutherland said.

"I should have figured. How did he do it?"

"Apparently, he didn't hear two martinis shaking."

Agnes stopped spearing olives for a second. "The Lakesong predinner drink changed. I wanted fruit juices with coconut water. No shaking."

Martha nodded knowingly. "Coconut water, bananas, olives, I think your baby is asking for potassium. You and I normally plan the menu week to week, but your little one may change things for a while. I can adapt."

"What about a name?" Darian asked.

"Too early," Sutherland said. "I do have a family full of oddball names that we can avoid."

"Milo brought up Freskin," Agnes said.

"Definitely off the list," Sutherland laughed. "He called it Finkel."

"He also suggested Murgatroyd or Octavious," Agnes said.

"Murgatroyd is a bit heavy for a baby, but Octavious might be good if the baby wants to be the emperor of Rome," Martha said.

Darian's robot suddenly came to life and zipped toward Martha, who stopped it before it flew off the table. Agnes looked at Sutherland. "Okay, Dad, stop playing with the toys. Let's go back home."

"Dad? Dad? My father was Dad."

Agnes touched his arm. "The torch has been passed."

§

Milo texted Sutherland, "I'm having wings and pizza delivered. In the billiard room. Packers are the second game. Sorry about the Vikings."

Sutherland was torn.

"Who's that?" Agnes asked.

"Milo. He's in the billiard room watching the game."

"What are you waiting for? Go join him."

"I thought you might need help with your dinner. It's Sunday night. No poker, no Martha."

Agnes smiled. "I'm fine. I want cereal and milk. We have all of that in our upstairs refrigerator. I plan to make my own dinner and find myself a sappy romance to watch."

"Are you sure?"

Pop-Up Dinner, Drop Down Dead

"Sutherland, go watch your game with Milo. I can pour my own cereal."

"I'm worried about the milk. Sure, you can pour your own cereal, but what about the milk?"

"You better leave now, while you can still hobble."

Agnes headed upstairs to a wonderful evening while Sutherland made his way to the billiard room. He stopped along the way to check the score. The Packers were already ahead 14-0.

Milo was sitting in one of three reclining leather chairs placed in front of a sixty-inch television. "Sit down. We have to discuss replacing this tiny television."

Sutherland grabbed a piece of pizza from the box and sat down. "It was as big as they came when we bought it."

"Times change, Sutherland. I was just talking to the ghost of your dad. He was shocked we were still trying to watch on this small TV."

"Not much shocked Dad," Sutherland said, taking a bite of the pizza. "Mmm, this is good."

"Well, how about this for shocking? The Packers just got a pick-six. Twenty-one to nothing."

"Yeah? Well, at least our coach isn't a flower."

Milo was about to munch on his third wing. He set it back down on his plate. "You're going to have to explain that one."

"Matt LaFleur. LaFleur, the flower. It's French."

"I should have taken French in high school," Milo said. "What did you take?"

"Woodworking."

20

"We should have played poker last night," Sutherland said. "As it is, I am bereft. The Vikings lost. The Packers won. If we had played poker, maybe I'd have my winnings to keep me smiling."

Agnes turned to stare at him. "Your winnings?"

"I think he's drifting into a fantasy world," Milo mumbled in between bites of his eggs and hash browns.

Martha came into the morning room. "What would you like, Mrs. McKnight?"

Agnes had to laugh every time Martha addressed her formally. "Well, Chef Gibbson, as we all know, I'm having difficulty eating my usual foods in my present condition. This morning, feeling better, I'm going to try—drum roll please—some dry toast and one of the herbal teas you suggested, maybe the raspberry."

"Good choice, madam. Just so you know, we have restocked the bananas, black olives, and dates, if you are so inclined."

The intercom announced a person at the front gate. Sutherland checked his app. "It's Sonja Johansen. At least she doesn't just walk in like Ed Patupick. I will do the honors. I want everyone to notice that I am leaving my scooter behind in favor of the boot." Rocking towards the foyer, he opened the gate and returned with Ms. Johansen.

"Good morning. Please join us. The coffee urn is on the cart," Agnes said.

Johansen poured herself a cup, put in two sugars, and a splash of cream. She sat down next to Agnes. Milo introduced himself.

"I'm reading a book about you," she said.

"I'm sorry. Ron Bello has to find better subject matter."

"Have you learned anything from the journal?" Agnes asked.

"The author has not identified himself. So far, he writes about leaving Norway for Canada, precisely Nova Scotia. Also, there are multiple mentions of specific carvings."

"Why would he end up in Lakesong?" Sutherland asked.

Johansen looked around the breakfast room. "This breakfast seating is not original to the house. Are there pictures of the original furniture?"

"I think what's left is stored on the third floor, on the north side of the house, or in the basement. Why?" Sutherland asked.

"I noticed in the parts of your house I've seen, your woodwork has distinct carvings. It was the style of the time to match the furniture carvings with the woodwork. I would like to see it, but not today. I wish to complete the journal first."

"You think this man was hired to carve woodwork and furniture?" Agnes asked.

"It's a possibility. Grand houses built in that time period often hired wood carvers. Matching the furniture to the woodwork was a sign of wealth."

"I'm happy when my socks match," Milo said.

"That's important," Agnes said.

Johansen finished her coffee. "Is there a room you would prefer I take my breaks and eat my lunch?"

"Wherever you feel comfortable would be fine," Agnes said. "I suggest the gallery or family room. We have a water and soft drink refrigerator in the family room. If you have any questions, please text me. I'll be in the house all day."

§

Gramm was stretching his neck. White was deciding if she really liked her chestnut praline latte, and Preston was experimenting to see if she could forget a police manual chapter she just read. She closed her eyes. She thought about a movie she was planning to see. The chapter disappeared from her brain. "Yes!" she shouted. With that outburst, the chapter came flooding back word for word.

"Sorry," she apologized, "I was trying to see if I can scratch my memory."

"Well, I'm definitely scratching this chestnut praline latte from my future," White complained.

All three were waiting on Milo.

"We've got to talk to Winterhausen again. He failed to mention he threatened Raf," Gramm blurted. "Preston, you and Milo talked to him last time. I want to get an impression of him."

White dialed him and talked for about two minutes before hanging up. "Winterhausen is currently on his way to lunch at the Marathon Restaurant. It's one of DeJong's."

"Let's meet him there," Gramm suggested. "I need to stretch my legs."

Preston looked dejected.

"Preston, I want you to find out everything you can about our victim."

"Kinda late in the game for that, isn't it?" White asked.

Gramm nodded. "We've had snowstorms and multiple suspects to keep us busy. I think we need to get back to basics. Who was this guy? Did he have money? We've been told he owed money to bad people. Did he really, or are we being lied to?"

"Where is Milo?" White asked.

Gramm looked at Preston. "Me?" she asked. "Why would I know?"

"You're sort of partners," Gramm said. "And speak of the devil, here's your partner walking in now."

Milo stopped off at the coffeepot, then wandered over to two of the younger cops and asked them some questions. Gramm grew impatient. "Get him in here!" he ordered Preston.

She leaned out of his office and yelled, "Hey partner! You're wanted!"

Pop-Up Dinner, Drop Down Dead

Milo looked confused but left the two cops and walked briskly into Gramm's office. "Partner?" he questioned.

"You needed to be here," White said.

"Yeah, you needed to be here," Gramm echoed. "Why weren't you here?"

"I was doing research," Milo defended his tardiness. "And I would like to point out it's Monday. I'm just getting up to speed on Monday."

"Milo, it's been a week and we're not close to a suspect for our make-believe murder."

Doug Odell, Gramm's counterpart, poked his head into the office. "How are you guys coming along?"

Gramm shrugged. "What's on your plate?"

"I just caught a fatal stabbing."

"Any witnesses?"

"No, but the perp left his phone at the scene. I got him in here now. He should be confessing before lunch." Odell disappeared.

Gramm's head dropped on his desk with a thud.

"Don't do that," White chided. "You could give yourself a concussion."

"It stretches the back of my neck…makes it feel better," Gramm said without lifting his head.

"Well, we got an easy one too," Preston said. "An out-of-work drug dealing chef that everyone hates is poisoned and sent flying down Mesaba in the middle of a snowstorm after being beaten up by loan shark muscle. Lots of motives and no witnesses."

"Don't forget, two suspicious members of the Duluth Police Department invading Canada," White said.

Gramm looked up. "All that sounds insane."

"On a personal note," Milo said, "I'm having a baby."

§

Milo arrived at the Minnesota Public Radio offices on time, but was forced to wait fifteen minutes until Ron Bello joined the interview from New York. Milo was alone except for an engineer who set him up in the studio—headset and bad coffee.

The host, Naomi Burjer, who was in the St. Paul studios, welcomed him. "We meet again, Mr. Rathkey. If I remember correctly, the last time you were on our program, you threat-ened to choke our author, Ron Bello, like a chicken. Are you still of that mindset?"

"Well, Naomi, I received a lot of pushback from chickens, so I am modifying my stance."

"Hold that thought, we are about to go on the air," Burjer said.

Milo could hear the engineer count down. "Three, two, one."

"Good morning. Welcome to Book Beat. We have a returning treat for you this morning. Milo Rathkey, famed detective, is the subject of another book by author Ron Bello. *Mind Lint. The Chaotic Cases of Detective Milo Rathkey* is the non-fiction account of Mr. Rathkey's solving of several murders in Duluth. Good morning, Mr. Rathkey."

Milo mouthed the words, 'good morning,' sending the poor engineer into a panic—Milo's entertainment payoff.

Concerned, but without missing a beat, Ms. Burjer con-tinued. "Along with Mr. Rathkey, we have the man who has captured the brilliance of the detective's work, author Ron Bello. Welcome back, Mr. Bello."

"Thank you, Naomi, good to be back," Bello said in his booming baritone.

"Before we went on, I was asking Mr. Rathkey if he was still going to choke you like a chicken, but he said he had gotten pushback from chickens. Care to explain, Milo?"

"Let me take this one," Bello said. "Milo has clearly offended a major source of protein. He feels bad about it. This brave man is all heart."

"I didn't say I felt bad about it," Milo protested. "I've never trusted chickens."

After a polite titter, Burjer began, "Let's discuss the book. Ron, what are these cases in the new book about?"

"One involved the death of an engaged couple who were shot to death with a bow and arrow," Bello said.

"Not your average murder," Burjer interjected.

"Their deaths involved an investment club scam, which Milo figured out and…"

"I would like to point out that my solving the case involved hours of work by the Duluth Police Department. I do not *solve* these things in a vacuum," Milo pronounced.

"But I read you have mind lint," Burjer said, "your peculiar way of looking at things."

Milo laughed. "Mind lint is a cute phrase invented by my good friend, Sutherland McKnight. It doesn't mean anything."

"I beg to differ," Bello said. "The Duluth Police homicide people work hard dotting the I's and crossing the T's, but it is Milo who sees what everyone else misses."

"Well, we don't want to give away the surprises in the book. Suffice it to say, Mr. Rathkey, mind lint or no mind lint, your mind sees things other minds don't. I will say this latest book details Mr. Rathkey speeding down a runway in a car to stop the murderer from escaping in a plane."

"Stupid move on my part. I was pretty beat up afterwards and my hearing has only recently recovered."

"He's too modest," Bello said.

"What?" Milo asked.

§

"Tell me again why we're meeting Reese Winterhaven at Marathon?" Gramm asked White as he drove to West Duluth.

"Winterhausen," White corrected. "He said he's having lunch there and was busy the rest of the afternoon."

Gramm lifted an eyebrow. "We could make him unbusy at our place."

"We have some omissions to…"

"Robin, just call them lies."

"Okay, lies. Besides, Kick DeJong may be there. It may give us a twofer."

"Is this place any good?" Gramm asked.

"I've eaten there twice," Milo said from the backseat. "Both times the food was great."

"You think egg foo yung is great," White said.

"And a meatloaf sandwich," Gramm added.

Gramm pulled into the half empty parking lot. "Not very busy. I don't think the public shares your review," he said to Milo.

Pop-Up Dinner, Drop Down Dead

"It's Monday, and only eleven o'clock," Milo shot back.

Walking into the restaurant, Milo's attention was taken by old black and white photos of runners crossing finish lines along with various running paraphernalia hanging from the walls and ceiling. White ignored the runner's theme as she spotted Reese Winterhausen and Kick DeJong sitting at a round table in the back of the room.

She led the procession up to their table. "Gentlemen, how good to see you again."

Kick DeJong looked in their direction. "Three of you? Really?"

Gramm introduced Rathkey. Kick gestured with his hand for the three of them to sit down. "What do you want now?"

White noticed that DeJong was calmer, but his hand had a slight tremor.

"We are here to ask Mr. Winterhausen a few questions, but we have some for you too," Gramm said.

Milo sat down as directed. Picking up a menu, he said, "I see you have sandwiches named after runners. The description of the Fred Lorz looks a lot like the Devil's Delight at your other restaurant."

"It is the Devil's Delight," Kick said.

White looked it up on her phone. "He took a car for eleven miles in the 1904 Olympics when he was supposed to be running. Should you name a sandwich after a liar and a cheat?"

Kick shrugged. "We also have a sandwich named after winners. Katherine Switzer completed the Boston Marathon when women were not allowed to compete. We put a lot of hot peppers on that one."

"Let's talk about Raf Bianchi," Gramm said. "Mr. Winterhausen, we have a source that quotes you as saying, 'Time for him to go.' That was in reference to the victim the night he died."

Reese sat back, smiling. "You've talked to Poppie."

"Do you deny saying it?" White asked.

"No, I said it." Reese picked up a French fry, dipped it in ketchup, and took his time eating it.

"What did you mean by it?" Gramm asked.

"I meant we should drop him. Time for him to go from the group."

Gramm turned to DeJong. "Have you talked to your lawyer? We are still waiting for an answer."

"An answer to what?" DeJong asked.

"What was the argument between you and Bianchi about? We know you threw him out of your restaurant."

"That's a lie!" Kick shouted. Reese gestured for him to bring it down a notch. "Who is this idiot witness?"

"Me," Milo said. "You comped my dinner because you thought I was upset."

"You got it all wrong."

"You threw him out. Not a playful chat among friends," Gramm said.

"Look, the guy saved my life. I owed him. He didn't make me happy all the time. We argued, but I still owed him."

Reese rolled his eyes.

"Now that's interesting, Mr. DeJong," White said. "Mr. Winterhausen just rolled his eyes. I bet he doesn't believe that. For the record, Bob Young doesn't believe it either."

Pop-Up Dinner, Drop Down Dead

Gramm jumped in. "We've heard a couple of versions of the day Raf saved you in the Deeps. What's your version?"

Kick folded his arms over his chest and closed his eyes. "It was summer. We were hot and jumping off the upper rocks all day. It was getting late. I was tired. I slipped and didn't get out far enough. Raf pushed me out further…saved my ass."

"Why wasn't Raf with you? Why was he on the lower rocks?" Rathkey asked.

Kick took a deep breath and mumbled about these questions being so dumb.

"It's not dumb," Reese countered. "Raf wasn't on the upper rocks because he was too busy being an ass. He saved your butt, Kick, because you were going to land on him. But we've told you this before."

Kick attempted to take a sip of his drink, which appeared to be a Coke, or perhaps a rum and Coke. His hand shook, and he spilled a little on his shirt.

"Have you ever heard of a boy named Percy Fleur?"

"No. These questions are so dumb. You're wasting everyone's time!"

"What about you, Mr. Winterhausen? Percy Fleur? Ever hear of him?"

Reese shook his head.

"Are you aware that Poppie Flower was visiting Bob Young up in International Falls?" White asked, hoping to get a reaction.

"Nope, and it's no business of mine. Maybe you missed the part where I referred to her as my ex. She can visit anyone she wants."

"Do you think Poppie had a reason to kill Raf?" Milo asked, looking directly at Reese.

"Poppie? I doubt it, but if she did have a reason, I think she would be capable of it. Pretty hard core that one."

"Mr. DeJong, would you put Poppie on your list of suspects?" Milo continued.

"Me? I barely knew her. She was Reese's flavor of the month," Kick said.

"That's cold bro." Reese smiled.

"But true," Kick said, standing up. "I have work to do. You people stay here and order. On the house."

"We can't do that, Mr. DeJong," Gramm said.

Kick shrugged. "Okay, stay here, order, and pay. I don't care."

Reese also stood up. "Not hungry anymore."

Kick sent a waitress over to the table, who dropped menus and took drink orders.

"This is getting us nowhere," Gramm said.

"I know I said this before, but tomorrow morning we need to look at the video to see who did what and when," Milo said. "The killer might be in plain sight."

21

Agnes' morning sickness had been replaced by early morning sickness. She lay in bed feeling queasy. The sun had yet to rise. Sutherland was sleeping peacefully, so Agnes slid into her slippers and grabbed her robe on the way into her living room to stretch out on the sectional. Her aim was to read herself to sleep. Every time she started to doze, a wave of nausea would send her rushing to the bathroom.

She heard Sutherland's alarm and his familiar sounds of rousing. Finding Agnes missing, he went on the hunt for her. She waved at him from the sectional. He joined her and attempted to be supportive, but Agnes told him to go and get dressed. When he was ready to go down to breakfast, she had been nausea-free for thirty minutes. Feeling brave, she rode downstairs with Sutherland, thinking of trying a cracker.

"Tough morning?" Martha asked as Agnes, still clad in robe and slippers, walked into the kitchen and sat down at Martha's desk.

Agnes nodded. "This morning sickness doesn't know how to tell time."

"I've done some research. Low fat, high carb foods and plenty of liquids."

"What would you suggest?"

"More crackers and water."

"Sounds delicious, Martha."

Sutherland entered the kitchen looking office ready. "I seem to have lost my wife."

Agnes weakly raised her hand. "I'm over here."

"Mrs. McKnight, do I deliver crackers and water to your present position or to your usual spot in the morning room?"

Agnes stood up. "Let me try the morning room. Could you put a cover on Sutherland's smoothie so I can't see or smell it?"

Sutherland guided her to the morning room, where Martha delivered several oyster crackers and water.

"Hot tea or hot chocolate?"

"Ugh, on the chocolate. I'll try a weak chai," Agnes said, sitting down.

As Martha was delivering the tea, Sonja Johansen buzzed in from the gate. Sutherland took care of ushering her into the morning room.

"Are you ill?" Sonja asked Agnes, surprised she was not dressed.

Agnes nodded. "In a way, morning sickness. First trimester. I thought it was over."

"I remember. Herbal teas."

"I'm trying Chai this morning but will try herbals later. Thanks."

"Would you like an update on my translation?" Sonja asked.

Milo and the cats strolled in. Milo poured himself a cup of coffee, sat down, and said hello to everyone. "Agnes, having a bad morning?"

"So far, so good," Agnes said with a weak smile and double thumbs up.

"Will the smell of my usual breakfast bother you?" Milo asked.

"I don't know, but thanks for asking."

"Wait," Sutherland said. "My healthy smoothie needs to be hidden, but Milo's cholesterol feast gets a pass?"

"Please stop talking about food. Sonja, I would love an update."

"I still don't know the man's name, but I've learned how he happened to be in Duluth."

Martha delivered Milo's breakfast. He immediately provided pieces of his bacon to Annie. Knowing his place, Jet waited behind Annie for his bacon.

"You feed the cats bacon?" Sonja asked. "That's not healthy for them."

"That's what I've been told. However, Sutherland's dad fed his cat bacon. She died—at age twenty-one."

"Back to the update," Agnes said, backing her chair up, preparing in case Milo's breakfast smells would cause her to exit.

In fact, it did the opposite. Reaching over the table, she used her teaspoon to steal a taste of Milo's hash browns.

Milo stared. "So far so good and getting better."

Agnes held up her hands. "We have to wait and see how it settles."

Sutherland was flummoxed. "Does our unborn child crave Milo's hash browns?"

"I don't know about our child, but I seem to, and it's staying," Agnes said.

"Martha! We need more hash browns!" Milo shouted, causing Martha to reappear in the morning room.

"Hash browns? Really?"

Agnes was scooping up another teaspoon full.

"Before you take any more of Milo's, I will make you some of your own. Milo gets extra butter."

"Those do look good," Sonja said.

"Two more plates of hash browns coming up," Martha said.

"Sutherland? Want to join the others?" Milo teased.

"I'll pass. Can my smoothie come out of hiding?"

"NO!" Agnes shouted.

"Hash browns good. Green smoothies bad. I'm beginning to like this kid," Milo said.

"If I can get back to it, our mystery man took a train from Nova Scotia to Fort William in search of work," Johansen said.

"I've never heard of Fort William," Sutherland complained.

"Fort William and Port Arthur combined to form Thunder Bay," Milo said.

Sutherland looked at him. "How do you know that?"

Pop-Up Dinner, Drop Down Dead

"My extensive knowledge of Canadian history."

"Did the Canadians make you learn things like that after they kidnapped you?"

"You were kidnapped by Canadians?" Sonja asked.

"Not really kidnapped," Milo admitted. "More like we invaded."

"Ignore them," Agnes said, as Martha came back with a cup of chai tea and hash browns for Agnes and Sonja.

"Our man spent a winter in Fort William, where he found a community of Norwegian ex-pats. He writes about how the community subscribed to a Norwegian language newspaper out of Two Harbors. He found a personal ad for a wood carver in Duluth. As soon as the weather warmed, he set off for Duluth."

"How?" Sutherland asked.

"Walking. He was picked up by several passing horse carts along the way. So far, he does not mention the name of the family that hired him, but he replaced their first carver who had died."

"So, they just hired him?" Milo asked.

"As opposed to what?" Sutherland questioned.

"I see him ringing the doorbell, asking if the people inside needed anything carved," Milo said.

Sonja thought that was funny. "No, he did an audition, which was the norm back then. He has begun to write in detail about what he carved." Sonja paused, then glanced at all the Lakesong owners. "I have a proposal for you. Currently, I am providing you with a strict translation of the journal. I can expand my role and give you a historical background of the people and places mentioned in the journal. However, the fuller history will double my fee."

No one spoke.

"You can think about it."

Agnes stood up, pushing back her chair. "Gotta go!"

Sutherland pushed back his chair and followed his wife. He turned back. "We'll get back to you on the history thing,"

Only Milo and Sonja were left in the morning room. "I love the history, mystery thing," Milo said. "Agnes and Sutherland can pay for the translation, and you and I will have a contract for the history and further research."

§

By the time Milo arrived at the station, Gramm and company were already ensconced in his office. They left an empty chair for Milo. Gramm was leaning back, stretching his shoulders with his eyes closed.

Preston began to detail the latest visit to the Tip Top—Darlene's problem with Morrie Wolf over the hiring of Leroy Thompson. "As we left the Tip Top…"

"Oh look," White said. "Milo has arrived…with bags of popcorn."

"Popcorn?" Gramm asked.

"What? I thought we were going to watch a movie," Milo said, explaining the popcorn. He tossed the hot bags on the desk.

White left the room.

Gramm scowled. "If we can stop folks from leaving the room, maybe we can get this done and solve our case."

Pop-Up Dinner, Drop Down Dead

Preston grabbed a popcorn bag and opened it with one pull. Milo did the same. Gramm huffed, but opened his bag, pouring out some of the popcorn on his desk. "I meant to do that."

White returned with a large monitor on a wheeled cart. "Much bigger screen," she said, as if it needed an explanation. She plugged her computer into the monitor, and after some trial and error, the video appeared.

Preston and Rathkey applauded. White grabbed the remaining bag of popcorn and opened it up. Looking at Gramm's desktop, she said, "You spilled some."

"I meant to," Gramm complained.

White started the video. "We are looking at everyone's movement during the dinner. Kate, write down the time code of everyone's movement around the table, especially anyone who came into contact with our victim, his food, or his drink."

The video began, as Preston had said, with Kick on one side of Raf and Bob Young on the other. Next to Young were Poppie and Reese and then Emma.

"Where's Jess?" Gramm asked.

"The empty chair between Kick and Emma is hers. She's just not in it," White said. "Look."

They watched as Jess returned to the table, saying something to Emma first, and then Kick. Kick shook his head. Jess leaned in again. Scowling, he downed his latest drink, pushed his chair back, and stood up before he stumbled over to the empty chair next to Emma.

Raf looked at this with a puzzled look on his face, saying something to Kick. Kick shrugged and waved at the waiter for another drink.

"That man does not need another drink," Preston commented.

Jess began to pull out Kick's former chair, but Raf put his hand on it to stop her. He bowed before pulling out Jess' chair for her, but he tripped or fell into Jess. She pushed him back.

White shook her head. "Our victim is an ass."

"I think Bianchi was just trying to be a gentleman. A drunk gentleman, but still…" Gramm said.

"Do you see his hands? He's almost groping her."

"Hold that. We have movement on the other side of Bianchi," White said.

Bob Young stood and pulled out Poppie's chair. Poppie scooted over next to Bianchi's empty chair.

"What was that move?" Preston asked.

"I think Poppie was getting away from Reese," White said.

Milo cocked his head to one side.

"Milo?" Gramm asked.

"Interesting move. I have no reason to suspect Poppie, but there is a commotion between Bianchi and Jess. Everyone is looking at that. It's an ideal time for her to get closer to our victim."

White smiled, a smile Preston immediately picked up on. Both were thinking this was part of Milo's mind lint game and he had plenty of reason to suspect Poppie—the death of Perry Fleur.

They rewound the tape and watched again, this time in slow motion. Jess pushes Bianchi back just as Poppie says something to Bob, who stands up and holds his chair for Poppie.

"Now that's a gentleman," Preston said. "He doesn't fall drunkenly into her."

The video continued. Servers began delivering drinks. Poppie's right arm moved toward Bianchi's glass. White froze the video. "Watch her hand!" White said.

"I'd love to, but you keep stopping the video," Gramm complained.

White ignored the criticism and hit play. A server walked in front of the camera. White groaned. By the time the person cleared the camera, Poppie's arm was no longer near Bianchi.

"No!" Preston shouted. "We don't see Poppie grab the EpiPen or spike anything!"

"Let's look at it again," Gramm said.

White scrolled through the video frame by frame.

"That arm is moving toward our victim's glass," Preston said. "Isn't that enough?"

"What about other cameras?" Gramm asked. "Is there anything anyone recorded that could help us?"

Preston shook her head. "I looked at all the phone video and social media. No one pointed a camera at this table. Not even in the background."

White paused the video.

"We got nothing," Gramm said.

"We know why Kick got into an accident," Preston said. "He's on his third drink since we've been watching. Who knows how many he had before? Raf is matching him drink for drink. Waiters are taking orders. Jess is talking to Emma over Kick. Poppie is still chatting with Bob, her back toward Raf. Reese is sketching."

"Ignoring everyone," White said.

"Artists," Gramm scoffed. "Start it again."

The waiter came by, placing a number one by each plate except Raf's, which already had a number two.

Suddenly, Raf jumped up and appeared to yell at the group about something. He was gesturing to the numbers all around the table. From the smiles and laughter, it appeared as if no one cared, not even Kick.

"I think this is where our victim is accusing his friends of trying to kill him," Gramm said.

"Everyone is eating the entrée with peanuts, except him, of course," Preston added

"Let me say it again. This video gives us nothing we didn't already know," Gramm said.

Milo shook his head. "Not necessarily."

"What mind lint did you get from this garbage?"

"No mind lint, just a person."

"What person?" White asked.

"That waiter who blocked our view of Poppie, maybe he saw something."

"Maybe," Gramm said. "Ask Martha for an ID. Do it!"

"Don't need to. I know him."

"Of course," White laughed. "You know everybody that serves food."

"I think he can be helpful." Milo almost smiled.

§

"I would say, whoever carved the crazy wild scenes in the vault did not carve the furniture and woodwork," Agnes said to Sonja Johansen as the two took a break in the gallery.

"What makes you say that?" Sonja asked.

Agnes, drinking her midday raspberry tea, said, "The styles and subject matter are so different."

Sonja nodded. "Carving furniture designs is much different from carving dragons and fighting wolves. However, there are a number of markers in these works which line up. I think they were done by the same person."

"Have you learned any more about our phantom carver from his journal?"

"I have. He writes about how he enjoyed his time here. He talks often about the lake and the boats and how it all reminds him of home."

"Where is home?"

"I haven't pinned that down exactly, but I'm getting there. I have to make a few calls."

Martha rolled a snack cart into the room. "I've made tea sandwiches."

"Wonderful!" Sonja said. "I forgot my lunch today. It's sitting in my refrigerator."

Agnes moved away from the sandwiches while inviting Martha to stay. "Sonja says she's getting close to naming our carver."

"Another Lakesong secret about to be revealed," Martha said.

Sonja asked about the history of Lakesong and the three talked about the big house as the minutes rolled on. Finally, Martha stood up. "If you are finished, I have some ordering to do. Mrs. McKnight, any request?"

Agnes shook her head. "Not at this time." She left for her office.

Martha returned to the kitchen, and Sonja departed for the upstairs library to call a colleague she knew from the Hjerleid School.

Sonja waited for several minutes before Liesl Berlage came on the line.

"Sonja! Hello! I'm in a rush, but what can I do for you?"

"I'll be quick. Are you still stalled in your research on Ragnvald Oldberg?"

"I am. I've traced him to Canada, but then the trail goes cold. Why?"

"I'm working at an estate in Duluth, Minnesota. I think I have found him."

22

Preston and White agreed to arrive at work early for a confab on their suspicion that Poppie Flower killed Raf Bianchi. White came armed with a caramel brulée latte. Preston took the rest of the overnight pot, known affectionately as 'the sludge' with cream and double sugar.

"You know that stuff will kill you," White said, pointing at Preston's coffee cup.

"I know, but I will die so much richer than you. Those fancy coffees are expensive."

White took a sip of her coffee, feigning extreme pleasure. "So, where are we on the Poppie front? Do we even have a Poppie front?"

"I think it's time we tell Gramm about our theory. It all fits. I think Raf Bianchi sent Poppie Flower's brother to his death in The Deeps."

"But when we looked at the video, we didn't see Poppie drop anything into Bianchi's food," White argued. "There's no evidence."

"Because the waiter was in the way. Who knows what went on in those few seconds? Bianchi was busy doing whatever to Jess DeJong. Poppie could have easily poisoned his food with peanut oil. She got her revenge," Kate rebutted.

"Does it make sense or are we too eager to out-Milo, Milo?"

"It does make sense and *out-Miloing,* Milo is only a bonus. We need to get our theory on the record with the Lieutenant before Milo gets a chance."

White slapped her hands down hard on her desk. "Let's do it!"

§

Gramm was signing papers as Preston and White filed in and sat down. Milo arrived with a fresh cup of coffee after Preston had cleared out the dregs and made a new pot.

"Ideas, people. What do we have?" Gramm asked.

White spoke first. "Even though the video doesn't show much, Preston and I have a theory. You might say we've gone in a Milo direction."

"Scary," Gramm said. "Details."

"We believe we have found a hidden motive, which makes Poppie Flower a prime suspect."

"Her motive is…?"

Preston picked up the narrative. "It's old. It comes from an incident at The Deeps when they were teens. Remember, our victim pushed a kid off the rocks. Given this information, we asked ourselves what would Milo fixate on?"

"I'm right here in the room," Milo said.

"Quiet," Gramm ordered.

"When we got the story of The Deeps from Bob Young, it centered on Raf and his buddies. However, there was one unnamed person we ignored. What happened to the kid Raf pushed?"

Gramm turned to Milo. "Did you investigate the kid?"

"I did," Milo said.

"And?"

"This isn't my story." He held out both hands to Preston and White. "Continue."

"We discovered the kid drowned, or at least we think he drowned. The body of a young boy named Percy Fleur was found in the lake several days after an incident at The Deeps," White said.

"Poppie Flower's brother!" Preston blurted.

"How do you figure?" Gramm asked.

"Poppie's brother was named Perry. We figure the newspaper, or the rescue people got it wrong, calling him Percy, but it was Perry," White said.

"Plus, his last name, Fleur, is French for…ta da…wait for it…Flower." Preston was excited.

"Milo?" Gramm asked.

"Great job!" Milo said. "My services may no longer be needed."

White and Preston did a high five.

"So, where is your number one suspect?" Gramm asked.

"I called her earlier," White said. "She's back in town. I set up an interview."

"Where?"

"Here. She's our number one suspect, motive, means, and opportunity."

"What time?" Milo asked.

"Noon," White said.

Milo stood up. "I've got things to do."

After Rathkey left the room, Preston was beaming. "We out Miloed, Milo and he couldn't stand it!"

"I don't know," White said. "He didn't ask any questions. He just accepted our hypothesis."

"Don't second guess our theory," Preston admonished.

"Ernie, what do you think?" White asked.

"You have an assumption that Percy Fleur is Perry Flower. Have you looked for Perry Flower?" Gramm asked.

"We have. We could not find any recent reference for a Perry Flower."

"What about a death certificate?"

"There is one for a Percy Fleur. We are thinking that's Poppie's brother, Perry," White said.

"We think after Perry was born, mom and dad changed the last name from Fleur to Flower," Preston explained. "Milo suggested he called himself Perry rather than Periwinkle. Maybe he changed it to Percy. What do you think, Lieutenant?"

"I think Milo didn't ask any questions."

Preston shook her head. "I think we figured this out. We'll find out at noon when we confront Poppie."

"Do you think we're wrong?" White asked.

"It all makes sense, but…"

"But what?" Preston asked.

"Why didn't Milo ask any questions?"

§

Sgt. White and Officer Preston anxiously awaited the arrival of Poppie Flower at the police station. She arrived with a tall, handsome, blond man. Once it was determined that the man wasn't Poppie's lawyer, he was asked to wait in the bullpen. Both White and Preston guessed he was a new boyfriend. Poppie was directed to interview room A and sat down, hands folded in front of her.

White and Gramm entered the room, while Preston and Rathkey watched from behind the one-way glass.

Poppie was looking at her reflection in the one-way glass. "What do you think of my change?"

White stared at her. "Change?"

"Oh, come on, you must have noticed. I replaced the copper eyeliner with this stark white." Her hands swept across her brow to add to the effect. "Look at my eyes. They're blue now. Contacts. Last time I was here, they were brown—my real eyes. Am I memorable?"

"She really is," Preston said to Rathkey. "That white hair and piercing blue eyes are striking."

White ignored the question and began the interview with time, date, and those present.

Gramm opened his folder. "We have called you in to…"

"The reason I ask," Poppie continued, "is I only have a few days before my audition."

Preston shook her head. "Last time she said it was an open call, not an audition."

"Is there a difference?" Milo asked.

Gramm started the interrogation. "Ms. Flower, at the end of this interview, you may very well be going to prison, not a modeling agency. Please sit down."

If he thought that was going to scare Poppie, he was wrong. She laughed. "Me? You think I murdered someone?"

"We do," White said. "Let me give you our scenario. Some fifteen years ago, a young boy was pushed off the rocks at a place called The Deeps."

"Oh yeah, Bob told me about that. That's why Kick thinks Raf saved his life. Bob doesn't think so."

"Let's center on the young boy," White said. "His name was Percy Fleur. He drowned."

Poppie looked up and scootched her chair over to once again examine her reflection in the mirror. "What do you think of the white hair? Too much?"

White thought this to be a rehearsed trick. A way of deflecting sensitive subjects. "Does the name Percy Fleur mean anything to you?"

Poppie shook her head. "No."

"Perry Fleur?"

"I heard you the first time. No."

"Not Percy Fleur, Perry Fleur."

Poppie looked at both of them as if they were crazy. "No! Percy, Perry, whatever."

"Do you know that the name Fleur is French for flower?" White asked.

Poppie laughed. "Are you giving me a French lesson? I have an audition in a few days and the police are teaching me French? This is nuts."

Preston looked at Milo. "This is not going the way we thought it would. Are we wrong?"

"Yup. Very wrong."

"Nooooo! No, no, no!" Preston closed her eyes.

Gramm, tired of the stalling, came to the point. "Percy Fleur was your brother. Raf Bianchi killed your brother at The Deeps and once Bob Young told you what happened, you took your revenge."

"My brother is not Percy Fleur. My brother was Periwinkle Flower. He changed that to Perry Flynn."

White looked back at the one-way mirror. "How do we know that's true?"

"Ask him! He's sitting in that room with all the desks."

"The tall, blond gentleman you came in with?"

"Yeah, that's Perry. He doesn't think he's dead."

White looked at Gramm, who turned to the glass. "Can we get Mr. Flynn in here, please?"

Preston ran out of the room and down the hall. She returned several minutes later with Perry Flower, aka Perry Flynn.

White scowled at him. "What should we call you?"

"Perry's fine. It carries more authority than Periwinkle."

"Do you have any form of identification that still bears the name Periwinkle Flower?"

The man reached into his pocket and pulled out his wallet. He searched for almost a minute before producing a ragged piece of paper. "My old Social Security card."

"Any ID with your current name?" Gramm asked.

He produced a driver's license. "What is all this about?"

"Perry, these people think I killed a man because he killed you years ago at The Deeps."

"The Deeps? That old swimming hole off Seven Bridges Road?"

"I don't know. I never went there. I only know they keep calling it The Deeps."

White interrupted. "A boy named Percy Fleur was pushed off the rocks fifteen years ago."

"Fleur? French for Flower?"

"Yes."

"Well, that wasn't me."

"Why are you here, in Duluth?"

"My little sister is…anxious about her audition…"

"Open call!" Preston yelled behind the glass.

"Down-girl," Milo kidded.

"She'll do great. She's as tall as I am, has no hips and is a size triple zero. She'll flourish in their bizarre world."

Gramm looked at White, who thanked them both for coming in and told them they could leave.

"What about the eyeliner?" Poppie asked. "Is white good? Maybe copper with blue eyes?"

"That's my choice," White said, "copper with blue eyes."

Poppie smiled.

"Do you think that was really Robin's choice?" Milo asked.

Preston just shook her head as she returned to the bullpen.

§

"Well, I think Poppie's motive has disappeared. Do we all agree?" Gramm asked.

Preston was dejected. "It all fit, sort of."

"I'm sorry to have wasted everyone's time," White offered.

"No harm, no foul," Gramm said. "But in the future, let's not be quite so rushed to out Milo, Milo."

"So, Milo, what have you got?" White asked.

"Dave Ferris," Milo said.

"Oh Dave Ferris," White mocked. "That explains everything."

Milo played along. "So, you know Dave."

"No, she doesn't know Dave!" Gramm yelled. "Who is Dave Ferris and why do I care?"

"Dave's a longtime buddy of mine. He's the waiter that blocked our view. I got him the gig. We are in luck."

White rolled her eyes.

"Humor me, Milo," Gramm said. "Why are we in luck?"

"Dave used to be a pickpocket. Quite a good one."

A light went on in Gramm's brain. "Dave the Dip? You recommended Dave the Dip be a waiter at your chef's dinner?"

Preston looked puzzled. "Dave the Dip?"

"Notorious pick pocket in his day," Gramm said.

Milo shrugged. "He's retired now. Arthritis."

"What did he see?" White asked.

"He told me sleight of hand and misdirection," Milo said, calling his friend Dave the Dip.

"Will he answer the phone, *Dave the Dip*?" Preston whispered to White.

"Milo, I was expecting your call," Dave answered. "Thanks again for putting me onto that job. Every little bit helps these days."

"Certainly, no problem. Dave, I've got Lieutenant Gramm and others here. Could you tell them what you told me about the DeJong table?"

"Sure. That table kept me busy. Ms. Nguyen said they were big tippers, so I hovered. They were also big drinkers."

"We saw that when we watched the video," Milo added. "We also saw that Jess, DeJong's wife, was changing places with her husband. At the same time, Raf Bianchi bumped up against Jess, who pushed him away."

"That isn't what happened. He didn't bump up against her. I know it looked like that, but she actually pulled him toward her, then made a big deal of pushing him away. She cussed him out, but it was her doing. He was kind of drunk, weaving. Nobody noticed but me."

"Why would she do that, Dave?"

"I can't do it anymore, but I recognize it when I see it. She was picking his pocket. She was good, real good. I was impressed. Unfortunately, I didn't see what got lifted, and I usually do. Like I said, she was good."

"Did you see anyone tamper with that guy's food?"

"No, but I wasn't there continuously. They kept me hopping getting them drinks—even during dinner."

"Thanks, Dave. Talk to you later."

"Goodbye Poppie, hello Jess," Preston said.

Milo nodded. "You thought Poppie used Jess' change of seats as a distraction to poison Raf's drink, but according to Dave, it was the other way around. Jess used Poppie's move to make one of her own. If Dave says she's good, she's really good."

"How does someone like Jess have those skills?" Preston asked.

"She told us she was a magician, apparently a good one," Milo said. "I think we need to check the car Kick DeJong was driving the night of the dinner."

"The one in the accident?" White asked.

"Yup."

Gramm picked up his phone and dialed Brenda Peinovich. "Gramm, congratulations. You and your people managed to miss all storm duty."

"Yeah, except our made-up murder turned out to be real. The night of the storm, a guy named Kick DeJong was t-boned on Arrowhead Road. Did we impound the car and do we still have it?"

"I'm sure we did. Let me check."

After several minutes, Peinovich came back on the line. "It's still in the impound lot, but you won't be able to get it out. We towed a lot of cars over the last week. It's jammed in there."

Milo leaned into the phone. "We don't want to move it. We want to search it."

"Sure."

"Can we do that without a warrant?" Preston asked.

Peinovich answered. "Just say you're inventorying the contents and oops, look what we found. Looking for a gun?"

"An EpiPen," Milo said.

"And I thought I led a dull life. I'll tell impound to expect you." Peinovich hung up.

"Milo, what makes you think the pen is still in the car?" Gramm asked.

"I think it went this way. She lifts the pen, plans to dispose of it later, only there was no later. By the time Jess leaves the hospital, the car is in the impound lot."

"She could have thrown it in the trash at the restaurant," Gramm said. "It's long gone."

"No, I'd hang on to that EpiPen," White said, "and dispose of it somewhere that has no connection to me. I agree. Before she could do that, she lost it somewhere in the car during the accident."

"Well, I'd put it in my pocket," Preston said. "But we don't have access to any of her pockets now. She's home."

"I'd throw it out the window," Gramm added.

"I'm with Robin," Milo said. "Let's start with the car. It's the only thing we got."

§

Sonja Johansen started to enter Agnes' office, noticed she was on the phone, and turned and walked away. Agnes finished her call, got up, and poked her head into Milo's adjoining office. Sonja was sitting in one of the fireplace chairs, admiring the woodwork carvings.

"Do you have something for me, Sonja?" Agnes asked.

"I do. I hope I have not created a problem."

"What problem?"

"I sent copies of a few of the journal pages plus pictures of the carvings to a colleague in Norway. One of her main interests is a famous Norwegian Carver named Ragnvald Oldberg. She knows he left Norway around the turn of the last century, went to Canada, and then disappeared. My colleague, Liesl, believes he disappeared because he was wanted by Norwegian authorities. At present, she has no proof, but based on what I sent her, Liesl believes our carver is her carver."

"So Ragnvald Oldberg might have been on the lam when he lived here in Lakesong?" Agnes said. "How exciting!"

"She is operating on that hypothesis. Liesl is also a distant relative of Oldberg. She would like to come to Duluth to examine the carvings in person."

"That would be fine."

Johansen looked uncomfortable.

"What else?" Agnes asked.

"If all of this proves true, the problem is these carvings will probably put this house on a national registry of historic places. People may request to see your home and it will limit what you can do with the vault and that upstairs room."

"We like people and have no plans to change any of it, certainly not to destroy the carvings. My husband is active in preservation. I'm sure he won't mind."

"What about Mr. Rathkey?"

"Milo has no plans to change anything about Lakesong. Trust me."

§

Milo was in the middle of a just Milo and Sutherland, Lakesong dinner when Gramm called. "Forensics went through the car."

"And?" Milo asked.

"They had to do some work on the t-boned side in order to get to the entire car."

"And?"

"They found an EpiPen wedged in the passenger door. We are checking it for fingerprints. Are you thinking just Jess or Jess and Kick?"

"I think Jess," Milo said. "She hated Raf and has the sleight-of-hand skills."

"I agree," Gramm said. "But I've talked to the DA. He says the current case against Jess is weak, but if her fingerprints are on the EpiPen, that helps."

"Don't get ahead of yourself. Is the EpiPen Raf's."

"We don't know. Let's see what the fingerprints tell us."

"See you in the morning," Milo said.

"Be in early."

Milo hung up.

"Sounds like your case is winding up," Sutherland said.

"It's getting there," Milo said.

"Are you going to have a dramatic reveal?" Sutherland smiled. "I am an available experienced sherry pourer."

"Thanks, but I don't think your services will be required. The dramatic reveal attracts a bad crowd."

"Ron Bello?"

"Exactly."

23

Milo arrived at the cop shop at the same time as White and Gramm. Preston was already at her workstation with a freshly brewed cup of coffee. Gramm and Rathkey made use of the Preston-made coffee. White held up her cup and said, "Golden caramel, white hot chocolate, with two shots of espresso. In case any of you are wondering."

"That should get you spinning," Gramm said.

"It's my imminent arrest drink."

"Let's gather in my humble office while we await the fingerprint report," Gramm said.

"I've got the report right here," Preston said. "It came over fifteen minutes ago."

"You should try to get in earlier, Ernie," Milo kidded.

Gramm led the way into his office. "Let's get this case closed. What does the report say?"

Preston knew her eidetic memory was disturbing to some people, so she usually pretended to read from her phone. Milo caught on to that trick and leaned over to see her screen saver. Preston put her phone into her pocket and continued.

"Preston, what the hell is in the Forensics report?" Gramm demanded.

"The EpiPen has three sets of prints: Raf Bianchi's, Jess DeJong, and a third set that was too smudged to identify," Preston said.

Gramm's bushy eyebrows rose. "I think that settles it. We get an arrest warrant for Jess DeJong. I'll call the DA."

"Do you think the arrest warrant will jog her memory?" White asked.

Gramm answered while beginning his morning stretching. "I don't care. She doesn't have to confess. We have enough evidence for once."

§

Agnes' love of hash browns was over. She was finishing her breakfast of ginger tea and dry toast. Sutherland had slurped the final drops of his covered smoothie and was putting on his coat to leave for the office.

"We have to think of names," Agnes said.

"Don't we have to know if he's a he or she's a she?" Sutherland asked.

"No," Agnes said, producing a baby name book. "There are a number of gender-neutral names that are cute. I was flipping through the book. Charlie and Quinn are nice."

"We could name her after our close relatives, your sister, Barbara, my mother, Laura, or my dad, John."

Agnes scrunched up her nose. "I'd like him or her to have their own fresh start. The name Ragnvald is growing on me."

"Great. Ragnvald McKnight it is," Sutherland smiled.

Martha walked into the morning room to remove the breakfast dishes.

"What do you think about Ragnvald as a name for the baby?" Agnes asked.

Martha laughed. "You said you were feeling better this morning."

"I am. That dry toast was really excellent, Martha."

"Yet you came up with Ragnvald for this poor child."

"We could call him or her, Rags," Sutherland said.

"Wrong on so many levels," Martha said, loading the dishes onto her wheeled cart. "Keep thinking."

§

"The arrest warrant has been signed. Let's roll," Gramm said.

"Roll where?" Milo asked.

"I called Jess, told her we wanted to talk to her," White said. "She's at home up on Skyline Drive."

"She's a neighbor of Feinberg? Such a bad neighborhood," Gramm joked.

"Let's go," Milo said.

Gramm and White took a police car, Milo drove his Honda. When they arrived, not only was Jess at home, but so was her husband, Kick. He opened the door and let them in.

"You people are such a pain in the ass. I don't know what else you can ask. Come in. Jess is in the living room," Kick said. "I'm calling my lawyer for real this time."

Gramm and White walked up to Jess, who was lying on the couch. She elbowed her way to a more upright position as the group entered. "The doctors say I have a concussion. All I know is I can't seem to wake up. I'm kinda groggy, and have ringing in my ears, so please speak up. Do you have some information that can help me?"

Gramm and White stood. Milo sat down in a plush chair facing the couch. "Help you, how?" White asked.

"I still can't remember anything from the night of the accident. People come to visit, you know, to see how I am, but none of them can help me remember much. They are exhausting."

Gramm held up the evidence bag holding the EpiPen. "Maybe I can help. Recognize this?" He handed her the bag.

She looked at the pen through the bag. "It's an EpiPen."

"It's Raf Bianchi's EpiPen in case he ingested anything with peanuts."

Jess shrugged and handed the evidence bag back to White. "Why am I looking at this?"

"We found this in your car and your fingerprints are on it."

"You need a warrant to search our car!" Kick blustered.

"Not if it's in our impound lot," Gramm said. Turning back to Jess, "How did this pen get in your car?"

"I don't know. I don't remember."

"We have a video of the dinner you all attended. There is a moment when Raf bumps into you, Mrs. DeJong. In that moment you lifted his EpiPen," Gramm continued.

"Ha!" Kick laughed. "How would she do that?"

Milo stood up. "The same way I have your wallet." He held it out for Kick. "I'm not nearly as good as your wife, but I'm not a bad amateur."

White went up to Jess. "Jess DeJong, I am arresting you in the death of Raf Bianchi. You have the right to remain silent. Anything you say can and will be used against you in a court of law."

Kick was already on the phone. "Saul? We have a problem. They're arresting Jess." He paused for a moment. "They don't have crap. Okay, thanks."

Jess stood up, but looked unsteady. Kick rushed over to her, putting his arm around her.

"I will drive her," Kick said.

Gramm nodded.

Kick's face hardened. "I am going to sue you and the city for false arrest and putting my wife's health in jeopardy!"

Gramm, who had heard that threat at least a hundred times, said simply, "Be my guest."

§

Milo's phone buzzed as he followed Gramm back to the police department.

"Rathkey here," he said.

"Mr. Rathkey, this is Ed Bewly of the Minneapolis Star. Is this a good time?"

"No."

"Oh sorry. When would you have a few minutes to chat with me?"

"Well, Ed, it depends on what you would like to chat about. If you're trying to sell me a car warranty, I'm afraid we already have a woman named Mr. Anderson who takes care of all that."

"What?"

"Mr. Anderson."

'The police PIO, Kevin Richards, said you might be a little difficult."

"Difficult? I'm very forthcoming. My mechanic is Mr. Anderson."

"I would like to talk to you about Ron Bello's latest book, which features you prominently."

"Ron has a small problem. I think they call it disassociation with reality in which he simply makes up entire books about me. There isn't much I can do about it. I tried taking out a restraining order, but it was denied. He's a charmer."

"When would you be available?"

Milo sighed. "Let's try tomorrow morning. Right now, I am helping the police arrest someone."

"Tomorrow morning it is."

§

Saul Feinberg met the police as they escorted Jess DeJong into the booking area. "I have arranged for a hearing in an hour to get my client out on bail. She was seriously injured in a traffic accident."

"We know," Gramm said.

"How did you get a hearing late on a Friday?" Milo was impressed.

"I am owed a few favors. Nice trick, arresting her on a Friday, so she spends the weekend behind bars."

"We really didn't plan that," White said.

Feinberg laughed. "A discussion for another day."

"I thought you were the lawyer to the poor," White said. "How did you end up being the DeJong's attorney?"

"We're neighbors. I try to help people on my block."

"Block?" White questioned. "Skyline Drive is not a block."

"We like to foster a neighborhood feeling." He stopped his client as she was about to get her mug shot taken. "Don't answer any questions other than your name and address. I have arranged a hearing to get you out on bail."

"Thank you, Saul," Jess said as she walked into the room, using Kick's arm to steady her.

Two hours later, they were all before Judge Walter Asuron, a judge who liked Feinberg. A rarity.

The Judge called the hearing to order. "I have looked at the evidence in this case. I understand the counselor is asking that his client be released on her own recognizance. Mr. Feinberg?"

Feinberg rose. "Your Honor, my client is well known in the community. The charges against her are circumstantial at best, with some of the evidence found in an illegal search."

The county attorney, Dutch Wilson, stood. "Your honor. The validity of the evidence is not up to Mr. Feinberg. The EpiPen in question was found during an inventory of the DeJong's car as it sat in the police impound lot. Standard procedure."

"Let's not argue the merits of the case here. Mrs. DeJong has been charged. She will get her day in court. I will set bail at two-hundred-thousand dollars."

Kick turned to Feinberg. "I need to get two-hundred-thousand dollars?"

"We'll go see a bondsman. Usually it's ten percent," Feinberg said.

"Twenty thousand dollars? That, I can do."

§

Saturday and Sunday were uneventful. Milo spent most of both days reading in his library. Both cats were in agreement with Milo's choice of activities and eagerly joined him in front of the warm fireplace.

The weekly Sunday night card game was at Creedence Durant's house. Sutherland and Milo drove together in Sutherland's Porsche. "So, I expect you will be turning this jalopy in for a minivan sometime soon," Milo stated.

"Jalopy? The man who drives an old, dented Honda calls my Porsche a jalopy."

"Dented? There is not even a ding on that classic Honda. So, the minivan? Yes or no?"

"No! Why would I buy a minivan?"

"Sutherland, you are going to have a child. That makes you a family of three. This jalopy has only two seats. Math is not your strong suit."

"I beg to differ. I'm a business person. Unless you have forgotten, we have the SUV, the Bentley, the Rolls, and, of course, the ever popular Vespa. Oh yeah, also there is Agnes' Mirage."

"And Goliath," Milo added.

"I'll take a pass on Goliath, if you don't mind."

"I want to watch you put a child car seat in the Rolls. In fact, I'll pay you to take it to a fire station and have the firemen install it."

"Fire station? Why fire station?"

"Fire people will install child seats for you if you need help."

"How do you know that?" Sutherland asked.

"I looked it up after you and Agnes made your announcement, just in case your future child and I needed to go out for a beer."

"I would thank you to not be taking our baby 'out for a beer.'"

"So overprotective. You do know the Rolls, being old, does not have seat belts."

"It does. Dad had them retrofitted."

"What ever happened to that old Lincoln that was in the garage when I first moved back here?"

"It required a driver. Dad sold it to a collector—made the deal three days before he died."

Sutherland parked in front of Creedence's barn-like house.

"I can get you a good deal on a used minivan," Milo said.

Sutherland set the parking brake. "Let's not make this imaginary minivan the subject of tonight's card game."

"Classic avoidance."

"Classic avoidance of minivans. If we found ourselves in need of an ordinary car with a back seat, we'll simply use your Honda."

"That won't work. People shoot at me in that car."

"It happened once! You would think you're dodging bullets every day," Sutherland said as they walked up the stairs to Creedence's front porch. "Why are you two always the last to arrive?" Creedence asked as he ushered them in.

"We like to make an entrance," Milo said. "Besides, Sutherland is refusing to buy a safe vehicle in which to transport his child."

"*In which to transport?* Who are you?" Feinberg asked.

"No big deal, you just trade in that sports car for a minivan," Gramm said. "I did, and it no longer even affects me when I think about it." Gramm began to sniff and dab his eyes.

"If you need a moment alone, the study is through that door," Creedence said with mock sympathy.

"I…I…I'll be just fine," Gramm continued his pseudo sorrow.

Sutherland held up his hands. "Okay, we're not going to play Milo's game all night. The estate has many cars that are suitable for transporting young children or old detectives." He walked over to the snack table, picked up a cream puff, making a show of eating it in front of Milo.

"You're a monster," Milo said, taking one for himself.

"Last week, I was in Paris for a paleontological conference," Creedence said. "So tonight, we have amuse-bouches, French appetizers: cheese puffs, prune wrapped in bacon, mushrooms filled with flavored cream cheeses, cream puffs…"

"Yeah, yeah, yeah, food," Gramm said. "Let's play."

Creedence picked up the cards and began to shuffle. "So, who took my place last week?"

"My partner, Robin White."

"Is she any good?"

Feinberg laughed. "She's a shark. Gramm brought a ringer to the game."

"In my defense," Gramm said, "I did not know that she had been a casino dealer."

Creedence started laughing and couldn't stop. Minutes went by before Gramm threatened to eat Creedence's prize dinosaur toe bone if he didn't deal.

"Seven-card stud, nothing wild," Creedence said.

"Good choice," Gramm agreed. As he looked at his cards, he said, "Saul, I guess we won't be able to trade information tonight."

Sutherland asked why.

"We have arrested Jess DeJong for the murder of Raf Bianchi, AKA Ralph Bing," Gramm said. "She is being represented by fellow poker player, Saul Feinberg."

Feinberg started the bidding at a dime. "Unfortunately, we can talk about it all night."

Milo, looking at a pair of duces down, upped the bid to fifteen cents.

"What?" Gramm demanded. "Are you no longer her lawyer?" He saw the fifteen cents.

"Oh, I'm her lawyer," Feinberg said. "She's just no longer your suspect."

Sutherland, pleased the conversation had moved on from imaginary minivans, upped the bid to a quarter. He only had the beginning of a straight. Not worth the bid.

"Please explain!" Gramm said.

"The DA offered her a plea deal and against advice of counsel—that would be me—she took it. She will plead guilty tomorrow."

"What's the problem, Saul?" Milo asked.

"Your case is weak. I could easily get her off. I told her so, but she insisted, said she wanted to get it over with."

"How much time does she serve?" Gramm asked.

"Two years plus probation." Feinberg shook his head. "It shouldn't happen."

"Did she admit to taking the EpiPen?" Milo asked.

"No," Feinberg said. "She doesn't remember anything. That in itself is a defense."

An uncomfortable silence swept across the usually affable group. Creedence and Sutherland tried to lighten the mood but were unsuccessful. Creedence spoke first. "This is usually where Milo gets us off on a tangent. I'm not as humorous as Milo, so I suggest we drop this and focus on the cards." Everyone agreed.

Gramm was actually the big winner. Saul was off his game. Milo came in second. Sutherland and Creedence were the losers.

On the way home, Milo was deep in thought. Sutherland tried his hand at lightning the mood. "Once again, I'll have to tell Agnes about my high stakes loss. I don't know if I can hide the $1.75 I lost tonight."

"Have I ever introduced you to Darlene Budack?" Milo asked.

"No, why?"

"She can lend you the $1.75. No one will be any the wiser. Payment is due every Tuesday at noon. Don't be late."

"I'm thinking I could win it back in the next card game," Sutherland said.

"Slippery slope."

24

Gramm was pleased to put this case to bed. What started out as a made-up murder turned into a complicated case that might have never been solved. White and Preston didn't like the victim, Raf Bianchi, so their sympathy was with Jess DeJong. Where Milo stood was a mystery.

"We got an attaboy from Deputy Chief Sanders," Gramm told White and Preston as they gathered in his office.

Milo was late. He looked somewhat troubled.

"What's your problem?" Gramm demanded. "We did our jobs. We caught the perp. Case closed."

"It all seems too easy," Milo said. "I feel like we've been setup."

"Look, you're the one who led us to her. Without you and Dave the Dip noticing she was a master of sleight-of-hand, we would be nowhere," Gramm said. "Smile. Cheer up. It's over."

White nodded. "Look at the evidence. We ruled Poppie out, so the only other person to even come close to Raf was Jess."

Milo shook his head. "We forgot one other person."

"No Milo, the case is closed. The perp has pled no contest. The Deputy Chief is happy. I'm happy. White is happy. Preston hasn't almost killed herself with a bomb or a motorcycle. Whatever you're thinking, drop it."

§

Milo did not drop it. First, he looked at the video going through it frame by frame. Just before she pulled Raf toward her, one particular frame showed a shadow in Jess' hand. Just one frame, but something was there.

"Son of a bitch!" he said to Jet, who was lounging in front of the fireplace.

§

Reese and Emma were having a quiet lunch at Marathon. "Kick checked into three months of rehab this morning," Reese said.

"That's great! No Raf, no Oxy, no problem," Emma proclaimed.

Reese gave her a stern look. "Not great! Jess is serving a two-year sentence. With Kick in rehab, you are going to have to help manage the restaurants."

"Me? I have a job."

"Yeah, you," Reese said. "You're going to have to take a leave of absence or quit. I don't care which, but we are going to manage the restaurants. You are doing the day to day."

Reese reached for his phone to put Kick's release date in his calendar. It was not in his pocket. "Not funny, Emma. Time to grow up."

She handed him back his phone.

§

Armed with a new theory, Milo Rathkey rewound the video to Raf Bianchi's entrance into the dinner. Bianchi ordered a drink from a passing waiter before making a beeline to Emma. The young girl shook him off and twirled around, painfully bending Bianchi's arm behind him. Bianchi was in clear distress until Emma let him go. He watched Emma shove her right hand into her pants pockets.

Milo looked at the scene many times, frame by frame. Was she putting something in her pocket? Was it the EpiPen? He couldn't be sure. Bianchi meanwhile lurched around the table to Kick, slapped him on the back and stumbled. Zooming in, Milo could clearly see him deliver a bag of pills to Kick's jacket.

Milo had a giant question, but it was answered when he watched Jess stand up, move to her sister, and hug her after Bianchi's assault.

Continuing to watch the video from that point, he saw the waiters come by with the food. Emma got up from her chair, bumping into one of the waiters, almost knocking him off balance. She reached out and steadied him.

Milo zoomed into the dish that the waiter carried. It differed from the beef stew served to the rest of the table. Only Raf ordered the non-peanut entrée in a pineapple half. The waiter Emma bumped into was carrying Raf's food.

Milo thought for a while before calling Feinberg. "I have a favor to ask."

"Ask away," Feinberg said.

"I need to talk to Jess DeJong."

Feinberg laughed. "I don't think that's gonna happen. She doesn't even want to talk to me."

"Give it a try."

"Why?"

"It's part of my education. I have some questions."

"Would these questions prove her innocence?"

"That's not my job. Tell her if she wants to go to prison, I have no problem with that. I just have a few questions."

"What are your questions and what will you do with the answers?"

"Nothing."

"Milo, I know you. You know who really committed the murder and why my client is willing to take the fall."

"Yes, on the first part. No, on the second."

"I'll see what I can do," Saul said. "In return, I want a dinner at Lakesong. It's been a long time since I tasted Martha's food."

"Deal."

"Jess is out on bail and is at home until she is formally sentenced."

"Thank you, Saul."

§

Jess was lying on a couch when Milo arrived at the house on Skyline Drive. Reese let Milo in, warning him that Jess was tired and to keep it short.

"Where's Kick?" Milo asked.

"Rehab," Reese responded.

Milo nodded to Jess as he sat down in a brocade chair opposite the couch. "I have a few questions."

"I told Saul, I'm not pleased you're here and I don't see why you have any questions. I must have done it. I hated him. I took his EpiPen and laced his food with peanuts," Jess said.

"Did you grind them up?" Milo asked.

"The man was a monster. He was keeping my husband in a constant state of oxy high."

"Well, I do admit you have a strong motive, but if you are determined to push this lie, you need to know that Raf ingested peanut oil, not peanuts."

Jess said nothing.

"You love your sister, don't you?" Milo stated.

Jess shifted uneasily. "Of course I do. What does that have to do with anything?"

Milo nodded. "Relax, I know it's all over. You're going to jail and everybody is happy."

"Okay," Jess murmured.

Reese, who had been lurking in the kitchen, sauntered back into the room and sat down in the chair next to Milo. "What are you getting at?"

"Humor me. Tell me about your parents," Milo asked.

Reese answered before Jess could. "They are none of your business. We've been taking care of each other for years."

"So, who raised Emma?"

"Us."

Jess remained quiet.

"How? You were children."

Jess finally spoke up. "Smart children. Our drunk dad left us after Emma was born."

"Where was mom?" Milo asked.

"Doing nothing for anyone," Reese said.

"She had her own problems. Reese and I were not in her world."

Milo nodded. "This is beginning to make sense. I didn't believe you would go to jail for a sister, but for a sister you raised as a daughter, that I can believe. Milo stood up. "That's all I needed to know. I looked at the video of the dinner. Your sleight of hand is fantastic."

"So, why the questions?" Jess asked. "You know I did it. You saw me lift the pen."

"I saw your sleight of hand, but you weren't making a withdrawal. You were trying to make a deposit. I suspect you realized what Emma was up to, and you tried to put the EpiPen back into Raf's pocket."

"That's your story," Reese said.

Milo pursed his lips. "Emma has crossed a line, intentionally taking a life. That's a huge jump. Are you going to be there every time Emma gets angry?"

Jess and Reese glanced at each other.

"We have so far," Reese said.

§

Agnes sat, legs curled, in the family room. Sutherland arrived with her new pre-dinner drink, coconut water, and a little mango juice. She smiled at him as he sat down next to her.

"What are you thinking?" he asked.

Agnes leaned back against the sofa. "I was just thinking about our baby. All of this, this house, is going to be normal to her. Her home."

"It was to me," Sutherland said.

"But now we know about some of the hidden doors and mystery staircases. Lakesong will be one giant adventure. Oh, and she will have one thing you didn't."

"What's that?"

"An Uncle Milo."

Sutherland laughed. "I think I'd find an Uncle Milo a lot of fun."

"Me too."

"This house isn't done showing us its mysteries," Sutherland said.

"Her mysteries," Agnes corrected.

"Sorry. Her mysteries." Sutherland asked Agnes about the status of the carvings.

"According to Sonja, our mystery carver is definitely Ragnvald Oldberg, a famous Norwegian carver who disappeared. Her contacts in Norway are excited. They say the carvings are exactly his style. We'll get a few visitors in the next month to look at them close up and verify."

"What about the journal?" Sutherland asked.

"I thought we could donate it to the Oldberg museum in Norway."

"There is an Oldberg museum?" Milo asked.

Agnes nodded. "He has enthusiastic fans."

"Have you agreed on a baby name yet?" Milo asked.

"I'm thinking toast," Agnes said.

"Toast?" Milo questioned. "What about my hash browns? You liked to eat my hash browns."

"That was short-lived. They went down but didn't stay long, but I have been able to eat toast three mornings in a row," Agnes bragged.

"Not Gofsmop. Toast," Sutherland mused.

§

Famed mystery writer, Dylan Abigail McKnight, known to her family as Toast, would lose her favorite unicorn lovey, Neigh Neigh, at age four. Her Uncle Milo joined her in the search, instructing the toddler on how to implement a successful investigation. She would later tell her biographer that this was her first lesson, followed by many more.

POP-UP DINNER, DROP DOWN DEAD

If you wish to contact the authors, email us at authors@dbelrogg.com or leave a message at www.dbelrogg.com.

If you enjoyed this book, please leave a review on Amazon.

BOOKS BY D.B. ELROGG

GREAT PARTY! SORRY ABOUT THE MURDER

FUN REUNION! MEET, GREET, MURDER

MISSED THE MURDER. WENT TO YOGA

MURDER AGAIN! HAPPY NEW YEAR!

SNAP, ZAP, MURDER

CLUES, CASH, PIECES OF MURDER

OLD MURDER, NEW MURDER, WHERE ARE THE COWS?

POP-UP DINNER, DROP DOWN DEAD

Made in the USA
Columbia, SC
12 July 2025